ROGUE LAWMAN
COLD CORPSE, HOT TRAIL

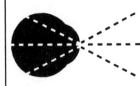

This Large Print Book carries the
Seal of Approval of N.A.V.H.

Rogue Lawman
Cold Corpse,
Hot Trail

Peter Brandvold

WHEELER PUBLISHING

An imprint of Thomson Gale, a part of The Thomson Corporation

THOMSON

GALE

Detroit • New York • San Francisco • New Haven, Conn. • Waterville, Maine • London

LIBRARY OF CONGRESS CATALOGING-IN-PUBLICATION DATA

Brandvold, Peter.
    Rogue lawman — cold corpse, hot trail / by Peter Brandvold.
      p. cm. — (Wheeler Publishing large print western)
    ISBN-13: 978-1-59722-632-5 (pbk. : alk. paper)
    ISBN-10: 1-59722-632-7 (pbk. : alk. paper)
    1. Large type books. I. Title. II. Title: Cold corpse, hot trail.
PS3552.R3236R65 2007
813'.54—dc22   2007028132

Published in 2007 by arrangement with The Berkley Publishing Group, a member of Penguin Group (USA) Inc.

Printed in the United States of America on permanent paper
10 9 8 7 6 5 4 3 2 1

For Frank Roderus,
the straightest shooter in the
whole dang posse!
(And a darn good writer, friend,
and mentor.)

1.

DEAD OR ALIVE

The wind was howling wolflike outside the tiny, smoky cantina, blowing up dust in the main street of Coyote Springs, Arizona Territory. It made the lamps sway and the batwings squawk. A bearded man with a gold eyetooth and shabby bowler hat set a wanted dodger on the table, and turned it toward Gideon Hawk.

With three greasy fingers, he slid the whiskey-stained parchment through the playing cards and cigar ashes, until Hawk's own sketched likeness stared up at him — a ghostly specter with dark, deep-set eyes, angular face, and hard, unshaven jaw.

The image took Hawk aback.

It couldn't be his. The face looked like that of a hardened, merciless killer, not unlike those of the men he himself hunted. But there it was, his own name, GIDEON HAWK, and the words ROGUE LAWMAN in large block letters beneath the even larger letters announcing, WANTED: DEAD OR ALIVE.

Hawk looked at the man with the gold eyetooth. The man smiled. Hawk glanced at the two other cardplayers, one on either side of him — both hard-eyed, broad-shouldered men clad in greasy trail clothes. Before they'd sat down, Hawk had seen the knives and well-tended revolvers on their hips. The man on Hawk's right wore a thin, rat-hair coat with the bulge of a shoulder holster under his left arm. When he'd reached forward to toss money on the table, the coat had opened slightly, offering glimpses of a big Le Mat.

"You think I didn't know you were bounty hunters?" Hawk said. "You three smell like an undertaker's privy."

"If you knew we was bounty hunters," said the man to Hawk's right, who had a thatch of unruly red hair and one wandering eye, "why you playin' cards with us?"

Hawk riffled his cards and puffed the long, black cigar between his lips. "Dead men's money is as good as any other."

The men glanced at each other, an indignant light in their eyes. The man to Hawk's left snickered nervously. He removed one hand from his fan of pasteboards, and began edging it off the table.

"I reckon you better keep both hands right where they are," Hawk advised him, staring straight ahead at the hombre with the gold eyetooth, but aware of the other two in the periphery of his vision. "And I reckon you boys better have another rye, forget about that wanted dodger."

The man on his right leaned over the table, growling, "You think we're scared of you? There's *three* of us, one of *you!*"

"And there's a thousand dollars on your head, Hawk." The man with the eyetooth grinned. "And we're hungry. If you wanna swap lead, we'll swap lead. But we ain't tin-horns fresh from over Alabamy way. You can't take all three of us. So, why don't you save yourself and us a lot of trouble and come peaceful?"

Behind Hawk, a floorboard squawked faintly. He didn't turn around, but kept his eyes on the man with the gold eyetooth.

"See," said the man on the left, pulling at his long, tobacco-stained chin whiskers, "if we mess the place up, get blood on the floor an' such, the bartender'll charge us for the cleanup and repairs . . ."

Out the corner of Hawk's left eye, a figure moved in the mirror behind the back bar.

". . . and there just ain't no need," the man with the spade beard added reasonably, his perpetually bloodstained fingers tugging on the whiskers, "when the only thing a lead swap can get you is —"

Hawk didn't hear the rest. He dropped his right cheek to the table, the impact knocking over the whiskey bottle and bouncing the scattered coins. A rifle butt sliced the air over Hawk's head, knocking his hat off and making a loud whooshing sound. Faintly, a man grunted.

Hawk glanced over his left shoulder. The man who'd swung the rifle stumbled with the violent force of the swing. With his right hand, Hawk slipped his nickel-plated Russian .44 from the cross-draw holster on his left hip, raised it to his armpit, and fired straight out from his side.

The gun's pop sounded inordinately loud in the closed quarters. The man with the rifle bellowed, dropped the long gun, and staggered toward the bar, clutching his right hip, into which a neat, smoking hole had been drilled.

Hawk was only vaguely aware of the indignant cries around him, as the saloon's other patrons scrambled to safety. His senses homed in on the table before him where his three poker companions, shaking off their surprise at Hawk's dodge of the rifle butt, reached for their own revolvers.

10

Hawk bolted to his feet, throwing his chair back and lifting the table with his left hand. With his right, he extended the Russian at the man with the wandering eye, who was pushing up from his chair and bringing the big Le Mat up from under his arm.

Hawk drilled a round through his brisket, blowing him back down in his chair. The man sat, gritting his teeth and throwing his head back as the Le Mat slipped from his fingers and blood geysered from his chest. The chair went over, the man's knees rising above the table, his back hitting the floor with a loud crack and a *whap!*

Turning left, Hawk stepped into the table, which he held before him like a shield, driving the other two bounty hunters back in their own chairs. He thumbed the smoking Russian's hammer back, fired through the bottom of the table.

The man with the gold eyetooth yowled. His chair barked on the pine boards.

A shot cracked to Hawk's left, the bullet splintering the table near his left hand and shattering a whiskey bottle behind him.

As Hawk continued pushing the table back and over, he drilled two more quick shots through the bottom, one on each side of the hole to his left.

"Ah, *God!*" groaned the man with the

11

spade beard as Hawk overturned the table and stepped back.

Spying quick movement out of the corner of his eye, Hawk turned toward the bar. The man he'd felled with the hip shot had retrieved his rifle. His back to the bar, grimacing and cursing, he jacked the loading lever and raised the barrel toward Hawk.

Gideon swung toward him, crouching and extending the Russian, popping off two more fast shots into the man's throat and heaving paunch. As the man screamed and dropped the rifle, collapsing against the floor, Hawk holstered the empty Russian and clawed the stag-butted Army Colt from the sheath on his right hip.

Raising it, he saw the man with the gold eyetooth crawl out from beneath the table, run crouching toward the batwings, then turn, blood pumping from a wound in his left shoulder.

Eyes spitting flames of fury, he bellowed, "You son of a locoed *shoat* — !"

Hawk popped a round into Mr. Eyetooth's forehead. As the man staggered straight back toward the batwings, firing his pistol into the low, smoke-blackened ceiling, Hawk turned to the man with the long whiskers.

He was pushing himself up from a broken

chair, grunting and cursing, sweat running down his cheeks and into the tobacco-stained beard.

His voice brittle with exasperation, he panted, "I'll . . . I'll . . . I'll . . ."

He was halfway up and turning toward Hawk when Hawk's Colt roared, plunking a .44 pill above the man's left ear. As the man gave a clipped sigh and hit the floor as though felled by a pugilist's haymaker, Hawk swung his gaze around the room, rife with the rotten-egg odor of cordite. In a situation like this, you never knew who else, compelled by the prospect of a thousand-dollar reward, might decide to throw in with the bounty hunters.

But all the seven or so other customers were cowering at the room's perimeters, under tables, or behind overturned chairs. A little Mexican whore, clad in only a spangled burgundy skirt and with several strands of bright Mexican beads looped around her pert, brown breasts, looked up from behind a large rain barrel mounded with empty bottles. Hawk looked twice, was surprised to see no cocked derringer in her hand, ready to earn the whore more money than she'd ever made in the mattress sack.

Hawk lowered the Colt and, swinging another cautious glance about the room, stooped to pluck a handful of greenbacks off the floor. He left several dollars for the barkeep and undertaker, then started toward the batwings. Movement out the dusty front window caught his eye.

He stopped.

Four soldiers in blue tunics, black pistol belts, and tan kepis were heading this way from the livery barn. A short, pudgy man wearing a marshal's star ran to join them, pointing at the cantina. Above the din of wagons, clomping horses, and barking dogs, Hawk heard only snippets of the marshal's words. ". . . four bounty hunters . . . they was gonna . . . rogue lawman . . . pshaw! . . ."

As the soldiers and the marshal strode toward the batwings, Hawk cursed. He wheeled, peered into the shadows at the back of the room. A low door was in the back wall, just beyond the bar. Hawk made for it, stepping over bodies and around the shattered table and chairs.

To his right, the Mexican apron moved suddenly, raising a double-barreled barn-blaster up from under the bar planks. Hawk crouched as the shotgun boomed, the flash lighting up the entire room. The double-ought buck careened over Hawk's head and smashed into the support post to his left, gouging a gourd-sized hole and splitting the post in two with a thunderous crack.

As part of the ceiling fell to his left, raining dirt and grass from the sod roof, Hawk straightened and emptied his Colt into the apron, smashing the man against the back bar, bleeding and screaming and shattering bottles as he fell.

Hawk opened the back door and glanced behind him. The soldiers bolted through the batwings, Army-issue pistols drawn and raking their gazes across the room.

"There!" a sergeant shouted, pointing at Hawk.

Hawk had turned to slip through the door when a small figure brushed past him and through the door ahead of him. It was the topless whore. Frowning, Hawk bolted through the door, closed it, then rammed a trash barrel under the knob.

He turned to the girl standing in the alley before him, arms crossed over her breasts, eyes slitted with fear. Barefoot, she leaned toward him beseechingly.

"Please, you must take me with you. The soldiers, they are very bad. They don't pay, only take. ¿*Comprende?*"

"Beat it!" Hawk shouted as the soldiers pounded the door from inside, jolting the barrel back from the jamb.

He turned and ran along the alley, hurdling trash and logs fallen from woodpiles. He turned on the other side of the post office and ran through the gap between the post office and a harness shop.

Hearing shouts and running feet behind him, he turned to see not only the soldiers and the marshal, but the girl. Running surprisingly fast on her dirty, bare feet, cupping her breasts in her hands, she was right on his heels.

"~~Goddamnit~~, I told you to get the hell out of here!" Having circled around the saloon, Hawk approached his horse, tethered with a handful of others to the hitch rack before the batwings. "You'll be a hell of a lot safer on your own than you ever will with me!"

"On my own, I'll be dead before nightfall!"

Hawk slipped his reins from the rack and cast a glance behind him. The soldiers were sprinting toward him. Several had lost their hats. A red-bearded sergeant was snarling like a rabid cur. He paused to aim his .44. The gun popped, the slug drilling into the awning support post six inches right of Hawk's shoulder.

"Hey, that ~~goddamn~~ *whore's* with him!" one of the other soldiers shouted as he and the others passed the sergeant, boots thumping the boardwalk in front of the post office.

Hawk swung onto the grulla and looked at the girl.

She stood before the hitch rack, staring up at him with terror and pleading etched in her wide, brown eyes. She couldn't have been much over sixteen. The hands covering her breasts were fine-fingered and delicate. Her straight black hair hung in her eyes.

"Come on then!" Leaning forward in his saddle, Hawk extended his hand to her.

She leapt forward and grabbed it. He swung her up easily behind him, then turned the tall horse west, nearly colliding with two saddle tramps riding leisurely along the street, and dug his spurs into its flanks. The grulla sprang off its rear hooves, lengthening out in a wind-splitting gallop, deftly swerving around mine dreys and ranch wagons.

Pistols popped behind, slugs plunking into the road on both sides of the horse. One ricocheted off a rock with an ear-ringing spang.

"After 'em!" shouted an Irish-accented voice.

Hawk urged the horse with another rake of his spurs. The girl wrapped her arms around his waist and pressed her head against his back. He could feel her Mexican beads and firm breasts through his black frock.

"Shit!" he raked out, tipping his hat to the wind.

2.
La Puta del Diablo

Following the stage road north into the high, desert benches and gaping canyons, the grulla split the wind as only a mountain-bred mustang can. This one was taken from a Colorado outlaw who had no more use for it when Hawk had drilled a .44 slug through his brain plate. The bare-breasted girl behind Hawk's saddle didn't slow the mount a hair.

In spite of the Arizona heat, the beast put its head down and enjoyed the wind in its mane, the fluid pumping of its heart, the grating clomps of its hooves on the red desert caliche.

Three miles from town, Hawk turned the horse off the trail, rode another twenty yards, then swung his right boot over the saddle horn and slid to the ground.

"What are you doing?" the girl asked.

Hawk flipped her the reins, shoved her bare left knee out of the way, and reached into his saddlebag for a small folding hatchet. With three deft blows, he chopped a limb from a piñon pine, then, branch in hand, walked back out to the stage road and began covering his tracks.

He covered only his own tracks where they began curving off the trail. He left the several overlaid sets of tracks of passing riders, and the four narrow furrows ground by the last stage's iron-rimmed wheels.

As he worked, he heard the girl clucking and grunting behind him. Saddle leather squeaked, and whipped reins whistled softly.

Hawk glanced over his shoulder. She'd slid onto his saddle and was batting her bare heels against the grulla's flanks, bouncing up and down.

"Come on, damn you," she urged, her thin, black brows furrowed with consternation. "¡*Vaya!* Go!"

Keeping its feet firmly planted, the horse glanced over its left shoulder at Hawk. It twitched an ear, then turned its head forward, lowered its head to crop grass, and swished its tail at flies.

Hawk snorted and continued rubbing out his tracks. Finished, he tossed some gravel and bits of dried horse apple over the needle marks in the road, then tossed away the branch and headed back to the horse.

The girl was still trying to get it moving, grinding her bare heels angrily into its ribs and swatting its neck with the rein ends, her small, round breasts and beads jostling as she bounced.

Hawk dropped the hatchet under the saddlebag's flap. "I trained him not to ride off with anyone but me in the hurricane deck."

When he'd secured the flap over the bag, he grabbed the girl's left arm, jerked her back to the horse's rump, then toed a stirrup, forked leather, and clucked.

The horse snorted eagerly, sprang off its rear hooves, and leapt forward in an instant gallop.

Jerked backward, the girl yelped, grabbed Hawk's coat, and flung her arms around his waist. She pressed her right cheek against his back as the grulla headed northeast through the manzanita grass and creosote, her skimpy skirt blowing back behind her knees.

"Bastardo," she snarled.

A few hundred yards farther, they forded the White Water River, then rode to a shelf halfway up the next sandstone ridge. The vast desert stretched away on three sides, like a rumpled, rust-colored quilt with haphazard patches of lime-green, and the blue of the river stitched through the middle.

Far to the south and west, horseback riders, most dressed in cavalry blues and tan hats, with sunlight winking off their trapdoor Springfields, galloped up a low ridge and disappeared down the other side. Their penny-colored dust sifted slowly.

"That takes care of them," Hawk said. He spat and turned his head to the left. "Now, what am I going to do about you?"

"Take me to Tucson."

"I'm not going to Tucson."

"Tucson is a nice town. Better than Coyote Springs." Behind Hawk, she made a disdainful spitting sound. "You take me there, I will make it worth your time."

"Enticing," Hawk said dryly, "but like I said, I'm not going to Tucson. I'll drop you in Benson and you can take the stage. I'll *lend* you the fare."

"The next stage doesn't run for three days!"

"I'm sure you'll find a way to occupy yourself."

She punched his shoulder with the backside of her fist. *"¡Bastardo!"*

Hawk reined the grulla up the ridge, following a faint game trail at a forty-five-degree angle. "So I've been called. What's your handle?"

"They call me La Puta del Diablo, The Devil's Whore," she said proudly, enunciating each word carefully, adding as though with a smile, "but you can call me Estella."

Hawk snorted. "The Devil's Whore, huh? How did you earn *that* attractive stamp?"

"Use your imagination."

"Had a feelin'."

He heeled the grulla over the ridge and down the other side. By the time he reached the dry wash at the bottom, the sun was nearly down, casting deep-purple shadows and dropping a sharp desert chill.

He vaguely remembered a spring from the last time he'd passed this way. He hadn't looked for it long when the grulla, smelling the water, jogged over a low ridge stippled with Joshua trees and saguaros. A few minutes later, it sunk its snout into the water bubbling up from the sand and rocks around which Mormon tea, manzanita grass, and yellow brittlebush blossoms grew thick.

Hawk gave Estella a hand down. While she drank, he unsaddled and hobbled the grulla, then spent a good fifteen minutes rubbing the animal down with a handful of dry grass.

He shuttled his saddle, rifle boot, saddlebags, and bedroll over to where the girl sat on a rock, between the cottonwoods and a sandy bank. As good a place as any to throw out a bedroll. He dropped the gear, then rummaged around in his saddlebags, tossed the whore a blue-checked shirt.

Estella caught it, glanced at him under her furrowed brows, and held the shirt out before her. Judging it worthy, she shrugged into it, covering her breasts and beads, throwing her long, black hair out from the collar.

"Gonna get chilly tonight," Hawk said, turning and moving off down the cut.

When he came back with an armload of mesquite branches and began digging a small fire pit, the whore sat where she'd been sitting before, leaning forward, rocking back and forth, the shirt pulled down over her bare legs. She'd buried her feet in the warm sand. There was a pensive, conniving cast to her features.

The Devil's Whore. He was liable to get a knife in his back before the night was through.

Hawk laid a fire, keeping it small, then wandered off to change from his gambling duds to his trail clothes — simple blue shirt, red neckerchief, tan denims, and cream duster. Before returning to the camp, he took a slow look around. This was Chir-

24

icahua country and, in spite of the reservations, Bronco Apaches were still raising hell with the white eyes.

Back at the camp, he set coffee to boil, then tossed the girl a few strips of jerky and hardtack from his saddlebags. When he'd shoved the gambling duds into his war bag, he leaned back against his saddle to wait for the coffee to boil.

Chewing the dried meat, he glanced at the sky, where one pale star flickered feebly. The sun bled down behind the purple western crags. "What'd you do to rile those soldiers?" he asked after a long silence.

Estella had sat down close to the fire, leaning back against the rock she'd been sitting on. She'd pulled her beads out of the shirt, and they glittered in the firelight.

Inspecting the hunk of jerky in her hand, she said, "I stabbed their friend with a hat pin." She lifted a shoulder, brushed sand from the meat in her hand, and popped it into her mouth. "He tried to get away without paying . . . after he bit me and slapped me half the night. He was an animal . . . even for a *soldado*."

The coffeepot boiled. Hawk grabbed a handful of Arbuckle's from a burlap pouch, tossed it into the pot.

"I know who you are," Estella said, hugging her knees and eying him accusingly across the fire.

Hawk returned the coffee pouch to his saddlebags. "You and half of Arizona, seems like." That's why he'd decided to head for Mexico.

"Lawmen came to the cantina a couple of weeks ago," Estella said, chewing another hunk of jerky. "They said you were an outlaw lawman. Vigilante. They said that you killed another lawman last winter." She smiled. "Your friend."

A dull blade prodded Hawk's heart. The pain must have shown in his eyes; Estella recoiled slightly and stopped chewing, the smile fading from her lips.

He hadn't killed Luke Morgan, but he might as well have. Morgan, a young deputy United States marshal whom Hawk himself had trained, had been gunned down by a county sheriff, Wick Haskell, who'd been trying to save Hawk's life.

The joke had been on both Hawk and Haskell.

Hawk hadn't wanted his life saved, and Haskell hadn't known he was killing a legitimate lawman who'd been trying to carry out a death warrant on a rogue — a death warrant signed by four territorial governors.

"Perhaps . . . they were wrong," the whore said haltingly, staring at him.

The coffee had started boiling again, brown bubbles churning up around the lip of the pot. With a leather swatch, Hawk removed the pot from the fire, set it on a cold rock, then fished two tin cups from his saddlebags. He filled both from the pot.

"If you want a cup of this mud, fetch it yourself. I don't deliver."

He took his own cup and sat back against his saddle, staring darkly into the brush, remembering.

Chin on her knees, Estella stared at him furtively. Finally, she rose, stretched like a cat, then moved around the fire. He turned to his left. The girl knelt beside him. She'd taken off the shirt again, revealing her small bare breasts encircled by the beads. Her tangled hair hung sensuously along both sides of her face.

She had a wild, lusty look in her eyes.

"I take your mind off . . ." She took his coffee cup, set it on a rock by the fire, and straddled his outstretched legs.

"No," Hawk said.

She planted her hands on either side of him and lowered her face to stare bewitchingly into his eyes. She smelled slightly salty, gamy. Her body radiated an intense heat.

Her nipples stood out from her breasts, firm as rubber posts.

Goose pimples rose on her skin. She gave a little shudder, making her breasts sway, the beads clacking together, then lifted the corners of her mouth in a smile of sorts.

"Come on," she crooned, grinding against him. "I make you feel good tonight . . . then we go to Tucson tomorrow. . . ."

She lowered her head closer, pressed her lips to his, parting them, sticking the tip of her tongue in his mouth. He didn't lift his hands to her, and he didn't return the kiss, but he didn't resist her. He couldn't deny her pull, and he hadn't had a woman in a long time.

Kissing him again, the young whore pushed her breasts against his chest. She clamped her mouth over his, drew his hands up the backs of her smooth thighs. Hawk closed his fingers over the twin, round globes of her buttocks, kneading them, the girl groaning softly as he squeezed. He opened his mouth, sucked at her tongue, turned his head to fit his mouth over hers.

A sudden image of his young wife, Linda, flashed in his mind. She was scooping eggs from a hot skillet to the plate of their son, Jubal, who bounced a small wooden horse across their kitchen table in Crossroads.

At the same time that Hawk brought his hands up to the girl's shoulders and thrust her away with an angry grunt, a rock thudded down the ridge to his left. He jerked his head that way. The rock tumbled a few yards west of the fire, bulled through the brush, and came to rest at the base of a low hummock.

The whore leapt off Hawk, sitting back on her heels as she grabbed the shirt and drew it across her breasts. "They've found us!"

"Get away from the fire," Hawk ordered, grabbing his rifle and ramming a shell into the breech.

Hunkered on his haunches, he peered up the ridge, the eroded sandstone face copper in the dwindling light. At the lip, a shadow moved.

"Keep your head down," Hawk told the whore, then sprang off his haunches and ran to the base of the ridge.

When he found a trough, he cast another look above, then took the rifle in his left hand and began climbing. Boulders were strewn halfway to the top, making the climbing relatively easy. The last twenty yards were the hardest, his boots slipping on the slippery, grooved face of the sandstone as he cast cautious looks above, ready to dodge a rifle shot.

He hoisted himself over the lip and knelt on one knee, taking the Henry in both hands and looking around, breathing slowly through his nose as he listened above the pounding of his heart.

Faint thuds rose from the other side of the ridge.

Hawk moved slowly forward and peered northward. The thin shadow of a horseback rider galloped a serpentine route through the chaparral, obscured by distance and the shadows leaning out from the rimrocks and saguarros.

The horse dropped into a shallow ravine shrouded in spindly brush, and was gone.

Hawk made his way back down the ridge face, half-sliding the first twenty yards, then climbing carefully down the boulders one rock at a time, turning his face to the ridge and feeling his way with his free hand and his feet.

Near the bottom, his right boot caught in a crevice between two boulders.

Cursing, he fell, his back smashing the ground. Wincing at the pain in his twisted ankle and his back, he looked up.

Two black rifle maws yawned down at him, close enough that Hawk could see individual scratches in the bluing. He ran his gaze back along the barrels, past the

Springfields' receivers and cocked hammers, to the two young men clad in cavalry blues cheeked up to the rifle stocks.

Behind and between them stood another bluebelly — a slender young man with lieutenant's bars on the shoulders of his blue wool tunic. To the lieutenant's right, a big, broken-nosed sergeant was bear-hugging the girl from behind, holding her off the ground and muffling her cries with his meaty left paw.

3.
DEAD TO RIGHTS

Hawk reached for the Russian on his left hip.

"Don't do it, mister," the lieutenant said, holding an Army-issue .44 straight out from his shoulder. "We have you dead to rights."

Hawk froze, slid his gaze from the young lieutenant to the two rifle-wielding soldiers, both wearing privates' stripes and holding the rifles a foot from Hawk's face. The campfire was behind them, so Hawk couldn't see them clearly, but he could tell that they were frowning under the pinned-up brims of their tan kepis.

They weren't the same soldiers that had chased Hawk and the whore from Coyote Springs.

The one on the right took one step back. "He's got a badge, Lieutenant."

The lieutenant stepped forward. He glanced at the ground. Hawk's deputy U.S. marshal's badge had fallen from his vest pocket, where he carried it when he wasn't hunting men. It lay faceup in the red desert caliche a few feet from Hawk's belly, the firelight playing across its polished, dusty surface.

With his left hand, the lieutenant plucked the badge from the dirt, inspected it between his thumb and index finger. He dropped it onto his palm and held it out toward Hawk.

"Sorry about the intrusion, Marshal. The spring there is about the only water in twenty square miles. I hope you don't mind if we share it with you this evening?"

"I don't own the water," Hawk said, taking the badge and slowly climbing to his feet.

"Are you hurt?"

Hawk worked his jaw, glanced at the girl still thrashing in the sergeant's arms, and shook his head. The lieutenant glanced over his left shoulder. "She's with you, I take it?"

"My . . . associate."

"Put her down, Schmidt."

When the sergeant complied, the whore spat at him, swore at him in Spanish. The sober lieutenant turned back to Hawk. "We thought she was with an outlaw gang. We're carrying payroll money to the Sibley outpost. Can't be too careful, you understand."

"I understand," Hawk said. He glanced at the girl again, still spitting Spanish epithets at the sergeant and the two privates walking into the gathering darkness south of the camp. "She, on the other hand, is probably gonna take some time."

The lieutenant studied her. "What brings you two out here, Marshal? She a prisoner or something?"

"An informant." Hawk picked up his rifle, brushed dust from the barrel, then turned back to the lieutenant. "You're heading to the Sibley post, you say?"

"That's right."

"Near Craigville?"

The lieutenant nodded, frowning.

"Mind if she rides along? I got business over east, don't have time to take her there."

The lieutenant hesitated, watching the girl sit grumpily down beside the fire, throw her hair out, and drape her shirttails over her bare knees.

Hawk added, "Her being an informant, and me needing to get to other chores, it *would* be official business."

The lieutenant tugged on his chestnut goatee, the firelight dancing in his brown eyes. Bemusedly, he said, "Rather *distracting* official business, though." He jerked slightly, adding, "To my men, I mean."

Hawk turned up a corner of his mouth. "I'm sure you have them well disciplined."

The lieutenant looked off. Five or six other horseback bluebellies were leading two pack mules and a saddled horse — probably the lieutenant's — toward the spring. Their shadows slid around the creosote and saguaros. The soft hoof falls and desultory voices carried softly on the evening breeze. Smelling the water, one of the mules brayed.

"Have her ready to ride at daybreak," the lieutenant said abruptly, and started away.

"You didn't post a scout on the ridge yonder, did you?" Hawk called.

The lieutenant turned and shook his head. "We scouted the springs in advance, but I didn't send anyone up that rimrock. Why do you ask?"

"A rock fell from the ridge a while ago. I climbed up, spied a single rider galloping north."

The lieutenant nodded. "I'll keep an extra guard posted."

He walked away.

Hawk moved to the fire, poured a fresh cup of coffee, and leaned back against his saddle. The girl was glaring at him.

"They are soldiers!" she spat. "They will rape me and throw me in a ravine."

"I got a feeling you can take care of yourself," Hawk said, and blew on his coffee.

Hawk finished his coffee, then strolled around the campsite. When he'd checked on his horse, he tossed another log on the fire and rolled up in his blankets.

Estella was already asleep, curled under Hawk's extra blanket, using her hands for a pillow.

Hawk lay awake for a time, hearing the soldiers chatting around their own distant fire, and their mules braying at the rising moon. The weariness of the long day caught up to him, and his lids closed down, shutting out the stars.

He didn't know how long he'd slept when soft footfalls startled him. His right hand jerked toward the pistol belt coiled beside his head.

"It is just me," Estella said in an angry whisper. She was kneeling beside him, her blanket draped across her shoulders. Brusquely, she peeled back Hawk's blanket, then lay down beside him, her hair fanning his face. Drawing both blankets over them both, she turned to him, wrapped a bare leg over his, and pressed her face against his chest.

"I am cold," she said. She lifted her chin to scowl up at him. "Only that, so don't get any ideas!"

She snuggled against him, and in a minute she snored softly into his chest.

Hawk was tense and embarrassed. He was reminded again how long it had been since he'd lain with a woman. Finally, he sighed, relaxed, and rested his head against his saddle.

It was going to feel damn good to get shed of this girl.

He woke when Estella stirred at the first wash of dawn. He blinked his eyes groggily as the girl rolled away from him, climbed sleepily to her feet, keeping one of the blankets draped around her shoulders.

Hawk kept his head on the saddle, watching her as she crawled to the dead fire, plucked some dried juniper branches from the pile beside the stone ring. Crunching the branches up in her hands, she leaned over the ashes and blew, gently coaxing a dull orange glow from the gray.

Continuing to blow, she fed the glow with bits of the dried juniper, until a match-sized flame licked up from the ashes, feeding off the tinder. Soon, a small coffee fire snapped and crackled in the fire ring.

Hawk sat up, stretching. "You do that well."

She didn't look at him, just continued to add bits of kindling to the smoking fire.

Hawk reached for a boot, tipped it upside down, and shook it to dislodge any night visitors. "You have anyone in Craigville?" he asked.

"My sister," she said snootily and without looking at him.

He didn't attempt any more conversation. When he'd pulled on his other boot, he and the girl had a cup of coffee and the last of Hawk's jerky and hardtack. Saddling the grulla under the cottonwoods, he could hear the soldiers chatting and chuckling as they rigged up their mounts, chains and buckles clanking, the smell of coffee and corn cakes wafting.

He led the horse back to the fire, where the girl sat, crouched over a tin coffee cup, one bare foot resting on the other as she stared glumly into the flames. Behind her, a horse blew. Hawk looked up to see the straight-backed lieutenant trotting his Army bay toward him, horse and rider looking crisp and official.

"We're about ready to start, Marshal," the lieutenant said, halting his horse a few yards from the fire and turning it sideways. "Is the girl still riding with us?"

"She sure is, Lieutenant."

Hawk looked at Estella. She glanced over her shoulder at the lieutenant and sighed. Lazily, she stood, tossed her coffee into the fire, and handed both the blanket and the cup to Hawk.

He took the cup. "You'll need the blanket till it warms up."

"And the shirt?"

"I grew out of it."

Estella shrugged a shoulder and walked toward the lieutenant, who extended his hand to her. She took it and swung up behind the McClellan saddle, resting her bare calves and knees against the bay's ribs. The lieutenant pinched his hat brim to Hawk, and reined the bay away.

He'd ridden only a few feet before he stopped and turned back.

Hawk tensed.

"I don't believe I caught your name, Marshal."

Hawk glanced at the girl. She was looking at him with one corner of her mouth raised.

"Hollis," Hawk said.

Estella turned away.

The lieutenant nodded. "Homer Primrose." He studied Hawk through slitted eyes, head canted to one side, as if trying to place him. Finally, he turned the bay through the brush. "Good luck with that job over east."

Hawk dropped the girl's cup into a saddlebag, and swung onto his horse. He sighed. It felt good already, being rid of that girl and those soldiers. . . .

With a glance at the rising sun, he heeled the grulla south, toward Mexico.

Two hours later, Estella Chacon walked through strewn, sunbaked boulders, then stopped and looked back the way she'd come to make sure the soldiers couldn't see her. She raised her dress above her waist and squatted down beside a bunchgrass clump.

"With alacrity, Miss Chacon!" the lieutenant called beyond the boulders. "We have a schedule to keep!"

Estella looked up as her pee hissed in the gravel. In Spanish she snarled, "Soldier bastard, you make me ride two hours without stopping, and then you expect me to pee as fast as a bird shits!"

Estella took her time.

When she was finished, she stood, dropped her dress and shirttails over her knees, and strolled with exaggerated nonchalance through the boulders. In a hollow,

40

the eight soldiers sat their saddles or stood holding water-filled hats from which their horses drank.

A couple smoked and chatted.

The lieutenant was staring toward Estella, an impatient frown on his face. "Come along, miss. We have —"

"*Sí, sí* — we have a schedule to keep," Estella grumbled, adding under her breath, *"Soldado bastardo."*

"Better let her ride with me for a spell, Lieutenant," said the big red-bearded sergeant, his sun-blistered cheeks bunching as he grinned. "Your gelding needs a break."

"I'll take her, Lieutenant," offered the private dumping water from his hat and squinting up at Estella. He ran his eyes up and down her body. "I don't mind a bit."

"Let her ride with me, Lieutenant," said a scrawny soldier who looked about twelve in his overlarge uniform and floppy-brimmed hat. Dung-brown chew dribbled down his chin. Chuckling, he grabbed himself. "She can ride right here!"

Several of the other men joined in the scrawny soldier's laughter. Blushing, the lieutenant admonished them all to calm down.

"You take her, Sergeant. Certainly you, the oldest one here, will be able to control yourself."

"Of course I can, Lieutenant," the sergeant said with a wink, leaning out from his horse and extending a hand to Estella. "You just let ol' Sergeant Schmidt take care of the lovely *puta*." He ran his small blue eyes across the round mounds in the blue-checked shirt. "Remember me? We met in Coyote Springs a while back."

Making a face and drawing the corners of her blanket across her chest, Estella looked at the lieutenant. "I would rather ride with you."

"My horse needs a break, miss," the lieutenant said.

"She'll be safer with me than the sergeant," intoned a blond private holding the lead of one of the pack mules. "You shoulda seen how the sarge acted in Contention last month. Why, I never seen such — !"

The soldier's eyes had found the sergeant's threatening gaze. Flushing, he cut himself off with a cough, then cleared his throat and, fidgeting, turned to look over the head of his bay.

Several others snickered.

"With haste please, miss," the lieutenant urged.

Curling her upper lip, Estella took the sergeant's hand, let him swing her up behind him.

"Well, it ain't no whorehouse feather mattress, miss," the sergeant said, chuckling. "But I hope you're not *too* uncomfortable!"

In Spanish, Estella called him a bearded sow. As the sergeant threw his massive head back, laughing, the girl reluctantly tucked her fingers behind his cartridge belt, bracing herself for travel.

The lieutenant spurred his horse to the head of the pack and shouted, *"For-ward!"*

Estella's butt bounced as the sergeant heeled his own mount ahead, riding left of the scrawny private, who led one of the pack mules.

As they rode through the twisting, scrubby hills, the scrawny private ogled Estella and made lewd gestures. She did her best to ignore him, but more dust rose on her left than on her right, so the best she could do was turn her head to the right and keep her eyes closed.

They'd been riding for nearly an hour when Estella opened them to see where they were. The private who'd been ogling her now rode slumped in his saddle, his expression bored, a wad of chew swelling his cheek. They were topping a low rise, boulders strewn along both sides of the trail. A high, broad scarp with a concave face loomed farther back on the right.

A bird called loudly from just ahead and left. It had a vaguely artificial ring to it.

Estella turned her head to look that way. As she did, a figure climbed swiftly onto a large, flat boulder and just stood there, fists on his hips.

Her hips.

In spite of the male clothing — snug denims, flannel shirt, and leather vest — Estella saw the womanly curves and the long hair falling from the woman's flat-brimmed hat. Silhouetted against the brassy sky, the woman held a long, thin cigar between her teeth.

Estella blinked disbelievingly. The woman had to be a hallucination or a heat mirage.

But then one of the horses whinnied, and a soldier uttered a shocked exclamation.

The sergeant moved his right hand to his covered holster. Estella watched as he unsnapped the cover, removed his revolver, aimed it straight out at the scrawny private on his right, and pulled the trigger.

The revolver jerked, popped, and smoked.

Estella started back in horror, but kept her fingers wedged behind the sergeant's cartridge belt, staring awestruck at the scrawny soldier.

A small, round hole appeared in his left

cheek. The kid flinched as if slapped, then tumbled headfirst down his horse's right shoulder. He hadn't yet hit the ground before the sergeant swung his pistol straight ahead, and fired another shot. His horse had turned so that Estella had a clear view of the sergeant's bullet plowing through the back of the soldier straight ahead.

As the horse leapt forward, the soldier tensed and threw his head back. Blood spurted through the hole in his tunic.

As if the sergeant's second shot had been the signal, gunfire erupted from the boulders on both sides of the trail, orange fire stabbing through smoke puffs. None of the soldiers had so much as touched their holsters before the bullets began thumping into them, evoking screams from the men as well as the horses.

As the sergeant's own bay wheeled and skitter-hopped, starting at the gunfire, Estella glanced left of the trail. The woman she'd seen a moment before was hunkered down on her haunches atop the boulder, firing a silver-plated pistol with each hand, the cigar still clutched in her teeth, gun smoke wafting around her head.

The sergeant's horse wheeled sharply left. Estella's fingers slipped from behind the big man's belt. She was tossed like a corn-shuck doll off the horse's left hip, hitting the ground hard on her left shoulder.

Gritting her teeth against the pain, she gained her feet and began scrambling off the trail — she was too disoriented from the smoke and the gunfire and the screams to know in which direction — when a fleeing, shrieking horse materialized from the smoke, and rammed its shoulder into her chest, knocking her flat.

The back of her head smacked a rock.

Lights flashed behind her eyelids and a shrill, inner screech tempered the din around her. Something fell over her legs. She raised her head, blinking her eyes and pressing her hands against the ground as if to keep it from pitching.

The blond-headed soldier, missing his hat, his face bloody, had fallen over her shins. He raised himself clumsily to his hands and knees. As he lifted his head and began crawling away, a bullet plunked into the back of his skull. His forehead exploded.

The soldier's ruined head bobbed furiously up and down, spraying blood, brains, and bone, and then his chest hit the ground a few feet away from Estella. His scuffed brogans jerked as though he'd been struck by lightning.

Estella watched him as if in a dream. Her

own limbs grew heavy.

The sun faded behind the wafting smoke. The world went dark and silent. She didn't know how long she'd been out before someone lifted her head by her hair, searing her entire body with nauseating pain.

The big sergeant stared down at her, grinning, his dusty face streaked and beaded with sweat. A woman's face appeared beside his — the pretty, oval-shaped face of the woman who'd been firing the silver-plated revolvers and smoking a cigar. Her cool eyes were turquoise blue. She no longer had the cigar in her teeth, but Estella knew it couldn't be far away. She could smell it beneath the rotten-egg odor of the gun smoke.

The woman's straight, honey blond hair blew about her dusty, suntanned cheeks.

"What the hell do we have here?" she said, scowling at the sergeant.

"This here?" The sergeant's grin broadened. "This is just a little something I picked up along the way."

Estella's eyes closed. She sank down, down through warm, black tar.

4.
Buzzard Bait

Gideon Hawk was riding high above the desert floor, traversing a broad jog of saguaro-studded hills, when he halted the grulla suddenly and turned to peer back the way he'd come.

In the pink, sunbaked basin below — several miles out from where the hills began rising from the desert floor — a shot had sounded.

He waited, listening.

Cicadas whined. To his right, a roadrunner or a rabbit rustled the sunbaked brush.

Another shot sounded, so faint it might have been a twig snapping just beyond the last rise he'd crossed. But the sound was too sharp, with a spanging, lingering echo.

Several more shots rose from the plain — angrily, hastily fired rounds. Too many to be those of a hunter. Indians, possibly, but Hawk hadn't crossed any Apache sign, had seen no smoke talk.

The shots had come from a long ways away. It would take him an hour to ride back to the base of the hills, and probably another hour, traversing cuts and low rim-rocks, to reach the site of the shooting.

By the time he got to the scene, the shooting would long be over, the shooters gone. Whoever they'd been shooting at would be gone as well. One way or the other . . .

Hawk stared out over the plain, sweat funneling through the blond dust on his sunburnt cheeks, soaking the thick mustache drooping down both sides of his mouth. His eyes were hooded, haunted, brooding.

The shots had come from the direction the soldiers had ridden.

The soldiers and the girl.

Hawk lifted his canteen from his saddle horn, took a few sips, draped the lanyard back over the horn. He adjusted his seat on the sweat-damp saddle, nudged the grulla's flanks, and continued along the trail, weaving through the heavy shrubs and cracked, clay-colored boulders.

After fifty yards, he pulled back on the reins, sat staring over the horse's ears.

"Ah, *hell!*"

He neck-reined the grulla around and trotted back the way he'd come, retracing the old Indian trail switchbacking across the knobs. Nearly an hour later, the flat, burning desert stretched before him. It took him another hour to cut the soldiers' sign.

The sun was nearing the two o'clock position when, weaving through the creosote and crossing dry arroyos, he came upon a horse standing hang-headed, reins drooping, at the bottom of a shallow wash. The horse stood sideways to Hawk, its eyes half-closed, as if sleeping. Something hung down from its saddle on the far side.

Hawk dismounted, dropped the grulla's reins, and walked over to the horse — dirty, scratched, and sweat-lathered, its breath raspy. It had run itself to exhaustion. Walking around the horse's rear, Hawk stopped beside its left hip. His breath caught in his throat.

Before him, a soldier lay facedown in the bloody rocks. His left boot was caught in the stirrup, the ankle broken and twisted. The kid's tunic was tattered and bloody, barely hanging from his skinny frame. The dragging wasn't what had killed him, however. The bullet that had been drilled between his shoulder blades, no doubt blowing out his heart, had done the deed.

Hawk kicked the private's foot free of the stirrup, then hurried back to his horse. He mounted up and followed the dead private's tracks through the catclaw, over the skeletons of fallen saguaros, across a dry wash, and up the side of a low, cedar-stippled knoll.

Hawk halted the grulla atop the knoll, a pipestem cactus angling a long shadow to his right. Below, in the brush between two vast boulder snags, buzzards fought and quarreled over and between the half-dozen or so bloody, blue-clad bodies and over the large brown humps of two fallen horses. The fallen soldiers were laid out side by side in a relatively rock-free patch of caliche.

Blood was splashed around them like paint.

One of the shaggy, black buzzards, perched on the head of a dead soldier, squawked and turned its grizzled bald head toward Hawk, a bloody eyeball dangling from its hooked beak. The bird leapt from the soldier's head and ran, bounding awkwardly and spreading its massive wings, into the dense chaparral beyond the dead men.

Hawk lifted his gaze as something moved in the brush down the grade ahead and left. A soldier backed toward him, crouching and stumbling as he dragged a body toward the six already laid out. He turned his head to one side, to see where he was going.

Suddenly, he stopped with a grunt,

dropped the dead man's ankles, and whipped around. He stumbled right and forward, and dropped to one knee, clutching his right side.

As the man looked up from under the brim of his battered kepi, the sweaty, blood-streaked face of Lieutenant Primrose shone in the harsh light. He reached for the pistol on his right hip. Apparently realizing Hawk was out of the six-shooter's range, he pushed off his knee and ran toward the carbine leaning against one of the fallen horses.

"Hold on, Lieutenant," Hawk called, gigging his horse down the knoll and touching his Colt's butt. "It's Hollis."

Frowning up the knoll at Hawk, his lower jaw hanging, the lieutenant slowed to a shambling, heavy-footed walk. Primrose grabbed the carbine by the barrel, then sat heavily down on a rock, laying the Spencer across his thighs. He watched Hawk with a wary, puzzled expression, as if he wasn't sure he could trust his vision.

As Hawk reined up before the man, the fear in the lieutenant's eyes abated. He removed his yellow kerchief, doffed his hat, and mopped his brow and sweat-soaked goatee. Blood dribbled down from a gash on the side of his head. More of it stained the right side of his tunic.

Something behind Hawk caught the lieutenant's attention. Suddenly, he dropped the kerchief, grabbed his carbine, ran past Hawk toward a buzzard pecking the back of a dead private, and fired.

The bird screamed as the slug blew it off the dead soldier. It flapped in a broad circle, wings beating the ground insanely, chortling and squawking as it ran down like a child's top, and died. Around it, several other buzzards barked and ran for cover.

"Bloody scavengers!" the lieutenant shouted, tears welling in his eyes as he ejected the smoking shell. He rammed a fresh slug into the Spencer's chamber, but held the gun low by his side, staring at the soldiers lined out before him.

Flies buzzed around the glistening blood pools. Cicadas whined. High up in the brassy sky, a hawk screeched.

"What happened?" Hawk asked.

The lieutenant sighed, set the rifle down against the rock, and walked back to the body he'd been dragging when Hawk had first spotted him.

"Ambushed," Primrose said thickly, staring down at the dead private. "They were waiting in the rocks." He turned to look at Hawk, his rheumy eyes slitted with fury.

"Sergeant Schmidt was in with them."

"How many?"

Primrose shrugged. "I had no time to count them, Mr. Hollis. They took me by surprise. Before I knew what was happening, my horse had unseated me. I crawled away and began returning fire with my revolver."

The lieutenant leaned down, grabbed the body by both ankles, and straightened. "A bullet ricocheted off my shoulder holster, burned my side. I went down, hit my head on a rock. They left me for dead."

He paused, head hanging. His shoulders jerked. He turned to Hawk, laughing coldly. "One was a woman. A beautiful, deadly woman. I froze when I saw her, thought surely she must have been a mirage!"

He laughed again, stepped back, and began dragging the body toward the others he'd positioned side by side for burial.

Hawk took another look around. "What happened to the girl?"

"I haven't seen her body, so I assume they took her."

Hawk turned his horse around, rode slowly back the way he'd come, scouring the ground for tracks. "Did you see which way they went?"

"No." Behind Hawk, Primrose's voice

sounded pinched.

Hawk turned. The lieutenant had fallen to his knees again, head bowed, holding his right arm taut to his bloody tunic.

Hawk cursed and rode back to where Primrose crouched beside a cholla. Dismounting, he looped his reins over the grulla's saddle horn, then squatted before the lieutenant. "Let me take a look."

"I have to bury my men," the lieutenant said weakly. "It's the least I can do. Should have sent a scout ahead." He shook his head. Again, tears filled his eyes. "Just didn't think we'd be hit out here . . . small group . . . traveling cross-country . . ."

Hawk pushed him back, quickly unbuttoned his tunic, and peeled the right side away from the shoulder holster decorated with a Union medallion showing an eagle with spread wings. The disc was dented and creased where the bullet had hit. Behind the holster, the ricocheting slug had torn a deep, bloody path about six inches long.

Hawk cursed again and looked around. He had to get on the trail of those bushwackers before dark, but the lieutenant looked too dazed and weak to tend to himself.

"Come on, Lieutenant," Hawk said, standing and grabbing the man's left arm. "Let's get you into some shade and wrap those wounds."

Primrose shook his head. "I have to . . ."

"You don't have the strength to bury them. The commander at Bowie will send a detail."

"There'll be nothing left of them!"

Hawk pulled the lieutenant to his feet, drew the man's left arm over his shoulders, and led him away from the growing stench of death. The soldier was too weak to resist. Hawk clucked to the grulla, which followed, rolling its eyes uneasily at the carnage and the persistent buzzards returning from the brush jerking cautious, hungry looks around the gap between the boulder piles.

"~~Goddamn~~ Schmidt," the lieutenant said as Hawk eased him down in the shade of a paloverde. "Murdering son of a bitch. I'm going to dog his murdering ass . . . *ahhh! That hurts.*"

As he'd leaned back against the tree, he'd pulled the wound open. He clapped his arm and head over his side, breathing sharply through his teeth.

"You think that hurt," Hawk said, returning from his horse with a roll of bandages he'd fashioned from an old sheet, and a bottle of whiskey. "Try this on for size."

He popped the cork, nudged the lieutenant onto his left shoulder, and tipped the bottle over the eight-inch gash. When the whiskey hit the burn, the lieutenant arched his spine, threw back his head, and bunched his face with misery.

"Oh, *mercy!*"

While the lieutenant still had his head back, Hawk poured more whiskey over the gash in his head.

"Oh, *Christ!*"

When Hawk had cleaned both wounds and wrapped bandages around the lieutenant's lower chest and his forehead, he mounted the grulla and ran down one of the soldiers' saddled horses. A canteen hung from the saddle horn. Hawk led the horse back to the lieutenant and, without dismounting the grulla, tied the reins to a branch of the paloverde.

"You have a horse, weapons, and water," Hawk said. "You best rest here overnight and head back to Fort Bowie in the morning."

Hawk began reining away from the tree.

"Where're you going?" the lieutenant called.

"See you around, Lieutenant."

"I'm going with you."

Hawk turned. The lieutenant was pushing himself to his feet. "Stay put, Lieutenant.

You're addlepated."

"They're my men . . . my responsibility . . ."

When the lieutenant, lips stretched with pain, sagged back down against the tree, Hawk gigged the grulla into a trot, began scouring the ground around the carnage for the killers' sign. Twenty minutes later, he'd found where the bushwackers had tied their horses. It wasn't hard to see which direction they'd headed after they'd gathered the payroll-bearing mules and the girl.

Due south.

Hawk turned toward the paloverde. Again, the lieutenant was trying to stand, holding his arm against his side, his gritted teeth white against the dark hollows of his blood-smeared face. He was a tough, young bastard, but Hawk doubted he'd be able to climb onto his horse before his concussion convinced him it was a bad idea.

Hawk turned the grulla south and gigged it into a trot, following the tracks of the ten shod horses down a rocky shelf and onto a low table surrounded by distant blue, red-tipped mountains.

He'd ridden an hour through a shallow, jagged-edged basin when, pausing to drink, he spotted a small purple figure moving behind him. Frowning, he lowered the canteen, reined the grulla up a low table of sandstone, and raised his binoculars.

As he adjusted the focus, a bay horse bearing a blue-clad, slump-shouldered rider took shape. The rider wore a white bandage under the brim of his tan kepi. The horse plodded along slowly, the rider's head dipping toward the bay's jostling mane. The brass buttons of his tunic winked in the west-angling sunlight.

Hawk was about to snarl a curse when more movement appeared behind the lieutenant. His frown deepening, Hawk again raised the binoculars.

He lowered them and cursed sharply.

Flanking the lieutenant were four war-painted Apaches.

5.
INDIAN TROUBLE

Holding his hands over the ends of his binoculars to prevent the sun from reflecting off the glass, Hawk stared past the hang-headed lieutenant.

Sure enough. Four Apaches. Young braves, judging by how straight they sat their saddles and how brightly their cherry skin glistened in the west-angling light.

And sure enough, the color on their faces was no trick of the sun. It was war paint. They were four renegades, no doubt, who, weary of hoeing potatoes at San Carlos, had decided to raise some hell with the white-eyes.

The lieutenant was about two hundred yards away from Hawk. The Indians were another hundred yards behind the lieutenant. Riding abreast, they trotted their horses around the towering saguaros and low stone scarps, casting quick, frequent glances at each other, as if unable to believe their luck

— a bluebelly traveling alone.

Hawk dropped the field glasses back into his saddlebags, then reined the grulla off the stone shelf, hoping the late-afternoon shadows had concealed him from the Apaches as they'd apparently concealed him from Lieutenant Primrose. Hawk heeled the grulla northward across the basin, then back the way he'd come.

When he figured he was within a hundred or so yards of the Indians, he dismounted the grulla, shucked his Henry, rammed a shell into the chamber, then off-cocked the hammer. Crouching and weaving through the paloverdes and cholla shading a shallow ravine, he moved toward the middle of the basin and, hopefully, into the renegades' path.

As he moved along a sandy swale, a horse whinnied ahead and left — probably the lieutenant's bay, which meant the four Apaches wouldn't be far behind.

Hawk continued forward, setting his boots down softly in the coarse, red sand. Ahead, a horse nickered. Hawk began running toward it. He'd covered only ten yards before a bare, copper leg lashed out from behind a boulder on his right, too quickly for Hawk to avoid it.

He slammed down hard on his belly, his

Henry bouncing off his right thigh and tumbling off to the side.

Hawk rolled onto his back as the young Apache leaned over him, grinning savagely and aiming a nocked arrow at his face. The ash bow squawked, the sinew chirped as the renegade increased the tension. The brave's right hand opened. At the same time, Hawk flung himself left, hearing the projectile thump into the sand where his head had just been.

Hawk reached across his belly for his Russian. He'd thumbed the hammer back and begun squeezing the trigger when the kid, fast as a panther, kicked the gun from Hawk's right hand. The Russian popped, the slug sailing skyward as the revolver spun into the brush.

Catching the brave's moccasined foot, Hawk rolled off his right shoulder, giving the foot a hard tug and lifting the kid off his other foot. Yelling savagely, the brave arced through the air, hitting the ground on his back.

Hawk gained his feet only a half second before the brave had scrambled back to a crouching position, black eyes slitted furiously, chapped lips stretched back from brown teeth. Thonged talismans jostled about his hard, flat chest.

As the kid tried to read Hawk's next move, Hawk kicked him, the toe of his right boot connecting soundly with the brave's breastbone.

The renegade only snorted, stumbled back, and flung himself straight forward and up, bulling Hawk onto his back. Hawk slammed his left elbow across the renegade's jaw, which made a cracking sound as the brave slumped to the left.

Footsteps rose to Hawk's right as he climbed to his feet. He turned. Another brave — shorter, stockier than the first — ran toward him raising an Apache war lance bedecked with tribal feathers and talismans. As the brave, screeching like a wounded lobo, flung the lance, Hawk dropped to his knees.

A thud and the sound of crunching bone rose behind him. Glancing quickly left, he saw the first brave stumbling straight back, broken jaw hanging askew, eyes wide, the stone blade of the lance intended for Hawk buried in his chest. He grabbed the lance with both hands, blood geysering over them, his eyes growing wider until he stumbled over a rock and hit the ground on his back.

Hawk turned back to the second brave, who continued sprinting toward him, his jaws set hard, long hair flapping across his shoulders.

Again, Hawk ducked. The kid's left knee slammed into Hawk's side. As the brave fell forward, Hawk rose, throwing the kid straight up and over his back, careening atop the first brave, who gurgled as he died.

The second brave bounded to his haunches, reaching for the stag-handled knife on his right hip. Hawk straightened, clawed his Colt from its holster, and shot the kid twice through the forehead.

The stocky renegade stumbled back over the first, who now lay still, and dropped to his back, his ankles crossed over the first brave's throat.

A fast-moving horse thundered behind Hawk, close enough that Hawk could hear the horse's labored snorts. A shrill, angry keening sounded beneath the hooves.

As Hawk wheeled and began to raise the Colt, he caught a glimpse of his rifle lying between a bunchgrass clump and an ironwood shrub. He ran, picked up the rifle, dropped to a knee, and peered up the shallow wash.

The horse and rider shot toward him, the brave hunched low over his horse's neck, his brightly painted face bunched with fury. A bow and deer-hide quiver jostled on his left shoulder.

As he approached to within fifteen yards, the brave raised the lance in his right hand. Hawk snapped the rifle to his shoulder, taking quick aim, firing, then throwing himself sideways as the horse roared past him, screaming.

Hawk wheeled toward the horse, ejecting the spent shell, then freezing as the horse disappeared down the wash, its blanket saddle empty, braided reins trailing along the ground.

In the distance, a rifle spoke, too far away to have been aimed at Hawk.

Turning up trail, Hawk cast his gaze about, looking for the third renegade. Nothing but brush, rocks, and sand. He shoved the rifle's cocking lever home, seating a fresh shell in the chamber, and walked slowly between the wash's low banks.

In the distance, several more rifle shots rang out, the lead no doubt being exchanged by Primrose and the fourth Indian. Hawk ignored them, for the moment wanting to make sure of the third renegade's fate.

Hawk continued forward. Ahead and slightly right, blood dripped down the side of a rock. Beyond was a mesquite tree, the branches hanging over the trunk like a dusty green tablecloth. Hawk moved to the tree, tightened his finger on the Henry's trigger, and swept the branches aside with the barrel.

His trigger finger relaxed.

The third brave lay before the tree, hands resting palms up at his sides. His head was propped against the mesquite's thin trunk, open eyes staring unseeing at his own still chest, the bullet through his forehead dripping bright red blood onto the bridge of his broad nose.

Hawk let the branches fall back into place as, in the distance, the rifle shots continued, spanging and echoing around the basin.

Hawk whistled for his horse and jogged up the wash. It didn't take the grulla long to catch up to him, reins trailing. Grabbing the reins and keeping the Henry in his right hand, Hawk swung into the hurricane deck and galloped toward the shooting.

Five minutes later, he halted the horse on a rocky rise.

Straight below in the sun-and-shadow-stippled basin, another Indian ran out from behind a low shelf, his upper left arm glistening red. As he headed for another shelf just ahead, a rifle rang out. The Indian dropped his bow and arrow and, grabbing his right thigh, fell, sliding several feet along the ground.

Looking west along the basin, Hawk saw

the smoke puff lifting from a yucca plant at the base of a broad, sandstone ledge standing about ten feet above the basin floor. A tan kepi appeared. The sunlight reflected off the lieutenant's carbine.

Screaming, the Indian bolted to his feet and ran toward the shelf. He hadn't limped five yards before the lieutenant's Spencer spoke again.

The Indian stopped, throwing both arms out, the bow and arrow flying high over his head. He staggered backward and fell, dust billowing, red showing amidst the sweat-glistening copper of his chest.

The lieutenant's rifle boomed once more, the slug making a dull thumping, crunching sound as it plowed through the Indian's skull. After a minute, the lieutenant lifted his head from behind the yucca, staring toward Hawk.

Hawk lifted his Henry. "I'm coming over, Lieutenant."

A few minutes later, he halted the grulla on the west side of the shelf from which the lieutenant had drilled the fourth Indian. Primrose was returning his carbine to his saddle boot, his implacable face streaked with sweat and pink dust, the bandage around his forehead spotted with blood.

Clumsily, he swung into his saddle, adjusted the bandage on his forehead, spat, and turned to Hawk. "We'd better make use of what little daylight we have left," he said, glancing at the sky and gigging the bay forward. "I know Schmidt will."

Hawk stared at the young officer's back, cursed silently the younker's mulishness. He slid his own rifle into the saddle boot and urged the grulla into the lieutenant's sifting, salmon-colored dust.

He'd ridden only a few yards when movement atop the high left ridge caught his eye. As he turned toward it, he caught a glimpse of a hatted head as it pulled back behind the ridge's lip. Again, he was too far away to see clearly, but the high-crowned Stetson bespoke a white man.

He ran his eyes along the sun-pinkened lip, spat, and gigged the grulla ahead, keeping pace with the obstinate Primrose.

When the sun had fallen so low that they could no longer see the tracks of the fleeing killers, Hawk and Primrose camped in a box canyon, picketing their horses amidst desert willows and Mormon tea.

Sitting on a rock beside the small, curl-leaf fire, Hawk reached for the coffeepot, intending to refill his tin cup for the second time that night.

He glanced at the lieutenant leaning back against his saddle on the other side of the fire. Hawk had felt the man's eyes on him, studying him. Now the lieutenant grinned shrewdly, his brushy, brown mustache forming a straight line beneath his nose.

Hawk watched as Primrose transferred his own steaming coffee cup to his left hand, and slid his Colt Army from his covered holster. Chuckling without mirth, Primrose aimed the revolver at Hawk, and thumbed the hammer back.

"I just remembered where I'd seen your face before."

Hawk dropped his gaze and continued plucking the pot from the fire, using a blackened leather swatch. He filled his tin cup with the coal-black, piping-hot brew. "You don't say."

"Major Devereaux at Fort Bowie passed a federal wanted dodger around to all us officers. Your face was on it . . . Gideon Hawk." Primrose curled his upper lip. "*Deputy United States Marshal* Gideon Hawk."

Hawk returned the pot to a hot rock within the fire ring. "I sure never expected to be so famous."

"And I never expected to find myself riding with a wanted vigilante. Rumor has it a death warrant's been issued on you. That true?"

Hawk sipped the joe, leaned back against his saddle. "That's what I hear."

"By rights then, I should kill you."

"I reckon you should."

Primrose canted his head to one side. "I don't understand — what's in this for you? Surely it's not just the doxy."

Hawk shrugged. "Maybe it's the money."

"I didn't think that was your style. Maybe you just need an excuse to kill."

"Killing killers would be a pretty good excuse, wouldn't it?" Hawk also wanted to get the girl back, though he wasn't sure why. Maybe, having sent her off with the doomed soldiers, he felt he owed her something. Certainly, it wasn't because of the few minutes they'd spent rolling around by the campfire. . . .

Or was it?

The lieutenant stared at him, keeping the revolver aimed at Hawk's chest. The fire danced in his heavy-lidded, brown eyes. Hawk stared back at him stoically, Hawk's own dark eyes set deep under heavy brows.

The fire snapped, pine smoke curling toward the stars. The coffeepot chugged. A coyote yammered from a nearby ridge as, to

Hawk's left, one of the horses lay down and rolled.

The lieutenant tipped up his revolver's barrel, depressed the hammer, and slowly slid the Colt back into its holster. "When this is over, I'll have to arrest you, Marshal."

Hawk sipped his coffee and crossed his ankles. "I reckon you'll have to try."

6.
A Hot-Blooded Woman

At the same time, and about twelve miles south of Hawk's and Primrose's campsite, Rance Jacobs stepped inside a small, knocked-together prospector's cabin at the base of Las Guijas Ridge in southern Arizona, and closed the rickety door behind him.

He stood before the threshold, his leather-billed hat in his hands, staring absently into the dimly lit interior, where his partner, Grover Caslin, was preparing javelina steaks and hush puppies on a sheet-iron stove.

The room was smoky and fetid with wild pig and the rancid grease Caslin was frying it in.

Caslin turned from the stove, a bloody apron around his broad waist, curls the color of iron filings hanging in his eyes, and the long scar on his cheek looking unnaturally white against the desert-seasoned skin around it.

Frowning, he looked his prospecting partner up and down. "What the hell's nippin' at your udders?"

"I hate this time o' day," Jacobs said, working his fingers along the brim of his shabby hat as his black gaze burned into the cabin's back wall. "Suppertime . . . when I got so many long hours ahead to sit here in the cabin or out by the wash before bedtime, thinking of all the pussy I'm missing over to Tombstone."

"Jesus Christ!" the portly Caslin admonished, flipping one of the steaks. "I've heard enough of your damn complainin' about missed pussy! Haven't I staked you to this damn claim? *My* claim? And ain't I done told you that when we strike it big out here, we'll go to Tombstone or Tucson or Prescott or any damn where we please, and dip our wicks to our hearts' content!"

Jacobs scowled and slapped his hat against his thigh, moving to the rough-hewn table as though trudging through mud. "Yeah, I've been hearin' your yammerin' fer the past two months. You an' the ~~goddamn~~ coyotes are all I *got* to listen to."

Caslin grabbed a bottle from a shelf, took a pull, then set it on the table before Jacobs. "Have you a swallow o' that, you ungrateful pup."

73

Moving back to the stove, Caslin said over his shoulder, "You don't get rich overnight. It takes hard work and isolation. A little time off from pussy!"

Jacobs took a long drink from the bottle, slammed it back down on the table, ran his hand across his mouth. "I'm a young man. I need to have my ashes hauled regular. You know what I mean, Grover? Hell, I'm startin' to think stage-robbin' wasn't such a bad way to make a livin'."

Caslin flipped a hush puppy in the sputtering oil, then pointed his greasy tin spatula at his taller, younger partner. "That's the problem with you young pups nowadays. You want everything, includin' pussy, to come easy. You don't think you should have to work fer it. Why, in my day —"

Caslin cut himself off as Jacobs turned an ear to the door, as if listening.

"What is it?" Caslin said above the popping of the grease in the iron skillet. "Pussy?" He'd opened his mouth to guffaw, lifting his right knee to slap it, when the door burst open.

Wood shards sprayed from the latch as the plank door slammed against the wall with a thundering boom, making the whole cabin jump.

As Jacobs bounded up from his chair with

74

a startled yell, knocking the bottle over, Caslin leapt straight back from the stove, terror etched on his sun-seared features, instinctively thrusting the spatula out like a weapon.

"What in Christ — ?" Jacobs exclaimed, blinking his eyes disbelievingly at the open doorway.

He and Rance had half-expected a bear to be standing there. Possibly a renegade Apache. Certainly, not the young, high-breasted woman who stood before the open door, feet spread and shuttling her cool, blue-eyed gaze between the two prospectors, gloved hands on the pearl-gripped pistols jutting from the cross-draw, *buscadero* holsters on both her lean hips.

She was dressed in a man's trail garb, long, gold-blond hair falling straight to her shoulders.

A cigar smoldered between her wide, full lips. Her hickory shirt was unbuttoned far enough to reveal a good bit of deep, suntanned cleavage. Amidst his shock and terror, Jacobs felt the automatic tingle of lust deep in his loins.

The woman stepped into the room, her face flushed with anger. "Why in the hell are you two sacks of hog crap talking about pussy?" She ran her disdainful gaze up and down each man in turn, squinting over the smoking cigar in her teeth. "Look at you! What woman in her right mind would spread her legs for two human dung beetles like yourselves?"

Young Jacobs and old Caslin stood frozen, mouths agape, casting tense, disbelieving glances between them, then back to the beautiful, albeit rough-hewn, young woman standing in their cabin's open door. Behind Caslin, the javelina continued sizzling, the grease popping and sputtering.

As she took two menacing steps forward, two men appeared in the doorway and followed her into the room, casting quick, wary glances about the hovel. Jacobs wasn't as frightened as disappointed that the girl wasn't alone.

One man was a big red-bearded gent with small, sharp blue eyes and wearing a cavalry uniform with a tan kepi. The other was tall, lean, long-haired, and flat-eyed, with a shaggy dark-blond mustache dripping down both sides of his mouth. The soldier carried a carbine, the other man a long-barreled Smith & Wesson, the shoulder holster under his open duster hanging free.

"Easy now," Caslin beseeched the interlopers. "I don't know who ya are, but —"

"The only woman who'd spread 'em fer

the likes of you two's a whore — ain't that right?" the woman snarled, her eyes glassy with rage. "You slip them a few dollars, or you slip their *pimp* a few dollars, then you climb out of those grimy duds that have never been cleaned, and crawl between their bought-and-paid-for legs. 'Cause that's all either of you could ever get . . . lookin' like you do . . . smellin' like you do . . . is a poor, down-on-her-luck frontier *whore!*"

"Come on, Saradee," complained the tall man with the gray eyes and mustache, who'd taken a position right of the door, his Smithy held out before him. "Let's not start sawin' on that old fiddle."

"As if that's what she was born to do," the woman said, continuing her tirade, shuttling her furious gaze between the two prospectors, both standing tongue-tied and frozen before her. "As if they weren't nothin' more but a warm hole to stick your dicks in . . . you pathetic piles of sunbaked *dog* shit!"

As she swung around, sauntering toward Jacobs, the younger prospector held both hands up, palms out. "Please, miss . . . now . . . we didn't mean no ha —"

"Didn't mean no harm?" the woman mocked. "Treating women like rented mules you can whip to your heart's content, and you didn't mean no *harm?*"

"Come on, Miss Saradee," said the big, red-bearded soldier standing on the other side of the door from the tall gent in the duster. "It's gettin' late and I'm hungry —" The other man reached across the doorway, slapped him with his hat, cutting him off.

As if she hadn't heard, the young woman called Saradee swung back toward Caslin. "You see, I know what it's like to be one of those rented mules. I was one for two *long* years." She threw her head back, holding her hair behind her ear with her right hand. "That's how I got this." When she'd given old Caslin a good look, she turned that side of her head toward Jacobs. A long, knotted pink scar angled down from just in front of her ear to her shoulder.

"Almost bled to death," she said, "lyin' in the middle of a fuckin' saloon floor with a broken bottle in my neck . . . left to die . . . like a rented mule that just couldn't take it anymore."

Jacobs winced at the ugly scar, took another step back toward the far wall. He kept his hands up before him. "I bet you're claim-jumpers, huh? That it? Well, hell, me and old Grover had enough of this isolated livin' anyways. Tell you what . . . you can *have* our claim. Right now, tonight." He glanced at Caslin. "Ain't that right, Grove?"

Caslin's eyes were bright as he nodded. "Sure as skunk shit under a —"

"We don't want your ~~goddamn~~ claims." Saradee moved toward the old prospector. "We just want a place to bed down tonight. And I'll be ~~goddamned~~ if I'll bed down anywhere near two stinky, greasy, ugly, limp-dick rock farmers like the two of you."

She crossed her arms before her belly, slid both silver-plated pistols from the cross-draw holsters, and thumbed back the hammers. Jacobs stared at her, wide-eyed, his jaw hanging.

"Look at that," she said disgustedly as she glared at Jacobs. "Your life is hangin'. by a thread, but you've still got time to look at my tits."

"N-no," Jacobs said, backing against the far wall, sweat dribbling down his cheeks, hands held to his shoulders. "I just dropped my eyes a second. I wasn't lookin' at anything."

"You looked at my tits, you horny little weasel!"

Jacobs looked at the men standing on both sides of the door watching the woman as if observing a theater play from behind the curtain, their expressions flickering between amazement and amusement.

"For the love o' Christ!" the young prospector shrieked. "Can't you stop her?"

"You're the one starin' at her titties," said the tall man with a laugh, keeping his pistol trained on the room.

He hadn't finished the sentence before the woman had extended her left gun and fired, drilling a slug through Jacobs's right shoulder.

As the young prospector screamed and clapped his hand to the bloody hole, and began sliding down the wall toward the floor, the woman turned her right gun to Caslin.

"Whoa there!" he cried, holding his hands and spatula before his face, as if to shield himself from a bullet. "You got no cause to —"

The second gun cracked, flames stabbing from the barrel, the bullet plunking into the old man's belly where the bulge split the shirt open to reveal his wash-worn balbriggans. The slug exited his back, blowing a good portion of guts and blood against the wall behind him.

"Holy shit!" shouted the red-bearded gent left of the open door, wide eyes bright with amazement.

As Caslin was punched backward, cursing and bending forward, cupping both hands to the wound, the woman spun again to Jacobs, who had dropped to his knees. Taking careful aim, she raked a bullet across the younger miner's right cheek and ear.

Again, he screamed as he fell back against the wall.

"Here she goes again," the tall man observed aloud, shaking his head.

The woman turned to Caslin, who was crawling toward a rifle leaning beside a nearby cot. She drilled him once through his right kidney and, as his spine arched and his head fell back between his shoulder blades, drilled him again through the back of his head.

The soldier clapped his hands and stomped a foot. "~~Gawd-damn~~, that had to hurt!"

Meanwhile, Jacobs was screaming and bleeding against the wall to her left. As he dropped forward and scrambled, crawling, toward the door, the woman shot him through his left arm. He grunted but kept moving, the other two men in the room scrambling from the line of fire.

When Jacobs was a foot from the door, the woman fired two more quick shots, one from each pistol. One slug drilled splinters from the door frame; the other took Jacobs in his left hip.

Sending up another scream and dragging his left leg, he pulled himself through the door. Adjusting her position and aiming down the barrel of her right-hand pistol, Saradee Jones drilled a neat round hole through the young prospector's right butt cheek. The shot threw him onto his elbows just outside the cabin.

She walked slowly toward the door, holding both smoking pistols down against her thighs.

Grinning as though at the most bewildering spectacle he'd ever seen, Sergeant Schmidt glanced at the tall man on the other side of the door.

Waylon Kilroy shook his head, as if to say, "What can you do?"

Schmidt looked at Saradee, standing in the open doorway, staring out at the dying prospector. Walking slowly toward the man, she lifted her left gun and fired. When Schmidt followed her out, he saw the younger prospector lying belly-down, ten yards beyond the door. Blood glistened from the hole in the back of his head.

Beyond Saradee, the other gang members were walking slowly, cautiously up from the dry wash — vague silhouettes wielding pistols or rifles. The horses and the two mules nickered and blew behind them.

"Everything all right, Miss Jones?" one of them called.

Saradee stared at them, bunching her lips, her heart still hammering raw fury. "Men!" she raged. "Everywhere I look, I see *men!*"

As she seethed at the men standing frozen a dozen yards down the gentle grade toward the wash, Schmidt and Kilroy moved past her toward the others. Giving her a wide berth, Schmidt muttered to Kilroy, "That's one hot-blooded woman, my friend. How do you put up with her?"

"When it comes to Saradee," Kilroy whispered, "you gotta take the horns with the hide."

"I heard that!" Saradee barked as they walked toward the others.

"Just joshin', my angel," Kilroy said, turning and throwing his arms out, then taking his reins from one of the other riders. "We'll go picket our horses by the spring yonder, then set up camp here in the wash."

"Who's sleepin' in the cabin tonight, Kilroy?" a spidery little firebrand named Gavin Childress yelled, his voice pitched with mockery. He was holding the reins of the two pack mules on the other side of the wash.

He and all the other gang members figured Kilroy would be sharing the cabin with Saradee Jones, as per their arrangement since, six months ago, Saradee's bunch had thrown in with Kilroy's gang and the cavalry sergeant, Arvo Schmidt.

Before Kilroy could answer, Saradee Jones called down from the cabin yard, "Me and the *puta* — and only me and the *puta!*"

"Hey," Schmidt growled, turning from the horse carrying the Mexican whore, her hands tied to the saddle horn, "she keepin' *me* company tonight. I'm the one that found her."

Schmidt's voice had stopped echoing around the wash before guns flashed on either side of Saradee's long-haired silhouette. The twin cracks followed a quarter second later. The .45-caliber rounds tore up sand and gravel on both sides of the big sergeant's mule-eared cavalry boots.

The startled horses skitter-stepped as Schmidt jumped higher than he'd jumped since he was twelve years old back in Pennsylvania.

"Jesus Christ!" he barked with fierce indignation.

The other men, knowing the ways of Saradee Jones, chuckled.

Schmidt touched his covered holster and inwardly cringed as the woman marched toward him, her men's undershot boots loudly crunching gravel. He considered drawing the revolver, but then starlight flashed off both barrels of her twin Colts, aimed at his heart.

He dropped his hand from the holster and stepped back against the whore's mount, the white-speckled roan stepping away from him as the woman approached with a distinct air of menace.

He flinched as Saradee Jones stopped before him and lashed out with her right hand. He was surprised when the hand, instead of connecting with his jaw, reached up and grabbed the whore's left arm.

As she urged the girl off the horse, Saradee pushed her lovely, angry face up close to Schmidt's. "I told you before, Sergeant, there will be no rape this trip. The girl is spending the night with me. If I catch you anywhere near her, I'll drill a hole through your black brain. Understand?"

"Hey!" Schmidt gruffly objected, taking one step back. "The whore is mine, god-damnit!"

Schmidt tensed again as one of the pistols jerked toward him. Waylon Kilroy had moved in fast, however, and closed his big hand over the gun, shoving it aside, before the woman could pull the trigger.

"Saradee!" the tall outlaw barked. "We're

gonna need all the men we got south of the border!"

"He's just a fucking soldier anyway. I'm gonna fill his ugly hide so full o' holes — !"

"You do, me and my boys are taking our cut o' the loot and riding out. Right now — tonight." Kilroy's voice was hard, uncompromising, his heavy brow ridged beneath his slouch hat's dipped brim.

The girl — she suddenly appeared more a girl now than a woman — looked up at him wide-eyed, the hard lines of her face flattening. Her voice was thin. "Y-you wouldn't really leave me out here, would you, Waylon?" She seemed sincerely surprised and heartbroken.

He removed his hand from her gun, set it gently along the side of her face, rubbing her cheek with his thumb. "Up to here, we've done it all your way, angel. It's my turn to call the shots."

She shook her head slightly, complaining in a little girl's voice, "But I hate soldiers. You know that, Waylon. Ever since they hanged my brother . . ."

"Angel," Kilroy said, gently admonishing, "we do this my way."

Schmidt said indignantly, "Let's not forget you wouldn't even *have* this money if I hadn't set up the ambush from the *inside.*"

"Shut up, Schmidt," Waylon said without looking at him, keeping his eyes on Saradee Jones. To her, he said, "We got us an understanding this evenin'?"

Saradee lowered her eyes, turning her face against his palm, and nodded. He smiled, ran his thumb across her cheek once more, then lowered his hand.

It seemed to release the girl from a trance. She turned to the whore, who'd been standing nearby, head down, a blanket across her shoulders, and gave the girl's arm a brusque tug. "Come on."

As she began walking back toward the cabin, jerking the whore along behind her, she paused and turned once more to the sergeant. "You stay away from her, you understand, or all bets are off. I'll be feedin' your balls come mornin' to the camp-robber jays."

Schmidt didn't say anything. He stood frozen, watching both women move up the grade toward the lantern-lit cabin.

"That girl's got a way about her," he said to Kilroy, who'd begun leading his and the women's horses toward the spring.

Schmidt had turned his own horse in that direction when the girl's voice drifted down from the cabin. "Waylon?"

Schmidt turned toward the trim figure

silhouetted by the cabin's lantern lit doorway, facing the wash.

Kilroy had paused, the other men continuing to lead their own mounts and the mules toward the spring. "What is it, angel?"

"Come visit me when you're done settin' up." Saradee paused. "We got . . . things to discuss."

The other men chuckled knowingly.

"I'll be there, angel," the tall outlaw said.

Saradee backed into the cabin and swung the door closed on the night. It latched with a wooden click.

Schmidt led his horse toward the spring. "Like I said, that girl's got a way about her."

"It's kinda like makin' love to a she-griz with the springtime craze," said Kilroy, moving ahead of Schmidt. Chuckling, the outlaw stopped and waited for Schmidt to catch up to him.

Kilroy looked around to make sure none of Saradee's men were near, then said across Schmidt's left shoulder, "Just between you and me, I'm gonna have to kill her."

He threw his head back, guffawing as he led the horses into the brushy darkness around the spring. "But by God, I ain't never gonna forget her!"

7.
FLAGG

Around noon the next day, Hawk and Primrose found the two prospectors sprawled at the bottom of their own latrine hole, another batch of quarreling buzzards enjoying a succulent feast.

The men followed the killers' sign until a monsoon gully-washer rolled in from the west, forcing them to take shelter in a notch cave. The rain pounded the baked clay like grape fired from two-pounder cannons, the storm's gray curtain closing down over the mountains. Thunder chased its own booming echoes across the canyons, the horses giving regular, frightened whinnies where they were tied amongst willows.

For an hour after the storm had lifted, the smell of sage and desert blossoms clung to the brimstone odor of the lightning, and the washes rushed like rivers. The men tended a small fire, roasting a rabbit Hawk had shot when he'd seen the storm approach.

They slept in the cave, rising at the first wash of dawn and finding the killers' trail thoroughly obliterated. They didn't find as much as a cigarette butt or a soggy horse apple along the vague game trace the bunch had been following.

The lieutenant cursed as much as his tender head allowed, and then he and Hawk continued south, making their own way, trying to anticipate the muddy washes and canyons the killers had followed.

Late in the afternoon, as the sun tilted purple shadows away from the dusty-green western mesas and rimrocks, they drew rein on a low ridge. They built and smoked cigarettes, staring south toward three separate north/south ranges divided by the same saguaro-stippled chaparral they'd been traversing. Below them, Sonoita Wash cut its deep, narrow canyon between *bosquecillos* of poplar and sycamore.

"Well, here it is, Lieutenant," Hawk said, exhaling cigarette smoke. "The end of the line."

Primrose turned to him. He'd donned fresh bandages that morning, and the one around his head showed no blood. At Hawk's insistence, he'd removed the brass buttons from his tunic and replaced them with leather ties. "What're you talking about?"

"Beyond the wash is Mexico."

"I know that. I was once stationed at Fort Huachuca."

"Last I heard, this country has an agreement with Mexico. Their *rurales* don't chase their outlaws to our side of the line, and we don't chase our outlaws to theirs."

Primrose stared at him wryly, shade slicing across the right side of his peeling face. "I suppose you'll be turning back then?"

"Not me."

"Then consider yourself a scout and a tracker for the United States Army, Mr. Hawk."

Hawk turned to the lieutenant with an expression of strained patience. "Fort Huachuca's about thirty miles the other side of that ridge, Lieutenant. Best you head over there and report what happened. Let the politicians take it from there." Hawk shrugged a shoulder. "In the meantime, when I run down those savages and turn 'em out with the coyotes, I'll send back your money."

Primrose drew a deep breath and rose up in his saddle. "I'm going with you."

"That'd be desertion and cavorting with a felon."

The lieutenant sipped from his canteen. "Bending the rules for a greater cause." Hawk opened his mouth to speak, but Primrose cut him off. "No one's going to stop me. Least of all, a kill-crazy vigilante."

Hawk studied the young lieutenant through slitted eyes, the man's insult having as much effect as a stray drop from a distant rain cloud. "The ambush was no fault of yours. Your sergeant's a traitor, and your men were outnumbered."

Primrose looked off, flushing beneath his sunburn. "You see, Major Devereaux at Fort Bowie is my father-in-law." He blinked into the light, took a deep breath. "He's always failed to see what Lucy sees in me."

Hawk turned away, chuckling dryly and shaking his head.

"So there you have it," said Primrose.

When Hawk didn't say anything, Primrose put some steel into his voice. "Now, then, shall we head to Mexico?"

Hawk turned to the young soldier, regarding him soberly, then directed his gaze southward. "See those three ranges yonder?"

Primrose looked where Hawk was pointing.

"The killers could have followed either of the two valleys between those ridges. To save time and our horses, I suggest we split up, each take a valley, and meet up again at the other end of the middle range."

The lieutenant slanted a look at him. "You're not trying to shake free of me, are you?"

"It's a chance you'll have to take, Lieutenant. If you don't like it, Huachuca's that way." Hawk canted his head eastward, then gave the grulla the spurs.

A few yards away, he stopped and hipped around in his saddle. "Keep in mind this is Yaqui country. Don't let your guard down unless, as they say down here, you want to join the blessed."

He turned away and urged the grulla south, angling toward the gauzy green range on his left.

The lieutenant watched him for a time, blinking against the dust. Trying to ward off the unease he always felt at the phrase "Old Mexico" — conjuring, as it did, a barbaric, mythic frontier of frontiers, where many a gringo had disappeared, never to be heard from again — he shucked his Spencer carbine, laid it across his saddlebows, and headed south.

Deputy United States Marshal D.W. Flagg lay in a ridge notch, following the man in the blue shirt, tan denims, and flat-brimmed black hat with his field glasses.

Flagg held the glasses near their ends, shading the lenses with his gloved hands. A man like Gideon Hawk, hunted by lawmen and bounty hunters for nearly two years, would detect the slightest flash of reflected light.

"Is it Hawk?" asked Mooney Gill, one of the two scalp-hunters riding with Flagg. Gill and his Mexican partner, Juan Ochoa, knew the border country as well anyone in the Southwest.

"No, it's Natty Bumpo."

"Who?"

Flagg turned his head right. Gill was frowning at him, a short quirley smoldering in his thin-lipped mouth.

"Of course it's Hawk," Flagg grumbled.

"No need to be insulting to *mi amigo,*" admonished Juan Ochoa, hunkered down on the other side of Gill. "You are in Mexico now." Ochoa tapped his chest. "*My* country."

Flagg scowled at the Mexican. The lawman's gray eyes — the same shade as his close-cropped hair and beard — were hard. A fly buzzed about his head, but he didn't react to it.

Flagg's mouth stretched into a broad smile, his eyes suddenly as warm as they'd been hard. "Come on, Juan. We're working together now, for chrissakes. Turn your horns in. Mooney, tell your friend to turn his horns in."

Gill glanced at Ochoa, still glaring at Flagg. "He has a hard time with that, Flagg, you havin' fixed his brother with a rope cravat in Tucson and all."

"Juan, you know that wasn't personal," Flagg said. "Alberto had it comin'. If I hadn't brought him in, a Ranger sure enough would have. I don't know what you're so proddy about. Didn't he cut one of your ears off?"

Ochoa automatically raised his small brown hand to the right side of his head, which was covered with straight, lice-flecked strands of dark brown hair. *"Sí,"* the Mexican allowed. "But I cut off one of his, so we were even. Alberto and me, we had, as you gringos say, buried the hatchet."

To Flagg's left and lying a few feet farther down the ridge, Spade Killigrew laughed his high-pitched, cackling laugh. "Buried the hatchet? What the devil's mercy are you idiots talking about? That's Gideon Hawk down there, and he's riding *away* from us. Call me a stickler for details, but maybe we should bury the hatchet ourselves and get *after* him."

"I've been tracking that son of a bitch for

six months, Sheriff," Flagg told Killigrew, the town sheriff of Coyote Springs. He and his part-time deputies, Gill and Ochoa, had thrown in with Flagg the same day the soldiers had chased Hawk and the whore out of his town and Flagg had ridden in, searching for the vigilante badge-toter. "He'll keep another fifteen minutes," Flagg continued. "I think it's important that I have a good working relationship with all of the men in my employ."

"In your employ?" said Gill. "What does that mean?"

"Who work for him!" Killigrew snapped, removing his black derby and running both his heavily veined hands through his wavy, pomaded hair. He wore an immaculate spade beard and mustache, both clay-caked and sweaty. "Christ, might we get this conversation finished?"

"We don't work for you, Flagg," protested Ochoa. "We signed on for the reward on that *hombre loco*'s head!"

"Hell," said Gill, "after seein' them soldier-boys slaughtered, I say we forget Hawk and go after the payroll money. Why settle for five thousand dollars split four ways, when two or three times that is right under our noses!"

"Mooney." Flagg gave Gill a fatherly

96

expression of disgust. "You're a part-time lawman, for the love of Pete. Are you suggesting we hunt down stolen money and keep it for ourselves?"

Mooney Gill frowned, his eyes uncertain, then glanced at Juan Ochoa on his other side, who merely lifted his left shoulder and stared after Hawk, only the man's dust scarf now visible in the southeastern distance.

"Flagg's right," Killigrew said. "If we go after the payroll money, we gotta turn it in. Keepin' all that money for ourselves . . . hell . . ." He shook his head as if trying to convince himself of a hard truth. "That just wouldn't be right."

"Good man," Flagg said, slapping the sheriff's right shoulder. "Our business out here is to hunt down and kill Gideon Hawk. Are we all of similar sentiment? I'd hate to think I was hunting down one rogue lawman with three more of the same ilk."

"Shit, Flagg," Gill sneered. "You just want your name in the papers."

"More than that," Killigrew said as Flagg, flushing, slipped his field glasses back into their felt-lined case. "He wants to be the chief U.S. marshal of Arizona Territory."

"I bet the hombre with that job gets *mucho* free pussy," Ochoa chuckled.

"I get all the free pussy I need," Flagg

said, and spat. Wiping his mouth, he added, "But you wouldn't fault a man for aspirating to a higher echelon, would you, boys?"

Ochoa looked at Gill. "Now what does he say?"

Before Gill could speak, Flagg added as he climbed to his feet, "I'm not going to promise anything, but if you boys help me take down Hawk, I might . . . and I said *might* . . . help you track the payroll money."

Killigrew looked at him. "And?"

"And," said Flagg, "if the thieves have hidden that money where, after a thorough, time-consuming search, we weren't able to find it . . . well, that's just the curse of Viejo Méjico." Flagg dropped his hands to his thighs, slapping dust from his whipcord trousers.

They all had a good laugh.

As they headed down the slope to where their horses were ground-tied in the ridge's shadows, Flagg draped an arm across Juan Ochoa's shoulders. "We got us a good workin' relationship now, Juan? In spite of my history with Alberto?"

Ochoa chuckled, then looked around with a mock expression of bewilderment. "Alberto . . . *¿quién es ese?*"

Who is that?

Ochoa laughed. "And I have good news

for you, Señor Flagg."

"What's that?"

"Señor Hawk appears to be heading for El Garabato, an abandoned mining village not far from here. I know a shortcut through a rimrock. We should get there well ahead of him. Prepare a little surprise maybe, yes?"

"Juan," Flagg said, squeezing the smaller man's shoulders as they approached the horses, "I'm growing right fond of you."

8.
DEATH IN
EL GARABATO

The sun had nearly set when Hawk halted his horse on the crest of a low hill and looked down on the thirty or so hovels scattered at the bottom of a rocky hollow. Private dwellings encircled a small business district and central square, the main feature of which was a stout, brown church.

Except for wheeling birds, there was no more movement in the *pueblecito* than there was in the three mines gaping in the southern ridge towering over it. The only light was the sun's dying rays receding across the cracked red roof tiles and buckling adobe walls. The only sounds, the dusky breeze rustling the brush and the tinny mutter of the sulfur-fetid creek curving around the town's western edge.

An old mining village, no doubt abandoned when the gold and silver pinched out on the ridge.

Hawk slipped his Henry from his saddle

boot, levered the rifle one-handed, depressed the hammer to half-cock, and laid the barrel across his saddlebows. He kneed the grulla slowly down the hill and into the eerily quiet *pueblecito,* raking his gaze from right to left across the narrow street grown up with sage and cluttered with tumbleweeds.

A thud sounded on his right.

Reining the grulla down, he swung the rifle barrel toward a two-story hovel with a balcony sagging down its west wall. The breeze caught one of the hanging shutters and knocked it gently against its frame.

Hawk continued past the *alcalde's,* mayor's, office . . . past a cantina with a small front courtyard under a crude brush arbor, past a livery barn and public corrals grown up with wild oats and yucca, and past a tall, narrow structure identifying itself in Spanish as the headquarters for the local *rurale* troupe.

As the horse plodded slowly along the street, an aroma of sweet Mexican tobacco smoke touched Hawk's nostrils. He halted the grulla before a dry stone fountain fronting the church, and looked around.

Movement before and above him caught his attention, and he lifted his gaze to the church's bell tower. A gray-bearded man in a low-crowned straw sombrero stood in the tower, waving his right arm slowly above his head. As Hawk watched, the man extended the arm left, indicating the boulder- and hovel-strewn hillside to Hawk's right.

Catching only a half glimpse of a rifle barrel, Hawk released his reins and threw his body hard down the grulla's left hip. The rifle exploded the same instant Hawk's right shoulder hit the ground, the slug whistling over the grulla's saddle and plunking into a wall on the other side of the street.

The toe of Hawk's left boot caught in the stirrup, and the bolting horse dragged him several feet, saving his life as a shooter behind him popped three quick pills into the dirt where he'd fallen. His boot slipped free, and he rolled up against the fountain's bowl, which partly shielded him from the hillside and the first bushwhacker.

He cast a look back the way he'd been dragged. His Henry lay in the street, cocking lever extended. Lifting his gaze above the rifle, he saw a tall, red-faced man with a thin silver beard step out from behind the *rurales* office, levering a fresh round into his Winchester. Another, indistinguishable face appeared in the office's front window.

At the same time, someone moved in the corner of Hawk's right eye.

Hawk bolted to his knees, clawing both pistols from their holsters. He triggered his first shot at the red-faced man, whose eyes snapped wide beneath his hat brim as he jerked back behind the wall. The Russian's hammer had barely dropped before Hawk triggered the Colt toward the movement he'd spied on his right.

A man yelped as, firing an errant pistol shot, he crouched behind a rain barrel.

As Hawk swung back toward the *rurale* headquarters, the hillside shooter burned a bullet across his right cheek. Hawk trained both pistols on the red-faced gent, who had just stepped out from behind the *rurale* building, raising his Winchester. Hawk and the furry-faced bushwhacker fired at the same time, Hawk's slug nipping the right shoulder of the man's duster, the man's bullet winging six inches left of Hawk's face.

Hawk fired two more quick rounds, both slugs carving adobe from the *rurale* office as the red-faced gunman withdrew behind it, a badge glinting on the right lapel of his long, gray duster.

The gunman on the hillside fired another shot, simultaneous with the man behind the rain barrel, both shots flying wide as Hawk ran a zigzagging course back the way he'd been dragged, firing his pistols from both hips.

The Russian and the Colt clicked empty. Hawk scooped the Henry off the street.

Ramming the loading lever home, he fired a round where the red-faced man had been standing, but the slug shredded only air. The red-faced man was gone.

Wheeling, slugs thumping into the street around his boots, Hawk ran to the other side of the street, leapt a one-wheeled hay cart, and sprinted through the weed- and rock-choked gap between the *alcalde*'s office and a harness shop. The shooting died off, the echoes bouncing around the hollow, as Hawk ran into the alley and straight on past a series of plank and rock shanties. Hearing disgruntled voices shouted from the street and from the hillside near the church, Hawk jogged a serpentine course through the rocks and shanties to the back of the hill.

A muffled, echoing voice rose from the street. "Keep an eye on your backside, Juano, he might be tryin' to flank ya!"

Hawk moved around a rocky knob about halfway up the hill. On the other side of the knob, a wiry, long-haired Mexican in a short leather jacket leapt back with a start, swinging his Winchester barrel toward Hawk.

The man didn't get the long gun leveled before Hawk's Henry barked twice. The .44/40 slugs, fired from two feet away into the Mexican's gut, just below his crossed cartridge belts, blew him up and back, his own rifle discharging when it bounced off a rock. The man's eyes rolled around in their sockets. Blood and viscera spilled from the twin smoking holes in his belly.

As his eyes focused on Hawk towering over him and extending the Henry straight out from his shoulder, the barrel angled down, the Mexican's eyelids snapped wide, brows rising into his forehead, his lower jaw falling to his chest.

Before the man could scream, Hawk's Henry spat smoke and fire, and a ragged hole appeared in the Mexican's forehead, slamming his skull against a rock with a loud crack. The man's eyes fluttered. His high-heeled, black boots jerked. Blood welled onto the rock behind his head, dribbling down his shoulders.

A voice rose from the street. "Ochoa?"

Silence. In the distance, hooves thudded. Two horses galloping east.

The same voice rose again in the street. "~~Goddamn you~~, Flagg!"

Hawk lifted his head from the dead Mexican, stared thoughtfully up the rocky slope nearly completely shrouded in darkness.

Flagg. That's who the red-faced, silver-bearded lawman was. D.W. Flagg. His friends called him Dutch. Hawk had never met him, only heard of him. Union Civil War veteran. He was said to be nearsighted, which would account for his lousy shooting in the street.

In spite of the bravado Flagg showed in saloons and brothels, he was also known to run from tight spots, to wait for a more opportune time to reintroduce himself to his quarry.

"Ochoa!" The voice echoed off the southern ridge.

Hawk stepped over the dead Mex and moved slowly toward two rectangular boulders at the top of the hill, over the top of which the Mexican had fired down on him.

When he'd hunkered down in the V-notch where the two boulders joined, he took his rifle under his right arm, tipped his head back on his shoulders, and cupped his hands around his mouth.

"Got him!" he yelled skyward, giving the two words a subtle Mexican flare.

The sun was well down, filling the hollow with dense shadows. The breeze stirred the brush slightly. Otherwise, it was so quiet that Hawk could hear the dead Mexican break wind down the hill behind him.

"Juano, that you?" came the skeptical voice from the street.

"Got him!" Hawk yelled again. He took the Henry in both hands, hunkered on his heels, ready to spring.

In the far distance, a wolf howled.

The gunman's voice rose, pitched low with skepticism. "Stand up, show me your pretty face, *mi amigo.*"

Hawk rose quickly, brought the Henry to his shoulder, and aimed down the hill.

The man was a vague silhouette crouched to the right of the fountain, his face a pale oval beneath his funnel-brimmed Stetson. Hawk snapped the shot. As the man began to rise with a start, bringing his pistol up, Hawk's bullet punched through his chest. He stumbled backward, throwing his pistol over his head, and hit the street with a grunt.

Hawk kept the rifle on him for a moment. Raising it toward the bell tower, he saw the slender silhouette of the old man, sombrero tipped toward the ground before the church. The old man shook his head, his snickers sounding like the wheezing of an old burro.

Hawk stayed where he was for several minutes, watching and listening for Flagg. True to his reputation, the good marshal appeared to have beaten a hasty retreat.

Hawk moved down the hill and around the church, trying to sniff out any more shooters in the thickening darkness. When he rounded the church's northeast corner, heading back toward the fountain, the stoop-shouldered, gray-whiskered gent from the bell tower was hunkered down beside the dead man, going through his pockets.

As Hawk approached, the man turned his head sharply toward him, a cigarette stub smoldering between his lips. Hawk held his left hand up, laid the Henry's barrel over his right shoulder.

"¿*Norteamericano?*" the man asked.

Hawk nodded. "Who're you?"

"Cisco Weber. I live in the church."

"Prospector?"

"When the Yaquis aren't on the prowl." Weber looked at the dead man and continued feeling around in his pocket. He looked up at Hawk again. "You don't mind, do you? It ain't so much lucre I'm lookin' fer as tobaccy."

"Whatever you find is yours. You see which way my horse went?"

"Think he headed down toward the creek."

"Obliged."

"Who are these boys?"

"Dry-gulchers." He'd recognized the

sheriff's deputies from Coyote Springs —
gut-sack vermin who should have been
thrown to the hogs before reaching maturity.

The old man hitched a shoulder. "Mind if
I ask who you are?"

Hawk's tall, dark figure was disappearing
into the darkness, his Henry resting on his
shoulder. He didn't turn back around, and
he didn't say anything. The darkness envel-
oped him, his boots crunching gravel.

"Tight-lipped son of a bitch." Weber
snorted, going through the dead man's back
trouser pockets.

D.W. Flagg and Spade Killigrew beat a
shambling retreat through the desert night,
Flagg cursing under his breath and pressing
his right hand over his bullet-burned left
shoulder. They rode through two short
canyons, then turned into a piñon-sheathed
box canyon, having to rely on God's grace
and sheer luck to keep their horses from
breaking a leg in the rough terrain, and to
keep themselves from running into Indians.

Fortunately, the box canyon proved empty,
though the scat smells told Flagg that a bear
had holed up there in recent days. The
marshal sat down, resting his back against a
ridge, while Killigrew turned out the horses
and built a fire, over which he set water to

boil for coffee.

When the firelight reflected off the red rocks behind him, Flagg shrugged out of his duster and peeled his bloody shirt down his bullet-burned shoulder. Killigrew's hands shook as he fed more branches to the fire, his pockmarked, elegantly furred features glistening wet in the firelight.

"You think the fire's a good idea?" he said, looking warily into the darkness. "What if he tracks us here? There's no way out."

"Hawk's a different breed, I'll give him that," Flagg rasped, dropping his jaw as he angled a sharp look at his shoulder. "But not even he can track in the dark."

Killigrew shook his head and whistled softly. "What the hell *happened* back there?"

"You tell me, Sheriff." Peeling the shirt from the bloody gash, Flagg winced and ground his right heel into the rocky soil. "Why didn't you *shoot?*"

"My rifle jammed. Brand-new repeater, just got it in from Lordsburg. Had it sighted in and everything, and I bear down on Hawk's head — had him right in my sights — and it *jams!*" He sat back on his haunches. "What happened to *you?*"

"Well, for starters, your ~~goddamn~~ bean-eater missed his shot. I thought he was supposed to be a sharpshooter."

"I took that on Gill's word."

"If you miss your first shot with Hawk, the kettle's gonna boil right quick. I heard it said he moves around like a boxed cougar."

"You missed all your shots too, I take it?"

"Fuck you, Killigrew."

"We could have stayed and boxed him in."

"You don't *box* in Gideon Hawk, Sheriff," Flagg spat. "You rile a rogue bear like Hawk, you pull out and try again later, when you can get another long, clear shot. Wipe that look off your face. It isn't cowardly. It's using your *head!*"

Killigrew spread his hands. "I didn't say anything."

"Why were you at your horse?"

"I was going to exchange my jammed gun for a good one. I intended to go back and get Hawk, not *run away!*"

"Shut up and tend the coffee. The water's boiling."

The sheriff dumped coffee into the pot, then sat back against a fir tree, glancing into the night, nervously smoothing his sweat-drenched mustache, the waxed ends of which now sagged to his chin whiskers. "I reckon I can assume my deputies are dead."

"No great loss."

"You know," Killigrew said, crossing his

111

arms on his chest and dropping his chin, chuckling, "I think they were funny boys. Caught 'em one afternoon —"

He stopped and dropped his eyes to the coffeepot. The coffee was bubbling out from beneath the lid, steam rising noisily.

"Shit."

Padding his hand with a folded scrap of burlap, Killigrew grabbed the pot's handle. He'd lifted the pot six inches above the flames when his hand opened suddenly. A rifle cracked. The pot dropped back to the coals, the coffee splashing onto the flames with a *whooosh.*

Killigrew cried shrilly, clutching his bleeding hand to his chest, face bunched with pain as he glared fearfully into the shadows.

Flagg reached for the big, ivory-gripped Remington on his hip. Before he could begin to slide the gun from its holster, the rifle cracked again, the slug drilling the overturned pot with a tinny clang, lifting it up out of the fire and bouncing it off the scarp between Flagg and the cursing Killigrew.

His fearful eyes searching the box canyon's tarlike darkness, Flagg eased his hand away from the gun. Killigrew grunted and sighed, blood dripping from his clenched hands and puddling on his white shirt and vest. The flames lifted as the coffee evaporated from the branches, the steam's hiss slowly dying.

"Flagg?" The voice drifted out of the darkness, irritatingly bland.

Flagg's eyes slitted as he probed the dark, wavering curtain beyond the fire, trying to see the tall, broad-shouldered figure he knew was there, no doubt on the opposite ridge, training his rifle on the bridge of Flagg's nose. Flagg felt like a butterfly on the end of a pin. Still, a part of him couldn't help admire the rogue lawman's stealth, and envy his sand.

"I'd offer ya a cup of joe, Hawk, but we're fresh out."

"That cocksucker!" Killigrew snarled, glancing from his bleeding hand to the shadows, sweat streaming off his chin.

"Go on home," Hawk said. "Next time it'll be more than java you're out of."

A rock fell with a thud. Spurs chinged softly away.

While Killigrew cursed and squirmed, fishing in his saddlebags for a bandage, Flagg stared into the darkness, half his upper lip curled above his teeth in a snarling grin.

9.
TRYST

"Oh!" Saradee Jones cried, lying prostrate atop a horse blanket, her jeans and her men's balbriggans bunched around her ankles, her knees spread wide. "Oh! Yes! Oh! Yes!"

Waylon Kilroy lay between her legs, hammering away like a stallion heading home to fresh hay, his own jeans bunched atop Saradee's. He grunted hard with each plunge.

"Oh, God, Waylon! Oh, *God!*"

Kilroy stiffened, lifted his head, and dropped his jaw, his sharp-featured face flushed and sweaty, his thick hair in his eyes. He exhaled slowly, and rolled onto his back. For a minute, the lovers lay there, breathing heavily.

Their own private campfire crackled nearby, shunting orange light and shadows about the hollow sheathed in ironwood shrubs. The other gang members were camped fifty yards down the arroyo. One of them was strumming a guitar, the slow chords rising faintly.

"Oh, Waylon, honey . . ."

He patted her thigh, chuckled, said in a voice thick from drink, "Not bad, eh, angel?"

"No one can screw like you, Waylon." Rolling away from him and pushing up on her hands, her hair hanging down both sides of her face, she rolled her eyes and wrinkled her nose, adding with what she hoped wasn't too much melodrama, *"No one!"*

Actually, she'd never had a shaft that soft. He was big enough, but he just couldn't get it hard. Must've been the two quarts of tequila he drank each night.

"Where you goin'?" he asked groggily, his organ wilting against his thigh.

Saradee sat on her butt and pulled her jeans up. "Gonna take a little walk. Get some air. After a ride like that, it's gonna take me a while to go to sleep."

Waylon's mustached upper lip curled in a grin, but his eyes remained closed.

When Saradee had buckled her belt, wrapped her gun and cartridge belt around her waist, and stepped into her boots, she knelt down behind Waylon, who was already beginning to snore.

"Hey, sleepyhead," she cooed in his ear.

"Unh . . . unh," he groaned, his eyelids fluttering.

She nibbled his earlobe, made her voice soft and girlish. "You gonna kill that big, ugly sergeant when we get to El Molina?"

"Why you want me to kill him so bad?" Kilroy asked, his head lolling on the blanket, keeping his eyes closed.

"I don't like the way he looks at me."

"How's he look at ye?"

"Well whenever I . . . hey, are you listening?"

Kilroy's head jerked. "Yeah, I'm listenin'."

"Whenever I lean over for something, I catch him starin' at my ass. And he's always lookin' at my shirt. I could swear he was a big dumb horse and my bosoms were sugar cubes!"

Kilroy's eyes snapped wide, the pupils expanding, his brows beetling angrily. "Really?"

Saradee nodded, running the first and second fingers of her right hand lightly through the curled, wet hair on Kilroy's chest.

"Goddamnit," he said, rising onto his elbows. "I've told all the men, includin' Schmidt, to keep their damn eyes off you!"

"Well, the sergeant ain't heedin' your warning."

Kilroy pushed from his elbows to his hands and looked around for his pistol. "Damn him!"

"Shhh," Saradee said, giggling into his ear and pushing his left shoulder back toward the blanket. "I didn't mean to get you all upset. Like you said, we need every man, including Schmidt, till we're through Yaqui country. But after we get to El Molina, I'd like you to kill him. Will you do that for me, Waylon?"

His cheeks red in the firelight, Kilroy slid his gaze to her, his eyes narrowing slightly. "Why do you want me to kill him? You're as good with a gun as me or any other man in the bunch."

She sat back on her heels and planted one fist on a hip. " 'Cause that's what a man does for a woman, ~~goddamn~~ you!"

"Easy, easy, easy," Kilroy said, grabbing her arms and smiling up at her nervously. "I was just joshin'. Soon as we get to El Molina . . ."

"You'll drill a .44 slug through his big, ugly head?"

Kilroy nodded. "You got it." He lifted his head and kissed her. "Now, you think I can get some shut-eye?"

"Thank you, Waylon." She kissed him and squeezed his earlobes, shaking his head gently. "You really do love me, don't you?"

He lowered his eyes to her amply filled shirt, the deep, suntanned cleavage. "How could a man not love a woman like you, Saradee Jones?"

She stood, smiling down at him. "Good night, Waylon."

"Good night, angel. Don't you stray too far." He gave her a wink. "I know you can handle yourself, but you need your shut-eye. We still got a good three-day ride to El Molina."

"I'll just be a minute," Saradee said, smiling her heart-wrenching smile, donning her hat, and strolling off through the brush.

Keeping watch on a rocky ridge above the arroyo, Sergeant Schmidt stuck his stogie between his teeth, raised his Spencer rifle in both hands across his chest, and turned to his right.

A young *buscadero* named Whiskey Thorne sat fifteen feet away, his butt perched on a boulder, staring over the night-choked gorge directly below, and over the star-capped desert beyond. Schmidt looked past the kid's right shoulder and down the grade from where the sound of a rolling stone had cut the midnight silence.

There was a quiet rustling, and a cedar

branch moved. The kid jerked toward it, snapping his Colt from its holster. "Who goes there?"

"Who goes there?" said Saradee Jones snidely, letting the cedar branch snap back and moving toward Schmidt and Thorne, swinging her hips, hair jostling about her shoulders. "Who says that anymore?"

"Sorry, Miss Jones," the kid said, sticking his cigarette between his teeth and slipping his Colt back into its holster. "You oughta announce yourself, though. Don't want to get shot by mistake."

Thorne turned his head back toward the gorge. He took a deep drag on his cigarette, removed it from his mouth, and exhaling a long smoke plume, cupped the quirley in his palm.

Saradee marched up behind him as though she were going to walk past him toward Schmidt. Schmidt's heart chugged, and he raised his rifle slightly, ready to defend himself. Directly behind the kid, Saradee stopped and turned casually toward him as, facing the gorge, he exhaled the cigarette smoke. She raised her right arm toward the kid, planted the heel of her hand between his shoulder blades, and pushed.

Thorne had been sitting at the very edge of the rock, the gorge yawning beneath his feet. The shove caused him to stand. There must have been a little ledge between him and the gorge. Digging his boots into it, he gave little grunts and ululating sighs as, teetering forward over the canyon, he flung his arms straight out from his shoulders and tried to bring himself back toward the ridge.

"Oh . . . whoah . . . oah . . . noo . . . ahhhhhh!"

He plunged headfirst into the gaping darkness as though diving into a river. There was a smack and a rasping grunt as he hit the first shelf thirty feet below. After that, all Schmidt heard was a slight whooshing sound followed, a second later, by another, quieter thump.

The sergeant peered disbelievingly into the gorge. Directly below was a pinprick of orange light from Thorne's cigarette. The glow died slowly, like the expiration of eternity's last star, leaving the darkness around it even darker than before.

His heart skipping a beat, Schmidt turned to the woman. He edged slowly around the rock he was sitting on, planting his feet firmly on the ridge and bringing his rifle up warily.

He had his cigar in his mouth. "What in the hell kinda stunt was that?"

"At ease, Sergeant," she said, stopping six

feet before him. She cocked a hip, shook her hair behind her shoulders, shoved her hands into her back pockets, and stuck out her chest. The full, twin mounds of her breasts heaved toward him from beneath the flannel shirt. "Just thinning Waylon's herd, is all. I'll have to do it sooner or later."

Schmidt glanced into the darkness below the ridge, then turned back to her, squinting an eye.

She shrugged a shoulder. "Once we get to El Molina, there's gonna be war. Our men can't stand each other. I see no reason not to even up the sides."

"What about the Yaquis we might need to dance with?"

"When he was thirteen years old, Whiskey Thorne put his ma and pa on trial, and hanged 'em in their own barn. But when you so much as mention the word 'Injun' around him, he pisses down his leg. We'll get by without him."

"What's Waylon gonna say about that?"

"Whiskey never could hold his whiskey. He got drunk and plunged to his death, poor boy."

"Ma'am, you're somethin' else."

"Has Waylon told you he intends to kill me?"

Schmidt didn't say anything.

She laughed. "Figured he might have. He's absolutely gone for me, but of course he could never trust me. I don't hold it against him. I can't trust him either."

"Ain't this sweet?"

"What did you think you were getting into, Sergeant? A children's theater play?"

"Ah, hell, I don't want to hear no more. No offense, ma'am, but you're trouble."

Saradee chuckled huskily. "That's what my grammar-school teacher told me."

"I bet he did."

"Can you stare at my breasts and think at the same time, Sergeant? I have something important I'd like to discuss with you."

Schmidt jerked his eyes back to hers, his heart thudding, his face turning hot. He squeezed the rifle. "Now, hold on . . ."

"Do you want me?"

Schmidt's face got hotter. He didn't say anything. He stopped puffing the cigar, let it smolder between his lips.

She gave her head an impatient toss, and cleared her throat. "I said, do you want me?"

"I don't mess with other men's women."

She quirked a confident grin and crossed her arms on her breasts. "I have a feeling that's about to change, Sergeant. You see, Waylon can't perform worth shit. Pardon my barn talk, but his shaft's like an overripe banana. Couple that with the fact he's going to try to kill me, and what do you have? A ghost. *¿Comprende?*"

Schmidt shook his head slowly, feeling as though he too were falling into the gorge.

"If you kill Waylon," she said, "you can have me for as long as you want me. We'll split the money between us and any of my men still kicking after the El Molina hoedown, and head to Juarez." She paused, ran her tongue across her lips, her eyes across the sergeant's broad, heaving chest. "We could have us quite a time in Juarez, you an' me."

Schmidt swallowed, saliva leaking out around the cigar and dribbling down his chin. "We have an agreement, me and Waylon. I knew him in the Army, ye see? We fought Injuns . . . side by side. . . ."

Saradee unfolded her arms and began unbuttoning her shirt. "You probably had an agreement with the United States Army of the Southwest too, didn't you, Sergeant?"

Her long, slender fingers moved to the next button and the next, until she had all the buttons undone and she was peeling the shirt off her shoulders. She wasn't wearing anything beneath it.

"I was jealous of the whore," she confessed. "I didn't want her to have you. *I* wanted you. We'll sell the whore down in Mexico."

She tossed the shirt to the ground, turned to him, shaking her hair back, her breasts standing proudly out from her chest — round and full. She threw her arms back, arched her spine.

Schmidt's blood boiled. His cigar had gone out.

"Why don't you kill Waylon yourself?" he growled. "If you want him dead so damn bad . . ."

She chuckled, stepped toward him, and grabbed the hardness in his pants. "I can kill any man I've a mind to . . . except those I've slept with. It's just a thing about me. Too bad too, because they're usually the ones who need it the most."

A minute later, against his halfhearted protestations, she'd peeled his as well as her own pants down and leaped onto his lap, facing him and wrapping her legs around his back. "What do you say, Sergeant?" She looked up at him, his face sweaty and flushed, his beard twitching nervously. "Have I convinced you to switch sides, or do you need more time to think about it?"

Schmidt cursed, dropped his rifle, grabbed her buttocks in his big hands, and slid her onto his organ. He was sliding her up and down, and she was tufting his hair in her hands and raking her fingernails down the back of his tunic, when she heard a sharp smack.

The sergeant convulsed beneath her, groaned. She'd had her eyes closed; now she opened them as the sergeant fell sideways off the boulder. She gave a clipped, startled cry as he pulled her down on top of him.

Disoriented, she climbed to her elbows and looked down. The sergeant was out, chin tipped to his left shoulder. Blood trickled down the side of his head, glistening in his thick red hair.

Blinking, Saradee saw a figure to her right, turned her head that way. A man in a blue uniform and tan kepi stood over her, feet spread, aiming a Spencer rifle at her face.

10.
PRIMROSE TAKES CHARGE

"If you yell, I'll kill you," Primrose said tightly, staring down his Spencer's barrel at the woman's head. He remembered her, crouched atop the boulder at Piñon Rocks, slinging lead into his men with demonic glee.

The woman glared up at him through the tawny hair in her eyes. She was straddling the unconscious sergeant. Her breasts heaved. She quirked a smile and lifted her hands, palms out, to her shoulders.

"Well, well," she said. "An officer."

"Be quiet."

The lieutenant's heart fluttered with anxiety and from the strain of climbing the steep side of the ridge from the shelf where he'd left his horse. He'd spied the gang's campfires nearly two hours ago, and had decided to sneak into the encampment and retrieve the stolen money. He'd decided he couldn't wait for Hawk, or count on another chance to secure the currency.

"Get dressed," he ordered the woman, keeping the rifle aimed at her head. "If you try to run or summon the others, I'll kill you."

The annoying smile fixed on her lips, she rose slowly and backed away, keeping her hands raised, proudly exposing her breasts. "Most men prefer me naked."

"Shut up."

Calmly, she squatted down, picked up her jeans, and straightened. She glanced at Primrose, smiled, and poked one foot into the jeans, then the other.

"How long were you watching?" she asked.

"Shut up."

"Did you come for your money . . . or something else?" Buttoning her trousers, she threw her head back, arching her spine and causing her full breasts to bounce.

Primrose swallowed. "One more word, and you'll get what the sergeant got."

She sighed melodramatically and stooped to retrieve her shirt.

Primrose followed her movements with the rifle, glancing around nervously but also with a certain glee. In the back of his mind, he imagined the expression on his father-in-law's face when Devereaux learned that his worthless son-in-law had secured not only the stolen currency but two of the killers who'd stolen it, including the double-crossing Schmidt.

He had rope in his saddlebags. He'd lead them down the scarp and tie them near his horse while he searched for the money.

What then? He had only one horse. . . .

"Are you sure you want me to cover these?" the girl said, holding her shirt in one hand, indicating her heaving bosoms with the other. "Most men prefer them exposed."

"I told you to —"

Behind him, Schmidt gurgled. Primrose glanced toward the sergeant, who remained unconscious beside the rock, his pants and issue underwear bunched around his boots, his heavy thighs appearing inordinately pale in the darkness.

Primrose turned back to the girl. She had dropped the shirt and was bolting toward him, grunting savagely, knocking his rifle wide with her right hand.

Having been a pugilist at West Point, Primrose was fast on his feet. He pivoted sharply right, swung the rifle left, and tossed the girl over his left hip. Hitting the ground hard, hair flying, she raised an angry wail. She got it only half out, however, before Primrose smashed the butt of the Spencer against her right temple.

Her head hit the ground with a thud. She lay still, on her right shoulder, hair shrouding her face.

Raising a hand to the scratch she'd clawed across his left cheek, he said, "Well, that's one way to skin a cat."

With neckerchiefs and the girl's own shirt, he bound and gagged her and the sergeant, then, taking the Spencer in both hands, began walking northward down the scarp. Meandering around boulders and desert brush, he followed the smell of smoke to a gully lip, edged a peek through a notch in the rocks.

At the bottom of the gulley, a small fire was dying down. Around the fire were five men, three asleep, the other two playing a quiet game of cards. Guns and knives were propped about like jackstraws. Spying no moneybags, Primrose scuttled back from the lip, then continued toward the light of the second campfire, another thirty yards down the ravine.

A half-dozen more men lounged about the second fire, snoring or humming or cleaning their guns. One man was trimming his fingernails with a bowie knife. There appeared no money pouches amidst the weapons and camping gear, so Primrose stole on down the cut.

He found the pouches nearly twenty minutes later. The two burlap sacks, stamped "U.S." and roughly the size of twenty-five-pound feed bags, were leaning against a rock in a narrow neck of the ravine. A saddle and rumpled bedroll lay nearby, as did saddlebags, a rifle, gun belt, and several articles of clothing, including a hat. Between Primrose and the money, the glowing pink ashes of a burned-down fire lay within a stone ring, an open-lidded coffeepot standing on a flat rock near the coals.

As he lay on the ravine's southern lip, goatheads and clatclaw nipping at his exposed skin, Primrose's heart raced and his mouth went dry. He was about to raise himself and move forward, when the sound of trickling water rose ahead and right. Looking toward the sound, he saw the silhouette of a man in long gray underwear standing between a barrel cactus and brush growing over a low rock pile.

Primrose returned his weight to his elbows and snugged his right index finger against his Spencer's trigger, setting that thumb on the hammer. Frustration nipped him.

The money was less than thirty feet away, and only one man was guarding it. But that man was awake.

The lieutenant uttered a silent curse.

The man across the gully bent his knees, shaking himself. He crouched slightly then, tucking himself back into his underwear, began shuffling stocking-footed back toward his bedroll. He stopped, swaying slightly, as if drunk. He swung his head around as if looking for something.

"Saradee?" he grunted. "Angel, where the hell are you?"

Right of the man's bivouac, a horse whinnied a quiet reply. The lieutenant saw the shapes of two horses in the brush across the ravine, both peering toward the man who'd called for Saradee.

The man staggered around the fire, peering up and down the ravine. He stopped, moved heavy-footed back to his bedroll, knelt down, and picked up a bottle. He uncorked the bottle and took a long drink. Primrose heard several healthy chugs. When the man had recorked the bottle and set it back against his saddlebags, he looked at the money pouches.

"Well," he said, his voice clear in the silent night, "at least the little bitch didn't get the money."

He set both bags against his saddle. Primrose stretched his lips back from his teeth with dismay as the man reclined on his blanket, resting his head in the crack between the two bags. He drew half his blanket over his body, yawned, spat, turned his head this way and that, getting comfortable, and entwined his hands on his belly.

In less than a minute, his jaw dropped and grumbling, liquid snores rose from his throat.

Primrose stared at the prostrate figure, the U.S. Army pouches pale lobes behind the man's head. The lieutenant's heart had slowed, but it quickened again as he considered his course of action . . . as, to his own surprise and horror, he found himself pushing off his elbows and knees, crawling forward until he was free of the brush, then slowly gaining his feet.

He stood, heart thudding, hands clammy, peering up and down the ravine. Steeling himself, he stepped forward. He didn't realize he'd stepped on a stone that floodwaters had left hanging over the lip's edge. It gave way beneath his right foot. He and the rock dropped two feet straight down with a sudden, crunching thud.

To Primrose, it sounded as loud as a rifle shot.

The jolt shook his innards around, but the lieutenant remained on his feet. Gritting his teeth, he looked at the man on the other side of the ravine. The outlaw threw his right arm out lazily, muttered several garbled words. He smacked his lips and resumed snoring.

Primrose blinked. A drunk, sound-asleep outlaw. What luck.

Holding the rifle straight out before him, he crossed the ravine, swinging around the near-dead fire, and hunkered down on the man's right side. He looked at the money-bags. The man was snugged up against them. There was no way to lift the bags without raising the man's head. Surely, even as drunk as he was, that would wake him.

Primrose winced and ran a gloved hand over his goatee. He should cut the man's throat, but that would be cold-blooded murder. Besides, there was always a chance the man would call out and signal the others.

Looking around, he saw the man's saddle-bags. Quietly, he picked up the bags, moved to the middle of the ravine, emptied both pockets, and refilled them with sand. Returning to the sleeping man, he squatted down, set the bags beside him, then unsheathed his knife and set it on a rock to his left.

The outlaw continued snoring, mouth open, a wing of black hair in his eyes. His head was canted slightly toward the lieutenant. His pockmarked right cheek twitched.

Primrose stared at him, his pulse drumming in his ears, rubbing his sweaty hands on his trousers. Finally, uttering a silent prayer, he placed his left hand on the back of the man's head and, wincing, shoved it forward.

The man grunted, his breath catching in his throat, both arms falling to the ground beside him. Quickly, with his right hand, Primrose jerked both money sacks out from behind the outlaw.

He grabbed the saddlebags by the broad middle strap, but they were too heavy to lift with only one hand. Standing quickly, he propped the man up with his left knee, then picked up the bags with both hands, and slipped them between the man's shoulders and the saddle.

Gently, he eased the man back against the saddlebags.

"You lynx!" the man said, suddenly shaking his head. "Where'd you learn how to do *that?*"

Head lolling back against the rounded saddlebags, the man grinned. His cheek twitched. The grin faded, his jaw dropped, and another gurgling snore rose up from deep in his chest.

Primrose sheathed his knife. The money pouches were joined by a four-foot rope. When he'd draped the pouches over his shoulders, he picked up his rifle, a lariat, and two bridles. Moving slowly and glancing back at the snoring outlaw, he walked around the fire and turned toward the two horses.

Ten minutes later, he'd bridled both mounts, draped the money pouches over the neck of one, and led them across the ravine. It took him nearly an hour to find his way back up the scarp, via a route wide of the other two outlaw encampments.

At the top, he tied the horses to ironwood saplings and looked around. The sergeant was where Primrose had left him, belly down, bare ass in the air, hands tied behind his back. He appeared to still be out.

The girl had crawled about twenty yards from where Primrose had dropped her. She lay on her side, lifting her head toward him, gagging against the neckerchief he'd tied across her mouth. Her breasts bounced and jostled as she kicked her tied ankles, trying to free them.

"That will do you no good at all," Primrose told her, leaning down and pulling her over his shoulder. "I was the knot-tying champion of Albany for three years in a row."

He threw her, belly down, over the back of the horse with the moneybags draped around its neck. She arched her back and thrust her head at him, grunting furiously, resisting. Primrose swung the back of his right hand across her left cheek. That took the starch out of her; her head sagged down against the roan's ribs.

Cutting two short lengths of rope from the lariat, he tied her hands to her ankles beneath the horse's belly. That done, he went to work wrestling the half-conscious Schmidt onto the back of the other horse — not an easy task with a man Schmidt's size. To keep from breaking his own back, Primrose led the dun over the ridge's lip, then dropped Schmidt over the lip and onto the horse below.

He led the horse back to the ridge crest, and was tying the sergeant the way he'd tied the girl when footsteps rose behind him. He turned, heart hammering, reaching for his rifle. Had he gotten too greedy, taken too much time?

A shadow moved toward him, weaving through the brush.

Primrose cocked the Spencer, aimed, and waited. Behind him, the girl gave a long, fierce groan from beneath her gag. The horse blew and shuffled sideways.

"Gringo bastard," a woman's voice snapped in front of him. The shadow moved toward him — a small, dark, long-haired figure taking shape, wearing a man's blue-checked shirt. "You were going to leave me?"

Primrose blinked. The prostitute, Estella Chacon, marched toward him. He lowered the rifle. Guilt pricked at him. "I . . . I'm sorry, miss, I —"

"Forgot about me. It's so easy to forget a whore, isn't it?"

"How did you get free?"

She stopped and scowled up at him. "One of the men took me off in the brush. While he was trying to stick it in, I grabbed his pistol and beat him over the head with it." She held up the Starr .44, which appeared ridiculously large in her small brown hand. "I was hiding in the brush, waiting for the others to go to sleep, so I could steal a horse. Then, I saw you."

Primrose felt a proud thrill travel through him. Not only had he secured the money, and two thieves, but a hostage!

"Come along, Miss Chacon," he said, turning, "you can ride with the other woman."

"Miss Jones and the sergeant, eh? How did you get them?"

Primrose helped her onto the bareback horse, behind the other woman, whose body fairly rippled with rage. "They were . . . otherwise disposed . . ."

"Fucking, uh? It figures."

11.
"BYE, BYE, LIEUTENANT!"

Primrose led the horses down the trough he'd climbed, to the shelf where his own bay waited, owl-eyed. He mounted up and led the other two horses to the bottom of the scarp where, dark as ink, the crazily cut desert stretched off in three directions.

He decided to ride south, turn east at the far end of the mountain range to which the scarp belonged, then head back north through the basin Gideon Hawk had traversed. It was his best chance of eluding the outlaws. When they woke up and found the money gone, they'd no doubt scour the west side of the mountains first. If they found his tracks, however, they'd be on him, as the old salts would say, like flies on fresh hog shit.

Hopefully, he'd run into Hawk. He could use all the help he could get — even that of an outlaw lawman.

Mid-morning, he handed the reins of the

sergeant's horse to the whore, and kneed his own bay to the crest of a low rise. He fished his field glasses from his saddlebags and scanned their back trail, seeing nothing but the same rocky chaparral he'd been traversing since leaving the outlaws' encampment.

He returned the binoculars to the saddlebags and rode back down to where Miss Chacon sat the roan behind the kill-crazy blonde. The outlaw woman had long since worn herself out and, tied belly-down across the horse's back, had fallen silent.

"Any sign of the bandits?" asked the whore. She wore a scarf around her head, to protect herself from the sun. She still wore Hawk's spare shirt, more like a smock on her small frame, but her copper-brown legs and feet were bare beneath the spangled skirt.

"I think we've eluded them," Primrose said with a satisfied, almost jubilant air.

He swung down from his saddle and adjusted the whore's pistol, which he'd wedged behind his cartridge belt when she'd found no convenient way to carry it. He approached the woman whom the whore had called Miss Jones. Her long hair hung nearly to the ground. Her bare back and arms were mottled pink from the sun.

Primrose squatted beside her. "I'll remove the gag and let you ride upright if you promise to stay quiet."

The woman lay still. Finally, she nodded her head.

Primrose removed the handkerchief, then reached under the roan's belly with his knife, and cut the ropes. Gently but cautiously, he helped the woman off the horse. When he released her arm and stepped back, raising his rifle, she dropped to her knees and elbows, like a puppet whose strings had been cut. Her thick hair hung to the ground in frizzy tangles.

Her shoulders rose and fell as she breathed. Her voice was pain-pinched. "Bastard."

"Get back on the horse. I'll let you ride astraddle, if you're good."

She lifted her flushed face, the skin chafed from the horse's coarse hide. "I need some water."

"I'll give you water once you're back atop the horse, with your ankles tied." Remembering how fast she could move, Primrose retreated another step, and thumbed back the Spencer's hammer.

Slowly, she stood, flipped her hair back, and glared at him. She glanced at the money pouches draped over the horse's neck, then turned back to Primrose. "That's a lot of money. You and me" — she stretched a wooden smile — "we could have quite a time with all that money in Juarez . . . Mexico City. Hell, we could go on down to Buenos Aires."

Unconsciously, he glanced at her breasts. He'd never seen breasts that full. Lucy, bless her heart, was relatively flat-chested.

As if she were reading his mind, the woman's eyes flashed darkly.

Primrose stared at her down the Spencer's barrel. "Get on the ~~goddamn~~ horse, Miss Jones, or I'll drill a round through your killing heart."

Her smile evaporated. "I'm burning up." She hefted her breasts in her hands, stepping toward him. "Look at these. That horse's damn hide is chafing my tits."

"Get on the horse, and I'll give you my tunic."

She glared at him for several more seconds, then led the horse over to a rock, stepped from the rock onto the horse's bare back, in front of the whore, who was regarding her distastefully. Jones looked at Primrose expectantly. Lowering the rifle, he slipped out of his tunic, handed it to her, watched as she drew the dusty, blue garment about her shoulders.

142

When he'd tied her ankles beneath the horse's belly, he gave her his canteen, then walked back to where Sergeant Schmidt lay across the third horse. Schmidt lay motionless, his dusty red hair glistening in the mid-morning light. His broad shoulders, straining his tunic's seams, rose and fell as he breathed.

Primrose slipped the gag's knot free from the back of his head, pocketed the neckerchief, then walked around to the other side of the horse. He unsheathed his knife, then stooped down to cut the ropes beneath the dun's belly.

He froze. The ropes were untied, dangling from the sergeant's ankles.

Primrose's heart lurched. Before he could straighten, the sergeant's right heel rose in a blur of motion, smashing savagely against the underside of Primrose's chin. The lieutenant stumbled back, his jaw on fire with several cracked teeth.

Regaining his balance, he lifted his rifle as before him the sergeant threw himself off the horse. He landed on both feet, pivoted, and shambled toward Primrose, a savage grin showing white on his big, red face.

Before Primrose could aim the rifle, the sergeant kicked the butt from the lieutenant's right hand. The rifle flew up and over

Primrose's right shoulder, hitting the ground with a crack.

The lieutenant dropped his stinging right hand to his holster, but before he could get the cover unsnapped, the sergeant was on him, the man's right fist hammering across his jaw, the blow rattling his brains and seemingly knocking his eyes from his skull.

He dropped to a knee. He'd just turned his head back toward the sergeant when Schmidt slammed his ham-sized left fist against Primrose's right cheek. Blood flew from the gaping cut.

Primrose was thrown sideways. He rolled off his right shoulder. With bells tolling in his head, and the ground pitching with nauseating swiftness, he rose to a crouch.

He remembered the whore's gun wedged behind his cartridge belt, and reached for it. The sergeant's big, bulky frame closed on him again with amazing swiftness and horrifying menace, fists raised, oak-sized legs spread for power and balance.

Abandoning the pistol — he wouldn't have time to aim and cock it — the lieutenant dropped his head and sprang off his haunches. He ducked under the sergeant's right haymaker and rammed his head and shoulders into the big man's belly.

Primrose hadn't pounced with as much

force as he'd intended, yet the sergeant, sapped from the ride, was bulled over backward. The lieutenant landed on top of him, wheezing with fear and fury. He pushed onto his knees and went to work on the man's face with a combination so desperate and feeble, they would have gotten him laughed out of his boxing club.

Drained as he was, Primrose hammered away at the man's face. He had to knock the starch out of him, hurt him deeper than the lieutenant himself was hurt. Then Primrose could crawl away and draw one of his pistols.

It didn't work.

With an enraged bellow, the sergeant blocked Primrose's left fist with his own forearm. He rolled sideways, sending a right pile driver against the lieutenant's upper left chest. The wind left Primrose's lungs with a whooosh! He flew several feet sideways. As he struck the ground on his shoulder, his head glanced off a sharp rock.

The sky went red, and the world went silent.

The quiet, red world slid this way and that as, on his back, Primrose stared up at Schmidt. The sergeant loomed over him, appearing to lean first one way, then the other. His face was dirty and bloody. He smiled brightly.

Primrose reached for the pistol wedged against his belly. Too slow. The sergeant bent down and swiped it from his hand, like grabbing candy from a toddler.

The sergeant's bloody smile grew. He raised the revolver in his right hand, thumbed back the hammer, squinted one eye as he aimed down the barrel at Primrose.

"Fuckin' lieutenant's gonna die," he sang. He waved good-bye with his right hand. "Bye, bye, Lieutenant!"

Primrose's eyes slitted as he stared up at the pistol's maw. The gun sagged, jerked slightly right. It coughed and smoked.

The slug ripped into the ground a few inches right of Primrose's head.

Startled and confused, the lieutenant canted a cockeyed gaze at Schmidt. The sergeant's face was bunched with pain, his mouth shaping an O.

The pistol dropped from his right hand as, sagging to his left knee, he reached down to his right thigh, from which the feathered end of an arrow protruded.

Schmidt fell to a shoulder, groaning. Behind him, several painted warriors scrambled down a boulder pile, howling like Satan on Sunday.

■ ■ ■ ■

Earlier, at false dawn, Waylon Kilroy's eyes snapped open. He'd been dreaming that Saradee had poked one of her beautiful .45s into his mouth and pulled the trigger, and that he was staring up at her, the hole in his throat spurting blood, insisting he'd had no intention of killing her, and how could she possibly believe such a thing?

He loved her!

Kilroy's heart hammered.

It slowed as he looked around. Saradee wasn't standing before him. He lifted his right hand to his throat. No hole.

He continued sweeping his eyes around the narrow ravine he and the wild outlaw woman had camped in, away from the others. Saradee's lovemaking screams were notorious.

She wasn't here. Her side of their bedroll hadn't been slept on. Usually, this time of the morning, with the faint pearl glow in the eastern sky dimming the stars, she'd have already gotten up to rebuild the fire and make coffee and slice salt pork into a skillet. He often teased that she'd have made a good squaw.

Apparently, she'd never returned to the

camp after they'd made love last night.

He leaned back against his saddle to ponder where she'd gone, worry nipping at him, when he felt the two bulging leather pouches behind him. Strange. He vaguely remembered propping the money back there.

He turned. It was the saddlebags, all right. His heart hammered and a low whistle, like that of a distant train approaching fast, rose in his ears. He stared at both flaps, lifted his heavy hands, undid the left flap, and reached inside.

Sand.

That bitch.

He bolted to his feet, the blankets flying, and whipped his head around.

That fucking bitch!

Still in his stocking feet, he leapt the fire ring and ran to where he'd turned out the horses. Both gone. Heading back to his bedroll, he dressed quickly, wrapped his pistol belt around his waist. He'd drill her through each breast, then each eye, then . . .

He donned his hat and, checking one of his revolvers to make sure all six cylinders showed brass, he jogged down the ravine, leaping the shadowy shapes of brush clumps, stones, and driftwood branches. He approached the next camp, a half-dozen men sprawled around a cold fire ring. He kicked the first man he came to — one of Saradee's own boys. The man's eyes snapped open, and his right hand reached for the revolver holstered beside him.

Kilroy clamped a boot down on the gun. "It's Kilroy. Get up, and wake the others."

"What the hell?"

Continuing on past the man, stepping around the others, several of whom were groaning and blinking their eyes, he continued on down the ravine. His own men were camped fifty yards beyond Saradee's. The two factions usually camped separately; it kept the fistfights, knife fights, and lead swaps to a minimum.

When the sprawled figures appeared, one man standing at the right edge of the bivouac, yawning as he peed on a flat rock, Kilroy whistled and called his name. Still pissing, Kevin Redmond turned to him, frowning.

"What's up, Boss?"

Several of the others jerked awake, a couple reaching automatically for their weapons. "Everybody up," Kilroy ordered. "That bitch ran off with the money. I want everybody at my camp in five minutes."

Turning and jogging back the way he'd come, Kilroy yelled furiously over his shoulder, "Five minutes!"

He took four more strides and stopped. Someone had called his name. He lifted his gaze up the scarp to his right. A man stood on a rock jutting above the ridge crest. He held a rifle high above his head, waved it slowly from left to right.

His voice drifted down the ridge. "Come on up! You gotta see this!"

12.
RED DEVILS

The sun was high, and Kilroy and his men had ridden hard for nearly four hours, when he halted his long-legged pinto suddenly and dismounted. He poked his hat back and crouched near a spindly mesquite shrub, squinting his eyes against the fierce desert light.

"Here we go," he said, picking up a horse apple and crumbling it between his fingers. "They came through here 'bout an hour ago, headin' that way." He nodded south, where the tracks of the three horses could be seen in the rocks and caliche rising gently toward a low, piñon-studded bench.

The sun hammered and cicadas screamed.

"Where do you s'pose they got the third horse?" asked Barnal Montoya, one of Saradee's riders — a squat Mexican with a predilection for sweet Mexican cigarettes. A former *revolutionario,* and known as one of the deadliest gunmen to hail from Sonora, he wore crossed bandoliers over his ratty brown poncho, which had gold zigzag designs stitched across the front.

"We done talked about that," Kilroy said evenly, looking benignly up at the Mexican sitting the tall, dun Arabian. "We said we didn't know where that third horse come from. But you, Bernal, can rest assured that Miss Saradee Jones will fill us all in, soon as we catch up to her."

Montoya glanced off, removing the black cigarillo from his lips, blowing smoke through his nostrils. He glanced meaningfully at one of his compadres, a half-Cheyenne and former gambling-hall bouncer named Jerry "J.J." Beaver Killer.

Beaver Killer shook his head and snorted. "I'd like to know how this ever happened in the first place." He chuckled without humor. "Shit, Kilroy, you know what a ~~goddamn~~ wolverine she is."

"That's what he likes about her maybe, uh?" said Montoya, grinning.

The others, including a few of Kilroy's own men, laughed.

His ears warming, Kilroy turned out a stirrup and swung into his saddle. He cut his eyes between Montoya and Beaver Killer, no longer caring if his voice betrayed his annoyance. "We done talked about all

152

this. She knocked me over the head with a tequila bottle and lit off with Schmidt. The sarge probably threw whiskey off the scarp to get him out of their way."

Kilroy adjusted his position on the saddle and leaned forward, crossing his hands on the horn. His blood sizzled. Here he was, being insulted by the men of the outlaw bitch who'd double-crossed and cuckolded him, made him look the fool before the eyes of his own men and hers!

"Not to turn this into somethin' ugly," he said, "but since we're all so fuckin' curious — I'd like to know how the hell you boys lost the whore."

"Yeah," said another of Kilroy's men, laughing. "How do you lose a whore — especially as one as perky and with such nice *cajónes?*"

Coloring behind his dark whiskers, Montoya looked over his right shoulder at the second Mexican of Saradee's group — Alberto Jiminez. The portly, bearded Jiminez sat sheepishly slumped in his saddle, head down, cutting his eyes at Montoya but not regarding the man directly. He'd ridden drag all morning, his features creased with pain from the two deep gashes the whore had torn in his skull with the butt of his own revolver.

"Why don't we all just agree that mistakes were made, huh?" said one of Kilroy's young firebrands, Dog-Tail Bascomb, squatting atop a hill shoulder behind Kilroy. He was training his field glasses southward, where the terrain dropped gently. " 'Cause I think we damn near run up the ass o' the shoat we been trackin' through the onion field."

Kilroy turned to the spade-bearded youngster wearing threadbare Confederate cavalry slacks and a pair of cross-draw, sawed-off Winchesters in custom-cut holsters. "You wanna speak English, Dog-Tail?"

Bascomb straightened, skitter-stepped down the hill, and leapt off a shelf onto the back of his ground-tied mustang. He grabbed the reins, turned the horse around, and gigged it south. "Follow me!"

Kilroy glanced around at the other men.

Seeing that none of Saradee's boys had tugged iron, he removed his own hand from his revolver's butt, and kneed his mount into Bascomb's sifting dust, weaving through the yucca, cholla, and ironwood shrubs. The ground rose gently, then dropped sharply toward a cutbank sheathed in ironwood and curl-leaf.

Kilroy halted his gelding off Bascomb's right stirrup, about ten feet from the cut bank's lip. Holding his hand up to warn the others back, he rose slightly in his saddle to peer over the lip and through the screening brush.

At the far side of the broad ravine, a half-dozen war-painted Yaqui braves milled around two women sprawled near the opposite bank. The women lay spread-eagle on their backs, their wrists and ankles tied to stakes. They were naked, their clothes strewn about the wash.

The braves were gathered around the women, obscuring Kilroy's view. He was pretty sure, however, that they were Saradee and the Mexican whore. When one of the women cursed loudly, he smiled.

"There's the lady I've come to know and love."

"What now?" Montoya asked, sitting his Arab to Kilroy's right, canting his head to peer between two desert willows.

Kilroy turned his horse around, jerking his head for the others to follow. He rode a dozen yards back from the wash, dismounted, and shucked his Winchester. "Montoya, Dog-Tail, Reynolds, Landers, and Jimbo. We're goin' in. The money's gotta be around there somewhere."

"I didn't see the sergeant," Montoya said, dismounting and tossing his reins to the rider beside him. "Maybe he slipped away from the red devils . . . with the lucre."

"Don't bet on it."

"How you want to do this?"

"Us six'll circle around, slip up on 'em from the west." Kilroy turned to the bulk of the men still saddled. "You boys keep an eye on our backsides. There only appears to be six or seven, but there might be more hidden or on the scout."

Kilroy and Montoya headed west behind the brush screening the wash, the other four men hustling along behind. Jimbo Walsh slipped shells into the pepperbox revolver he carried in a deer-hide sheath just above his left knee.

Kilroy glanced at Montoya, then angled the look behind. "No one kills Saradee. I want her alive."

"She's our ramrod," said Jimbo Walsh, closing the pepperbox and slipping it into the sheath. "I'd say she double-crossed us as bad as she double-crossed you. You just look dumber 'cause you could have prevented it."

Kilroy stopped and wheeled, rammed the barrel of his Winchester to the underside of Walsh's fleshy jaw, thumbing the rifle's hammer back. Walsh stopped, tensing and wincing, tipping his head back on his shoulders.

"I've had about enough o' that horseshit," Kilroy spat through gritted teeth. "Now, the girl's mine. You see? You got that?"

Cheeks balled with pain, Walsh nodded.

"You sure?"

Walsh nodded again.

"It sure would be foolish for us to get into a lead swap out here in Injun country." Keeping the rifle barrel snug against Walsh's jaw, Kilroy glanced at Montoya. "But if I hear any more of the bullshit I *been* hearin', that's just what's gonna happen. May the last man standing get the loot . . . and try to get to El Molina alive."

Kilroy lowered his rifle's barrel, wheeled, and continued west along the wash, knowing his own man, Dog-Tail, would watch his backside if Montoya's boys were crazy enough to start something with the money and the red devils a hundred yards away.

When they'd followed a bend halfway through its curve, they crossed the wash, mounted the opposite bank, and headed back toward the Indians. The red devils were chattering like churchwomen at an ice-cream social, their guttural tongue sounding like total nonsense to the outlaws' monolingual ears.

Kilroy and the other men hunkered down in the brush on the wash's southern bank and stole peeks through the rocks. Below, a small, Yaqui-style fire crackled in the shade of several boulders and desert willows jutting around a spring. Several Indians were cutting strips of meat from the hip of a dead horse and laying it over a makeshift spit. One man — short and muscular, with ochre paint making a ghoulish mask of his face — rose from between the whore's spread legs.

Looking down at her and grinning savagely, he pulled his loincloth up to his waist. Beneath him, the whore's head was turned to one side, her lips puffed and bleeding. Her closed eyes were purple and swollen. Kilroy couldn't tell if she was breathing. He'd heard that Yaquis, like Apaches, would as soon ravage a dead woman as a living one.

Another Indian was still working away between the spread legs of Saradee. She was spitting and cursing at him, raging like a demon. Kilroy chuffed a laugh. She was spewing more filth than he'd heard even her utter before. The girl could write a dictionary.

The Indian between her legs stopped thrusting his hips and gave her a dirty look, barked a warning. She jerked her head up, spat in his face. He laid the back of his right hand across her jaw, hard enough for the crack to reach Kilroy's ears. A half second later, the brave had a knife in his hand.

"No, you don't," Kilroy heard himself shout as he stood and raised his Winchester. "That bitch is mine, you gut-eatin' son of a sow!"

Kilroy's rifle barked before the last word had left his mouth. The Indian atop Saradee had lifted his head toward the cut bank's lip, as if purposely giving Kilroy a better target. The bullet plunked through his left temple with an angry *thwunk,* brains and blood spewing onto the sand and gravel behind him.

As the other outlaws rose to their knees or feet, several yipping like lobos as they snapped their rifles to their shoulders, Kilroy drew a bead on the Indian who'd just finished with the whore. The brave dropped to a crouch, cutting his own black-eyed gaze at the cut bank. As he bolted right, toward a sheltering boulder, Kilroy drilled him through the stomach, punching him back and sideways. The brave dropped to his knees and threw his head back, screaming like a mountain lion in heat.

Kilroy levered a fresh shell and gazed into the wash. His and Saradee's men were triggering their own Winchesters, one shot after another, shredding several Indians where they stood, sending the others either diving for the sheltering rocks and their weapons, or running up the arroyo, toward their horses picketed in the shade of an overhanging scarp.

The outlaws had caught the Indians with their pants down, both literally and figuratively. In less than a minute, all were down, only one having managed to fling an arrow toward the outlaws. Kilroy and the others held their fire, peering through the wafting powder smoke as they scrutinized the bodies strewn about the wash.

"Never thought it'd be so easy to kill Yaquis," muttered Montoya.

Kilroy ordered the men to spread out, to scour the wash and surrounding ridges for more of the red devils. He doubted they'd find any. The Yaquis were known to travel in small, coyotelike packs, thus raising little dust or noise as they snuck up on their prey, which included virtually anyone not from their band.

When the men had drifted off, Kilroy and Montoya stepped from boulder to boulder as they descended the wash. Kilroy had gained the bottom, and was moving toward the staked women when something moved in the corner of his right eye. One of the braves had been playing possum. Now he bolted to his feet and ran, limping slightly, toward the horses.

Kilroy casually raised his Winchester, dropped the kid with one shot between the shoulder blades. The Indian flew straight forward and hit the ground belly-first, dust puffing.

"Waylon." Saradee's pinched voice rose on his right. He turned to the woman. Straining at her ties, she canted an awkward glance at him. Her face was bloody, wisps of her filthy hair stuck to her cheeks. "Oh, Waylon, thank God it's you."

Kilroy stood over her, his shadow angling across her naked body. He glanced at the whore. She appeared unconscious, but her chest rose and fell slightly, and her eyelids fluttered.

"It's me, all right," Kilroy said, returning his gaze to Saradee. "Your loyal Waylon."

"The lieutenant," she rasped, moving her puffy lips. "He caught me in the brush . . . forced me to go with him."

Kilroy squatted down, holding the rifle barrel up between his knees. "The lieutenant?"

"The one from the detail. We didn't kill him."

Kilroy frowned, but before he could ask

his next question, a voice rose. "Boss, lookee here!"

Kilroy looked up the wash to his right. The half-Delaware with Negro blood, Rufus Bunkmeyer, held up one of the money sacks in one hand, his sawed-off shotgun in the other, a big grin on his cherry-red face. His green eyes flashed in the sun.

Kilroy straightened. "Praise the Lord and whistle 'Dixie.' "

"There's moah," Bunkmeyer said, jerking his head up wash. "Betta come have a look, Boss."

Kilroy glanced down at Saradee. She frowned up at him, bending her right knee, pulling at the ties. "Untie me, please, Waylon."

Kilroy turned and walked toward Bunkmeyer. The woman called his name, her voice gradually acquiring an edge until she yelled, "Goddamnit, *you limp-dicked fuck, untie me or I'll gut you like a fucking pig!*"

"That's my girl," Kilroy muttered, giving his head a single shake as Bunkmeyer turned and led him around a bend.

As he stepped out of the shade of two towering cottonwoods, he saw what appeared to be two oval, sun-blasted rocks in the middle of a sand wash. When he walked closer, however, he saw they were human heads — men's heads, one with a trimmed cap of brown hair parted on one side, the other with thick red hair and matching mustache and beard.

The latter belonged to Sergeant Schmidt. The former, apparently, belonged to the lieutenant whom Saradee had mentioned.

Both were cut, scraped, bloody dirty, and sunburned. If they hadn't been wincing and squinting their eyes and gritting their teeth, Kilroy would have thought the heads had been hacked from bodies and thrown to the buzzards.

"Well, I'll be a monkey's uncle." Kilroy laughed, jerking his pants up his thighs and hunkering down between the two men. "Schmidt, you son of a bitch, where's the rest of ya?"

Schmidt stretched his lips back from his teeth, grunted, groaned, sighed. "Get me outta here, Waylon. For the love o' God . . ."

Kilroy laughed. "Those devils sure had a time with you. You got all your parts down there? Damn idiot!"

"Come on, Waylon. This weren't my fault. It's the ~~goddamn~~ lieutenant. He tracked us down, took me by surprise." Schmidt blinked sharply, licked his chapped, sandy lips, and rolled his gaze to the soldier beside him. "Dig me up and put a bullet in his head. Let's get outta here."

"Well, now wait a minute. I know the whore got away on her own. But how in the hell did the bluebelly here end up with you and Saradee?"

Schmidt blinked. It was hard to tell under his sunburn and patches of peeling skin, but Kilroy thought blood rushed to the man's face. "Hell, I don't know. Dig me up, damnit. We got us a deal, you and me!"

The lieutenant cleared his throat and lifted his head slightly at Kilroy, slitting one eye. "Before you do that," he rasped, swallowing, "you might want to consider the fact that I found the good sergeant and the lady copulating atop a boulder."

"Now, whoah!" Schmidt interrupted. "Just wait a ~~goddamn~~ minute!"

"That's how I was able to sneak up on them so easily," the soldier added.

Schmidt spat. "He's lyin'!"

Kilroy slid his gaze to the sergeant. "Why would he lie?"

"He's lyin', I say! ~~Goddammit~~, Waylon, I wouldn't do somethin' that low. Why, that's . . . that's . . . *low!*"

"Just about as low as double-crossin' your own soldier boys," Kilroy said, giving his head a quick, wistful shake.

"He's just tryin' to turn you against me,

164

Waylon. Don't you see?"

"Yeah, I see," Kilroy said, straightening. "He's doin' a good job."

"Waylon, please. For the love o' Christ, get me outta here. I can't breathe!"

The mulatto, Bunkmeyer, chuckled behind Kilroy and extended his sawed-off shotgun toward Schmidt's head. "Want me to shut him up, Boss?"

"No," Kilroy said. "Leave 'em. We'll leave them both here to fry and for the buzzards to pick at. Buzzards gotta eat too."

Bunkmeyer shrugged and lowered the shotgun. Most of the other men — including those who'd remained on the opposite side of the ravine — had gathered around Kilroy, the mulatto, and the two buried men.

Montoya said, "And the women?"

Kilroy looked at him. He bunched his lips angrily, pushed past Montoya and the others, heading back toward where Saradee was staked out with the whore. "Mount up and move out!"

Behind him, Schmidt shouted, "Waylon, don't leave me here, ya son of a bitch!"

As the other men headed back to their horses and the sergeant continued screaming until his voice cracked, Kilroy squatted down beside Saradee. She looked up at him uncertainly, glancing at the knife in his hand. "Waylon . . . ?"

"You've been through a lot, haven't you, angel?"

She watched the knife blade wink as it moved past her face, within an inch of her nose — so close that even through her swollen eyes she could see its razor edge — then down past her belly and legs, to the rawhide thong binding her left ankle. It slit the thong as though it were no more than a thin string.

"I sure have," she sniffed.

He grunted slightly as he cut the thong on her right ankle. "I'm just gonna have to treat you extra special for the next few days, ain't I?"

As he moved the knife up slowly past her face again, and cut the thong binding her left wrist, she watched him apprehensively, her bare breasts rising and falling sharply. "That'd be nice."

When he'd freed her other wrist, Kilroy ran his thumb across the knife blade, checking its edge. He sheathed the knife, bent down, and scooped Saradee up in his arms. "Let's head south, angel. I'm gonna arrange a very special treat for you in El Molina."

"A treat?"

"Why, of course, a treat."

As he carried her across the draw, she

draped her arms around his neck. "Waylon, you ain't mad about nothin', are you?"

He didn't look at her. "What would I have to be mad about, angel?"

She didn't say anything. Her shapely legs flopped over his arm as he climbed the ravine's opposite bank.

She stared at him uncertainly.

She had a feeling that, sometime in the very near future, she was going to wish he'd left her staked out with the whore.

13.
HUNGRY VISITOR

Two hours after the outlaws had left, Lieutenant Primrose licked his lips. He'd been so long without water that his tongue had no moisture in it. The maneuver only burned the cracks and scrapes, reminded him how sore his eyes were. They too were dry as stones.

At least, the Indians hadn't gotten around to cutting off his lids. He'd seen that before, and it wasn't pretty. Men's eyes turned to charcoal.

The sun had angled westward, canting shade out from the brush and rock scarps at the ravine's western edge, giving him and Schmidt some relief from the blinding rays that had made the lieutenant's eyes feel as though they'd been rubbed with sandpaper.

There was a sound like wet sheets flapping in a breeze. Shadows flicked across the sand before Primrose.

"Ah, shit," Schmidt said to his left. "Here

those mangy buzzards come again."

Primrose tipped his head back as far as it would go and lifted his aching eyes. Buzzards were careening above the wash, waiting their turn at the dead Indians around the bend to the west. Several occasionally swooped low for a better look at Primrose and Schmidt. The sergeant shouted curses, trying to hold the birds at bay, but by now his voice was so hoarse, it barely carried even to Primrose ten feet to his right.

The birds would get braver as the night descended. The thought churned the bile in Primrose's gut, and he again tried to move his arms and legs. It was no use. His wrists were tied behind his back, his ankles firmly bound with knotted rawhide. Even if the limbs were free, he doubted he'd have been able to move against the sand encasing him here like wet cement.

"Why the Jehovah couldn't they have just shot us?" Schmidt wheezed. "I'd have done as much for them."

"Speak for yourself, Sergeant."

"What? You enjoy the prospect of buzzards eating out your eyes before you're even dead?"

Again, Primrose tried to move, grunting with the effort. It made him somewhat breathless. "I haven't yet given up hope."

"Well, that's real admirable. My hat's off to you. But we're dyin', Lieutenant. And there ain't nothin' all your West Point schoolin' can do —"

"Oh, hell," Primrose said, cutting Schmidt off.

Schmidt rolled his eyes around. "What, what?"

Primrose stared at the gap in the brush where he'd seen the brown shadow slink. "Something on the bank . . . just moved."

"I don't see anything," Schmidt said after a minute.

Primrose's eyes scoured the brush. There wasn't a breath of breeze. Seventy yards down the ravine, the birds barked and quarreled. Gray-blue shadows leaned out from the bank.

The lieutenant peered into the gap in the brush marking a game trail. His heart leapt, and he stopped breathing. In the shadowy gap — actually a tunnel in the ironwood and willows — was the round, snub-nosed head of a mountain lion. Unless Primrose's fried brains and eyes were playing tricks on him.

He hoped against hope they were.

Behind the head, a tail swished. It was one of those wily, catlike whips. The mountain lion's ears stood up, then flattened back down against the head.

Shit.

"You see it?" Primrose said, expending himself again by trying to move against the ungiving sand.

Schmidt didn't say anything for a moment. He exhaled sharply. In his voice there was no venom, only hopelessness. "Son of a two-bit whore."

"Maybe he'll bypass us for the carrion farther on down the ravine."

"You tinhorn son of a bitch. Just had to trail us, didn't you? Showin' off for the major. Now you not only don't have the money you rode down here for, but you've widowed the major's daughter . . . and got me killed in the bargain!"

"I fail to see your logic, Sergeant. Your greed compelled you to kill your own soldiers. To back-shoot them. Now, you've gotten yourself killed as well."

"It pleases me no end that you're gonna die too, Lieutenant . . . with that corncob still rammed up your tight West Point ass."

"If you'd be quiet, he might leave."

"That ain't the kinda luck I've been havin'."

The cat lay there for a long time, staring at them, occasionally giving his tail that little insouciant thrash, like a barn cat waiting outside a mouse hole. Gradually, cool night shadows filled the ravine. The buzzards squawked like old ladies fighting over a parasol.

The cat rose to a crouch and padded toward the men, its dun coat flecked with dust and seeds, the tail swishing stiffly, the tufted end curled slightly, like the popper at the end of a bullwhip.

"Oh, Christ," wheezed the sergeant. "Here he fuckin' comes."

The lieutenant kept his voice down. "Hold still."

"Where might I be goin'?"

"Hold your head still and try to contain your fear. They can smell it."

Schmidt snorted.

Primrose drew air slowly into his pinched lungs, shaking off his fear as he stared at the cat padding toward them, crouched low, its tail straight out behind it now and about six inches above the ground. Six feet away, it stopped and slid its gaze between the two men, its translucent copper pupils slowly opening and closing in its yellow eyes.

Primrose could smell the animal's gamy peppery odor. A low, keening growl rose from deep in its belly. The fur at the back of its neck stood on end, and its long whiskers vibrated, as if brushed by a breeze.

The lieutenant breathed slowly in, then out. . . .

"Shit," groaned the sergeant.

"Shhh."

The cat hunkered down on its belly, rested its chin on its front paws, drew its back legs tight against its ribs.

Primrose gritted his teeth. His stomach clenched. The cat rose up slightly, stretched out its front paws, clawed at the earth, making faint scratching sounds in the sand.

"Oh, for chrissakes, just get it over with!" Schmidt bellowed as loudly as his damaged vocal chords allowed.

The cat dashed toward him, its jaws opening wide. Only six inches from the sergeant's face, it jerked and screamed.

The cat suddenly appeared to swerve away from the sergeant and head for Primrose, who gritted his teeth and closed his eyes, knowing his time had come and wishing, like the sergeant, that the beast be mercifully swift.

He felt the wind of the beast's diving body.

The cat squealed. There was a thud.

Sand sprayed the lieutenant's face, sticking to his bared teeth and bloody cheeks.

Perplexed, he opened his eyes slightly, peered through the slits.

The cat lay before him, on its right shoulder. It blinked its eyes several times, kicked its back legs, propelling its head closer to Primrose. Then the legs stopped moving, the light left the cat's yellow and copper eyes, and its lids dropped halfway closed. Blood trickled out the right corner of its gaping mouth.

The shot, which Primrose only now realized he'd heard at the same time the cat had screamed, chased its own, flat echo around the ravine.

Neither Primrose nor Schmidt said anything. Both men stared, awestruck at the dead cat lying between and before them, the half-open eyes staring up at the lieutenant. After several minutes, the thud of hooves rose up the ravine. They grew louder until horse and rider appeared in the corner of the lieutenant's left eye. The horse was a grulla covered in red desert dust. The rider wore a long, cream duster over a faded blue shirt, tan denims, and a flat-brimmed black hat. A green neckerchief was knotted loosely around his neck.

Hawk reined the horse up before Primrose and Schmidt, peered down at them over his right stirrup. The high, broad cheekbones, lake-green eyes, and dragoon-style mustache were shaded by the hat brim.

Primrose was giddy with relief. "Oh, for

pity sake," he said through a long sigh. "Hawk . . ."

"Who?" asked the sergeant.

Primrose shook his head as much as the sand allowed. "Get us out of here, Hawk."

Hawk swung down from his saddle, dropped the reins, and removed his folding shovel from behind his blanket roll. He hung his hat on his saddle horn and began digging, throwing the sand behind him. When he'd dug down to the lieutenant's waist, he cut the man's hands free. His legs were still buried. Hawk offered his canteen.

"Not too much."

Primrose took a breath and drank, wincing when the water hit his parched lips.

"I said not too much," Hawk said. "You'll puke it back up."

Choking, water dribbling down his chin, the lieutenant lowered the canteen. "You don't know how good that tastes."

Schmidt growled, "You might get me out of here and give me a shot of that."

"How'd you end up with him?" Hawk said, nodding at the sergeant, taking the canteen back, and ramming the cork in the lip.

"I stumbled onto their camp last night. Got Schmidt and the outlaw woman. The doxie was about to escape herself. I even got the money." Primrose looked around at the dead Indians upon which the buzzards eagerly fed.

Hawk had slung his canteen over the saddle horn, ignoring Schmidt's pleas for water. He turned to Primrose, picked up the shovel, and resumed digging the sand out from around his knees. "What happened?"

"Indians," Primrose said with a weary sigh. "Then . . . the outlaws. They got the money back."

Hawk slung a load of sand behind him. "The women?"

"I don't remember a thing between the initial Indian attack and waking up right here, beside the good sergeant. For all I know, the women are dead. Maybe the outlaws took them back."

Hawk rammed the shovel in the sand. "Finish digging yourself out." Turning, he toed a stirrup and swung onto the grulla.

"Hey, what about water for me?" Schmidt called weakly.

Ignoring the plea, Hawk gigged the grulla down the ravine, tracing the gradual bend as several buzzards scampered away from their carrion, screaming angrily. His horse shied at the scattered, bloody corpses and the viscera strewn by the birds.

Amidst the bodies and body parts, Hawk looked for the girl. He hoped he wouldn't find her here, that the outlaws had taken her back.

He was riding west along the darkening wash when he stopped suddenly. A slender, long-haired, blood-smeared body was staked out at the base of the southern bank, near a dead horse and a cold fire upon which strips of meat lay charred. A buzzard was perched on the girl's bare right knee, staring at her — a bald, hook-nosed demon awaiting another soul.

Hawk clawed his Russian from his hip and blew the bird's head off. He dismounted, knelt beside the girl, touched a finger to her neck. Her pulse was faint.

He cut her limbs free of the stakes, grabbed his canteen from his saddle horn, and cradling her head in his left arm, held the flask to her mouth. A few sips passed her lips; most dribbled down her chin and neck. She coughed and winced, shook her head and moaned.

She opened her eyes with a start, and glanced fearfully around the ravine. She looked at the headless buzzard lying beside her, then slid her gaze to Hawk.

Her voice was thin, nearly inaudible. "Please don't leave me for the scavengers. . . ." Her eyelids closed, and her head sagged to the side. Her chest fell still.

Hawk shook her gently. "Estella."

Dead.

The night breeze swept her hair across her swollen, bloody face. Cradling her head in his arm, Hawk smoothed her hair back from her cheeks.

"You'll be avenged."

He gentled her head to the ground, stood, and retrieved the dead horse's saddle blanket. He shook it out, wrapped the girl in it, tied it with rope, and eased the body facedown across the grulla's rear. Swinging into the saddle, he rode back around the bend.

In the gathering night, Lieutenant Primrose was digging the sergeant out of his would-be sand grave. The lieutenant had dug down to the sergeant's chest. He'd removed his tunic. He was dusty, sunburned, bloody, and nearly asleep on his feet, grunting with each toss of the sand.

"What the hell are you doing?" Hawk asked, halting the horse before him.

The lieutenant stopped, turned to him. Breathing hard, holding the shovel in both hands across his thighs, he glanced at the blanket-wrapped body behind Hawk's cantle. He looked at Hawk. "What's it look like I'm doing? I'm digging up my prisoner.

I'm taking him back to Bowie to face a court-martial."

Hawk drew the Russian. He thumbed back the hammer, extended the gun at Schmidt. Primrose stared, disbelieving, mouth agape. Schmidt's own mouth and eyes snapped wide.

"Wait . . . *no!*"

Hawk's revolver cracked. The bullet plunked through Schmidt's forehead, just above his left brow. The sergeant's head snapped back, then sagged to his left shoulder.

Primrose had flinched and leapt back at the shot. Now he stared at Schmidt. As Hawk holstered the Russian, the lieutenant turned to him, his face turning wine-colored behind the sunburn and bruises. His voice was raspy and brittle. "Y-you had no right to do that. That man was my prisoner. I was taking him back to stand trial."

"I saved you the trouble." Hawk reached down, grabbed the shovel from the lieutenant's hand. "I'll be needing this." He hooked the shovel's lanyard over his saddle horn and kneed the grulla forward.

Primrose watched, bunching his swollen lips with rage, as Hawk rode up the ravine and disappeared in the purple dusk.

■ ■ ■ ■

Hawk buried the girl on a knoll above an ancient riverbed lined with cottonwoods. He mounded the grave with dirt and, to keep predators out, stones.

He fashioned a crude cross from driftwood. He said no words over the grave, because he didn't believe in such things anymore. He merely held his hat before his chest for a few quiet moments, the dark night gathered around him, several coyotes howling from ridges.

He swung up into his saddle, descended the knoll, rode along a wash for a mile, and made camp on a sloping shoulder of ground angling out from a high, chalky butte. A spring bubbled out of the rocks, feeding some short grass and spindly brush. The water trickled down the slope and disappeared in the wash.

Hawk kept his fire small. A half hour after he'd hobbled his horse, he was sitting by his fire, eating beans and drinking coffee. A horse blew and kicked a stone.

A tired voice rose from the darkness. "It's Primrose."

Hawk said nothing. Knees raised, his boot heels snug in the dirt near the fire ring, he continued to eat.

The horse nickered, and Hawk heard hoof falls coming along the wash. Behind him and to his right, his own grulla lifted an answering whinny. Through the shrubs and boulders, a shadow moved. Tack squeaked as a man stepped down from a saddle. Boots clacked on the rocks. A figure appeared — Primrose, his tunic torn and bloody, his hat misshapen, his face so swollen it appeared round in the dim light.

He was leading a horse — one of the Indians' short-legged mustangs, with a saddle that must have been worn by the mount the Indians had been roasting. The horse looked about as comfortable with the saddle as the lieutenant looked with all those bruises on his face.

He stopped in the shadows on the other side of the fire, his shoulders slumped with fatigue. "You're still going after them?"

Hawk nodded and forked more beans into his mouth.

Primrose studied him, lines spoking his eyes. "The girl?"

Hawk lifted a shoulder and swallowed the beans in his mouth, dipped his fork for more. "I've come all this way, I'm gonna finish the job. Those killers don't deserve to live. They're due a reckoning, and I'm gonna serve it up raw."

Primrose studied him skeptically, saw the deputy U.S. marshal's badge pinned to his vest. The lieutenant shook his head. "You're not a lawman anymore, Hawk."

"That's where you're wrong, Lieutenant." Hawk chewed. "I am a lawman. I'm the *only* lawman anymore."

Primrose looked off, turned back to Hawk. "I think you're pure-dee crazy, Hawk. But I reckon you're my only hope of getting the money back. I'm going with you." He turned and led the Indian pony around the fire, toward where Hawk had hobbled the grulla.

Hawk sipped his coffee and stared into the fire.

14.
"WHY BUY THE COW . . . ?"

Seven days later, Waylon Kilroy sat in a stone crevice on a low rimrock above a narrow, boulder-strewn, sun-pummeled arroyo in southern Sonora. He trained his field glasses on the parched valley that he and the gang had traversed a few hours ago.

"Jesus, you do that well," he said, taking steady, deep breaths. "I swear, girl, you must be part-French."

Below the ridge's rocky lip, Kilroy's jeans were pulled down and bunched around his boots. He was half-sitting on a rock thumb protruding from the nook's wall. Between his naked knees, Saradee knelt, her gloved hands resting on Kilroy's thighs. Her straw sombrero — which she'd taken from one of the three Mexican miners she'd killed a few days earlier — bobbed slightly as she worked.

There was a wet sound as she lifted her head, the sombrero's brim tipping back to reveal her face, which still bore the scabbed abrasions and partial swelling of the Yaquis' savagery. "Any sign of Valverde?"

Kilroy shook his head. "I know that was him I seen earlier, though. After all these years, I can recognize that ugly bastard from five miles away. I swear he can *smell* me just as soon as I cross the Rio Grande. Comes runnin' like a dog with his tongue hangin', sniffin' around for a bone."

"Let's kill him," Saradee said, looking up at Kilroy from the shaded nook, his member in her gloved hand. "I don't want to share our hard-earned money with these damn greasers."

"He can sure make life miserable down here, but killin' him might do us more harm than good." Waylon glanced down at Saradee, frowning. "Snap to it, girl. I'm losin' my pleasure."

When she'd gone back to work, Kilroy lifted his gaze above the ridge, stopped as a vagrant thought struck him, and looked back down at her bobbing hat. Crouched there between his knees, she was in a rather vulnerable position. He could draw the big Remy from its shoulder holster and pop a pill through her beautiful, cunning head before she knew what was happening.

He wouldn't do it now, of course. Not

only was she working her sweet bliss on him, but both their gangs were waiting fifty yards down the canyon wall, near the opening of an old mine shaft.

Staring at the girl's shabby straw hat, around the steepled crown of which a bluebottle fly buzzed, Kilroy lifted the corners of his mustache. It was a good idea. He'd hold on to it for later, when her men were out of the way and he'd finally gotten his fill of the bewitching outlaw princess.

He tensed suddenly, tightening all his muscles and throwing his head back on his shoulders. "For the love o' *Jesus!*"

It took nearly a minute for his blood to settle.

"You must be half-French," he repeated through a long sigh, his heart slowing gradually. "Christ."

She looked up at him from between his knees, smiling coquettishly and running the sleeve of her calico shirt — also stolen from the miners — across her mouth. "Did you enjoy that?"

Kilroy shook his head and swallowed. He glimpsed something in the corner of his left eye. Twisting his head northward, he lifted the field glasses. He stared through the glasses, adjusting the focus.

Saradee remained kneeling between his

spread knees, his wilting member only inches from her face. A very vulnerable position. She remembered the threat in his voice when he'd rescued her from the Yaqui savages. She glanced at the pistol butts poking up from her holsters, and absently lowered her right hand to the polished grips of a .45.

"Yeah, it's him, all right." Kilroy's voice broke her reverie. "They took the bait now — headin' away from us. For now," he added dryly.

Rising, she reached for the glasses. "Let me see."

"Keep low."

"Yeah, yeah, just give me the fuckin' glasses."

Handing over the binoculars, Kilroy rose awkwardly and pulled his pants up. Saradee peered through the glasses, adjusting the focus until a dozen or so swarthy men in dark-blue uniforms galloped around a rocky mesa less than a mile away, heading south, their blond dust rising behind their sweat-lathered horses.

The lead rider was a big, broad-chested, heavy-gutted man with a flat, pocked face and large, black eyes. He wore two pearl-gripped pistols in shoulder holsters, cartridge belts crossed on his gold-buttoned, epaulette-decorated tunic.

To his left rode a tall, slender, hatchet-faced Mexican in the same blue uniform with red-striped slacks, but with a gaudy sombrero strapped beneath his chin, and with the sleeves of his tunic removed to reveal his dark, corded arms. Long, grizzled hair streaked with silver flew back in the wind. Saradee counted three knives and three pistols in various visible sheaths.

When she'd scanned the other riders — all younger versions of the two lead riders, and all armed as if for war — she lifted her cheeks in a scowl. The *federales* were a good three or four miles away. Still, she could sense their dark, fearless, south-of-the-border savagery that made even her look tame in comparison.

"Yep," Saradee said, lowering the glasses and turning a glance to Waylon buttoning the fly of his trousers in the nook behind her. "They're gonna have to go the way of all bad greasers. I won't have it any other way."

"That might be easier said than done, my flower."

She jumped down to the nook's floor, tawny hair bobbing on her shoulders. She slapped the glasses against Kilroy's chest, tipped her hat back to offer a mocking grin.

"You leave it to me if you're scared."

"As good as you are at French," Kilroy growled, glaring at her, her wiles having left him still feeling disoriented, "your English leaves something to be desired."

Saradee glanced down at the trough in the rocks leading down to the canyon floor. She extended her hand. "After you, my love."

"After you, my flower."

"I insist."

Side by side, hand in hand, they picked their way down the trough, like two young lovers on their first spring outing. Cutting cautious glances at each other, their taut smiles in place, they strolled along the shoulder of a low hill to the base of a rocky scarp, where the rest of the gang — twelve dusty riders — and their horses lounged in the shade of several mesquite shrubs and saquaros. A couple of men stood in the cool opening of a long-abandoned gold mine shrouded in desert willows. The horses were tied together under a sprawling cottonwood.

"Don't you two look handsome?" said Kevin Redmond, grinning like a bridesmaid at the happy-looking pair.

"Hansel and Gretel out fer a stroll," said Turkey McDade, sharpening his bowie knife on a whetstone. His voice was crisp. "While the rest of us sweat it out here, so damn thirsty we can smell the tequila in El Molina."

"Let the bee out of your bonnet, Turk," said Saradee, releasing Kilroy's hand and casually swiping McDade's hat from his head. "We're within an hour's ride."

"Any sign of the *federales?*" asked Dog-Tail Bascomb, running a greasy cloth over one of his sawed-off Winchesters.

"Does shit run downhill?" said Kilroy. "I told you I sensed their presence. I been down here enough times, I get a belly burn when one o' them chili-chompers is within ten miles."

McDade stooped to retrieve his hat, grumbling, "What're we gonna do about Valverde?"

"Cross that bridge when we come to it." Kilroy moved to the horse over which the money sacks were draped. He opened one of the pouches, dipped out a wad of greenbacks. "Time to part company with the lucre for a few weeks." He counted out several bills into his right hand, extended the money to Redmond, then moved on to Butch Reynolds, who was lounging against a low hummock near a barrel cactus. "A hundred dollars per man should tide us each till we can make the final divvy and part company."

"A hundred dollars?" said Bunkmeyer. "Shit, I can go through a hundred dollars in one night, Boss!"

"Rein in, fool!" snapped Saradee, rolling a smoke. "We can't go showing a bunch of money around El Molina without raising Valverde's suspicion. As long as he thinks our take in the States was small, he'll ride out and leave us alone."

She paused and glanced at Kilory still divvying up the cash. "At least, that's what Waylon thinks. Personally, I think we should kill the son of a bitch. We're gonna have to sooner or later, and I see no reason to put off for tomorrow what you *should* do today."

"There's plenty snakes from Valverde's hole," Kilroy said, slapping a wad of bills against the mulatto's vest and glancing affectionately at Saradee. "You kill one, they all come slitherin' out."

Saradee looked up with a cunning grin, poking the cigarette between her slightly swollen lips and striking a match to life on the buckle of her cartridge belt. "We'll play it your way, pet." She touched fire to the quirley, puffing smoke. "For now . . ."

"Look at how sweet they get along," said Kevin Redmond, cutting his eyes to Kilroy. "Boss, I think you should marry that girl."

"Keep your bloomers on, boy," sneered

Saradee, taking a deep drag off her cigarette and fixing her gaze on Kilroy. "Why would I buy the cow when I can get the milk for free?"

The others laughed as they stuffed their money into their pockets. Flushing, Kilroy grabbed the money sacks off the packhorse. He slung the sacks over his right shoulder and headed for the mine.

The others frowned as they watched Kilroy push through the shrubs before the mine portal.

"Hey, where you goin', Boss?" said Omaha Landers, cuffing his derby hat back on his head. His father was a Lutheran minister, and with a nod to the old man's honor, he always wore relatively clean broadcloth trousers and suspenders over a nice shirt, which looked a little ludicrous with the sawed-off ten-gauge hanging down his back.

"Stand down, Omaha."

The slender, well-dressed outlaw flushed with fury. "Stand down, my ass!"

"Can't think of a better place to hide stolen greenbacks than this mine shaft. Only a couple miles from El Molina, but Valverde'll never find it." Kilroy turned toward the group, a smug smile curving his dark-blond mustache. "In a few weeks, when we're sure we haven't been followed and our trail's grown cold, we'll come back and get it. All of us together" — he grinned from ear to ear, his blue eyes slitting cunningly — "like one big happy family!"

Kilroy turned, lowered his head a few inches, and disappeared into the dark mine portal, the others except Saradee frowning. Saradee eyed each rider, watching her man's back, ready to shoot if the need arose. It wouldn't have broken her heart to see Waylon gutted with a .44 slug, especially by his own men, but she needed him now. He'd dealt with Valverde before. She hadn't. In good time, however, he'd end up the way she'd fantasized up on the ridge, with his pants bunched around his boots, screaming like a nun in the devil's own whorehouse.

Saradee's men turned to her, eyes sharp with incredulity. Bernal Montoya, standing near the horses with the other Mex, Alberto Jiminez, was clutching the horn handle of his bowie, snugged in his shoulder sheath.

Saradee gestured for the men to stand down. She shucked her Winchester from her saddle boot and sauntered up to the low, round opening in the rock wall. All the men, including Waylon's boys, were watching her now. Waylon's scoundrels shunted their wary, angry gazes between her Winchester and her face, spreading their feet and lowering their hands to the six-shooters.

Rufus Bunkmeyer said, "What are your intentions, Miss Saradee?"

Saradee turned to the man. She remembered the three Yaquis who'd savaged her, scratching her breasts, grunting like mules, and slathering her face with their sweat and saliva. One had even tried biting her tongue off.

She kept smiling, meeting the half-breed's gaze. When Waylon was dead, she'd gut this savage with his own Arkansas toothpick. She didn't think Bunkmeyer had any Yaqui blood, but one red nigger was pretty much the same as another, and this one would pay for the others.

Saradee and the half-breed were still trying to stare each other down when Kilroy walked out of the mine and straightened up. "Safe and sound."

Jimbo Walsh poked a finger at the opening. "What's to prevent some drifter from wanderin' in there to have a look around . . . or — not to be suspicious, ye understand — one of us?"

Saradee hefted her Winchester, turned, and rammed the rifle's butt against the bottom of a square-hewn entrance joist. The joist was already gray and splintered, its top end leaning precariously out from the mine.

Saradee gave it three hard licks, and the bottom end of the timber slid inward with a crack and a groan.

The lintel gave. Saradee and the others backed away as the entranced disappeared in falling rock and billowing dust.

"What do you think?" Saradee said as the others choked on the dust. "We're gonna leave home without locking the doors?"

15.
EL MOLINA

An hour after leaving the mine, the Kilroy/ Jones Gang topped a rocky shelf and rode down into the pueblo of El Molina, sprawled along a hillside and bordered on the south by a small lake sparkling in the afternoon sunshine.

"Easy, boys," Kilroy warned, sweeping his gaze from left to right along the curving cart trail and noting the several slamming window shutters. "The good folks of El Molina take some warmin' up to. They ain't used to strangers. Don't let your guards down."

"We won't let our guards down, Boss," said Turkey McDade. "How 'bout our pants?"

Riding just behind Kilroy, the skinny hardcase was watching a full-hipped young woman stroll through a narrow door onto a second-story balcony of a run-down saloon and throw her thick hair out enticingly. She wore only a corset and frilly pantaloons buffeting in the cool wind off the lake.

Dogs barked and seagulls screeched. The ungreased wheels of several carts and ore wagons squawked, maneuvering to and from the few mines still showing color in the area. Mexican as well as American miners lounged about outside the cantinas, smoking and laughing. The air smelled like fish and spicy meat and tortillas.

"You come down with a bad case of the pony drip, don't beg me to shoot you," Kilroy told McDade. "I won't waste the bullet."

High-pitched voices rose suddenly, and sandals slapped the ground. Kilroy reined his horse up, his right hand closing around his pistol butt, jerking his eyes to the left. Two boys, both under six, one considerably smaller than the other, ran out from a crumbling, sod-roofed shack. Their fists were filled with bright red wildflowers.

They ran past Waylon and stopped beside Saradee's horse, yelling and extending the flowers in their dirty brown hands.

Saradee had drawn her own pistols. As she looked down at the boys, a celestial smile spread across her face. She sheathed her revolvers, fished out a coin from the trousers she'd stolen from the prospector she'd killed, and bought all the flowers for a dollar.

As the boys ran off, fighting over the silver, Saradee stuck several flowers in her hair, trimming her horse's bridle with the rest. She reached over and punched Kilroy's arm.

"Even the little ones know how to treat a woman down here, you cheap son of a bitch."

They'd ridden only twenty more yards when the gang checked down their horses again, this time at the snap of a small-caliber pistol.

Guns drawn, they watched a stocky, red-haired Yanqui with an upswept mustache run bare-chested and stocking-footed from a cantina on the right side of the street. His lips stretched back from his teeth, his blue eyes flashing fearfully, he bolted across the street, heading at an angle for an alley on the other side.

Inside the cantina the man had just vacated, a woman shrieked and cursed in Spanish. A moment later, the batwings burst open and out she ran, bare breasts jiggling, thin cotton skirt buffeting about her legs. She was barefoot, and she held a pearl-gripped .36.

"¡Bastardo!"

The following stream of Spanish was too

fast and garbled for Kilroy to fully understand, but he gathered the Yanqui hadn't paid her for services rendered. She stopped just outside the cantina, extended the pistol in her right hand. The gun snapped and smoked. The whore's full brown breasts bounced from the kick.

On the street, the red-haired Yanqui dodged the slug. He slipped in fresh horse plop, hit the ground on his right hip. As he heaved himself up and resumed running toward the alley mouth, the whore stepped off the boardwalk and triggered another shot. The slug plunked through the Yanqui's left shoulder blade, blood spraying as the bullet exited his chest and broke the window of a dry-goods shop.

The man groaned and dropped to his left knee, slapping his right hand to his shoulder. The pajama-clad men loafing on a bench before the store scrambled for cover.

As the red-haired man began to rise once more, the whore strode toward him, holding the pistol straight down at her side. She angled past the gang, Saradee and the men watching with bemused grins on their faces. They held the reins of their frightened mounts taut.

"*¡Bastardo barato del yanqui, dado!*" she cried, raising the pistol, thumbing back the

198

hammer, and squinting down the barrel.

The man had run another six feet and was entering the alley's mouth when the pistol popped in the whore's hand. His head flew back on his shoulders as he stumbled forward, then dropped to both knees.

"*Puta* bitch!" he wailed, the words echoing hollowly off the adobe walls lining the alley. A fresh bullet hole had appeared in his sun-browned back, just right of his spine.

As the bare-breasted whore walked up to him, he dropped to his hands, sobbing and cursing. "You shot me, you *bitch!* I was gonna pay you next week."

"*Sí, amigo.*" She smiled, aiming the pistol at the back of his head, clicking the hammer back. "But I don't extend credit to assholes!"

The gun popped once, twice, the man's head jerking with each round. It sagged between his shoulders. His arms collapsed, and his chest hit the dirt.

The whore lowered the pistol, spat on the dead man's back, wheeled, and retraced her steps to the cantina, before which several customers from inside now stood — a handful of rugged-looking Mexicans in dirty denims and hobnailed miners' boots — laughing and cheering and saluting the whore with their beer mugs and tequila glasses.

Ignoring them, the whore proudly pushed through the batwings. The miners staggered in behind her.

In the street, the male gang members sat their glassy-eyed mounts in stunned silence. Gigging her horse forward, Saradee turned to Waylon, and winked. "I like that girl."

Saradee led the gang around a bend in the narrow street and entered the main square encircled by the Banco National, the local *rurale* headquarters, the blocky beige church with bell tower and looming wooden cross, and several more saloons and brothels.

A couple of local *rurales* lounged on a dilapidated wicker sofa before their tin-roofed office, one smoking a corncob pipe, the other with a clear bottle in his fist. Both were hatless.

The one with the bottle was shirtless. His suspenders hung slack from his shoulders. Behind them, fishing rods and tackle hung from the office's buckling front wall. The *rurales* watched the gang with grim interest, but did not rise from the sofa.

Tipping their hats to the local policemen, the gang drew up to the largest saloon in the square. The tavern had a broad, brush-covered patio furnished with a dozen wooden tables. The gang's men hit the ground running and whooping like desert horses smelling water, several leaping the low wall onto the patio while others jogged through the building's main entrance. Saradee rode Waylon piggyback through the front door.

When Kilroy had sent two tavern boys outside to lead the mounts off to a livery stable, he and Saradee sat on the patio, at a table by the square. The skinny, turkey-necked bartender brought their drinks — two tequila shots and a bottle of the local *aguardiente* — on a wooden tray. He was setting the glasses and the bottle on the table when Saradee caught Waylon winking at one of the three whores sitting with Bascomb, McDade, and Montoya.

McDade had a hand in her blouse, massaging her right breast. Giggling and lolling her head against Montoya's shoulder, she winked back at Waylon, blushing, then cracking a quick, sneering grin when her eyes met Saradee's.

Kilroy paid the waiter, tipping him generously and instructing him to keep the tequila coming. He glanced at the whore again, then looked across the table at Saradee. The moment his eyes met hers, what felt like a blade tip poked through his jeans, pricking his balls. The sting and the threat of what the blade could do down there brought tears to his eyes.

Saradee leaned toward him across the narrow table, her chin about six inches above the scarred planks. She smiled icily. "Go ahead, wink at her again."

Beneath the table, she nudged the knife a sixteenth of an inch farther through his jeans. Kilroy's right eye twitched as ice flooded his bowels.

"Easy, now," he rasped.

"Go ahead," Saradee said. "Wink at her again."

Kilroy tried to slide back slightly in his chair, to ease the blade's pressure, but Saradee's hand was firm. "I know her from *before* you and I threw in," he said.

"Reckon I'll go over there and have a little talk with that *puta,*" Saradee said.

She removed her knife from Kilroy's crotch and, shoving her chair back, stood.

Kilroy glanced over at the whore, who was staring back at Saradee, her smile gone. Chuckling nervously, he grabbed Saradee's wrist. "You can't kill the whores in Mexico. They're like Mary Magdalene, for chrissakes. Sit down."

Saradee was still glaring at the whore. The

whore stared back at her, the whore's eyes apprehensive. The men at her table were talking and laughing, swilling tequila.

"Please, angel," Kilroy said, smiling stiffly. "Have a seat, drink your tequila. . . ."

"Fuck you."

"Sit down, Saradee."

She looked down at him. Holding her wrist, he smiled up at her. "We don't need a commotion, my flower."

Saradee wrinkled her nose. "I reckon I got my point across. Wouldn't doubt if she just peed her bloomers — if she's wearin' any."

"I wouldn't doubt it at all," Waylon said wryly, releasing her wrist and throwing back his tequila.

Saradee sat down and slid her chair close to the table. She threw back her tequila, then popped the cork on the *aguardiente* and splashed several inches into her water glass. She was about to take a sip when, glancing into the courtyard, she frowned.

"Uh-oh."

At the same time she'd spoken, Kilroy had heard the clomp of hooves on the square's crumbling cobblestones. He looked over his riqht shoulder, and his gut tightened slightly. The *federales* he'd spied through his field glasses earlier were riding in two separate groups around both sides of the fountain, heading toward the cantina.

They rode slowly on sweaty, dusty horses, most of which were smart-stepping Arabians. Major Valverde rode point. Close behind was Lieutenant Juan Soto, known as one of the most sadistic men in northern Mexico. Rumor had it that when Valverde had found his wife in bed with another man — another of Valverde's lieutenants — he'd had Soto torture her to death slowly, her screams echoing for days around the village in which Valverde kept a sprawling casa outpost housing his men and his whores.

Valverde had dealt with the betraying lieutenant himself. Another rumor had it that what remained of the man's body was still hanging from a cross out front of Valverde's quarters, as a warning to other would-be double-crossers.

"Señor Kilroy!" Valverde exclaimed, his fat, pocked face cracking a broad, toothy smile, his booming voice echoing around the square. "What an honor it is to see you again!"

"Major Valverde," Kilroy said, leaning back in his chair and spreading his hands, as though the joy at seeing the *federale* again was too great for words.

Valverde said, "I thought it was you. Oh, but the tracks we found! That many tracks,

I tell Lieutenant Soto, must mean that Señor Kilroy has once again blessed our beloved Méjico with his presence."

The portly Valverde glanced at the concave-faced Soto sitting to his left. Soto smiled, but his eyes were dull. His teeth were small, tobacco-stained stilettos, and he needed a shave. His bare, corded arms boasted a dozen tattoos.

"We follow, but somehow you gave us the slip!" said Valverde. He wagged an admonishing finger at Kilroy. "It is not nice to try to trick your friends, Señor."

"Trick?" Kilroy said, turning his hands palm up. "What trick? I didn't know you were back there!"

"Of course you didn't." Valverde laughed. His eyes had found Saradee when he and the others had first ridden up to the cantina. Now they lingered over the buxom, tawny-haired outlaw, and glistened with appreciation. "This one here — she belongs to you, uh?"

Kilroy glanced at Saradee, who regarded the soldiers without expression. "Major Clarinado Valverde, please meet Miss Saradee Jones."

The major lowered his head in a gallant bow. "Miss Jones, I am honored. I would dismount and kiss your hand, but as you see, I am filthy."

Saradee smiled woodenly. "Don't trouble yourself."

Valverde's own smile tightened as he kept his eyes on Saradee but spoke to Kilroy. "This one has some — how do you say? Pluck."

"I like my women with pluck," said Kilroy. "They can stay mounted longer."

Valverde frowned, uncertain. Understanding flashed in his eyes. He threw his head back, laughing and throwing an arm out toward Soto. Both men laughed as though at the funniest joke they'd ever heard, the lieutenant's arm flexing long, taut muscles from biceps to wrists.

Though most of the other men, sitting their own horses behind them, hadn't heard the joke, laughter began to ripple down the line. Chuckling, Kilroy glanced at Saradee. She returned the glance. She wasn't smiling. Kilroy glanced at his and Saradee's men spread out across the patio. They shuttled their own gazes up and down the line of *federales,* expressions tense, hands not far from their guns.

When the laughter died, Major Valverde leaned forward, crossing his forearms on his saddle horn. He ran his eyes lustily across Saradee's well-filled shirt, then licked his lips and turned to Kilroy.

His eyes hardened. "Now that we have enjoyed a good laugh together, it is time to talk business."

"Ah, gee, Major," Kilroy said, wincing. "I'm afraid it's gonna have to be a short talk this trip."

Valverde glanced at Soto. The lieutenant stared coldly at Kilroy from under the brim of his dusty, gaudy sombrero. His eyes reminded the outlaw leader of tiny, round dung beetles.

"Oh?" said the major. "And why is that?"

"Our last venture didn't go as planned. Turned out the bank we robbed didn't have near as much money as we figured. Unfortunately, we spent nearly all of the loot just getting down here."

Valverde clucked. "That is too bad."

"That's the way it goes sometimes."

"A few you win . . ." said Valverde.

"A few you lose," said Kilroy. "Just the same, though, I'd like to buy you a drink."

"Perhaps it should be me who buys you a drink, Señor." Valverde smiled.

Kilroy looked at him. "Oh? You run into a little extra *dinero* recently, Major? I never knew you to be so generous."

Juan Soto spread a smile, showing the

small, sharp teeth between his thin, cracked lips.

"A little extra, you might say," said Valverde, raising his right hand and snapping his fingers.

A rider moved up from mid-column, hooves clacking on the cobblestones.

"Just after we lost your trail, we came to the old mine which Juan's *padre* used to work. We found the entrance collapsed." The major scratched his head. "That seemed odd, because when we rode past the mine just a few days before, it was wide open."

Juan Soto's smile broadened, black eyes closing down to slits. Several of the men behind him and Valverde smiled as well. The rider he'd summoned approached Valverde's right stirrup.

Kilroy's gut tightened. He slid a quick glance to Saradee. Her face had become drawn and pale. A single bead of sweat trickled down her jaw.

"We suspect something funny is going on," Valverde continued, "so Juan and I order the men to open the mine back up again. And what do you suppose we find?"

Kilroy's face had turned to stone. His heart thudded painfully against his ribs.

"No," a small voice said in his ear. "Please,

Christ, no."

As if through a thick layer of fog, as if time had slowed by three quarters, he sat his patio chair stiffly, hand squeezing his whiskey glass. The young *federale* turned his horse so that its left hip faced the patio. A burlap money sack hung over the hip.

At the same time that Kilroy's eyes found the U.S. stamp on the pouch, the major glanced furtively around the square, then leaned toward Kilroy and cupped a fat, brown hand to his mouth.

"Thirty-six thousand American dollars!" he whispered through wheezing laughter.

16.

FLAGG'S
MERCENARIES

Not long after their reunion, Hawk and Primrose lost the outlaws' trail in a rain squall. When they came upon a forlorn little prospectors' cabin along a gurgling stream nestled in cottonwoods, with three dead men lying in the shaded yard, half-eaten by buzzards and coyotes, they figured they'd found it again.

The prospectors had been shot, probably ambushed from the trees lining the stream. The smallest had been stripped of his shirt and pants. Nothing except food appeared to have been taken from the thatch-roofed casa. The cabin and adjoining barn and stable hadn't been burned, the bodies hadn't been desecrated, which told Hawk the killings hadn't been the work of Indians.

"Prints down here," Primrose called from the trees along the stream. "A dozen or so."

Hawk looked at the youngest of the three dead prospectors. Shot twice in the head so the clothes hadn't been torn by bullets. Damn practical. He'd been carrying a shovel, which lay nearby.

"Prints down here," Primrose called again, louder.

Hawk glanced back at the young lieutenant, standing at the edge of the yard, holding his horse's braided rawhide reins.

"I heard you."

"Well, what're we waiting for?"

"We're gonna bury these men." Hawk stooped to pick up the shovel.

As he stepped the blade through the thin sod pocked with yucca and sage, Primrose walked up and stood beside him. "I don't understand you. Why bury them, when you wouldn't let me bury my detail?"

"We have time." Hawk tossed a shovelful of sod aside and again stepped the shovel into the ground. "I know where they're heading now. We're not far from a village rumored to be a haven for gringo outlaws — as long as they pay a tribute to the local *federale* troupe, that is. We're only about a day away."

He was breathing hard as he dug. "These poor bastards were killed through no fault of their own. We have time, so we'll bury them, and then we'll ride."

Primrose watched him, incredulous. He

shook his head, then tied his horse to a sycamore and tramped off to the stable in search of his own shovel. "You're an odd one, Hawk. Damn odd . . ."

They dug three shallow graves and covered each with rocks from the creek. Into the rocks they poked oak branches resembling crosses. Hawk stood before the graves, removed his hat, and bowed his head. Watching Hawk with a vaguely bewildered expression, the lieutenant followed suit.

After a minute, Hawk donned his hat, spat, and turned to where the horses were tied in the trees.

"Hawk."

He stopped and turned to Primrose. The lieutenant glanced at the rocky ridge behind the casa, golden brown in the mid-afternoon light, each rock and piñon standing out clearly against the slope. Primrose lowered his head with feigned casualness, hooked a finger across his nose.

"In the past hour I've seen three sun flashes off that northern ridge. Something tells me we're been spied upon through field glasses."

"We are." Hawk moved toward the horses.

Primrose hurried up beside him. "You've seen?"

"For the past three days we've been followed by eight men."

Primrose stared at him, jaw hanging. "Who?"

Hawk stopped before the tree to which the grulla was tied. "When we split up, I had my own little adventure. A deputy U.S. marshal by the name of D.W. Flagg and a sheriff named Killigrew tried to blow out my candle. I warned them to go on home, but I reckon they haven't cleaned their ears in a while. Somewhere, somehow, they found a dozen or so men — scalp-hunters, by the looks of them — to help hunt me down." He slipped the reins loose from the sycamore branch and swung onto the saddle. "I glassed them day before yesterday. They've been gaining on us steadily . . . by my design."

Primrose stared up at him. His face was now more brown than red, his goatee sun-bleached, but the peeled skin made him look diseased. "Why the hell didn't you tell me?"

"To tell you the truth," Hawk said, "I've been riding alone so long, it never really occurred to me." Chuckling wryly, he gigged the grulla southward along the stream.

Primrose jogged over to his Indian pony. "What're we going to do about it?"

"Fork leather, Lieutenant," Hawk called

without turning around, walking the grulla downstream. "And fill that empty chamber you've been keeping under your pistol's hammer. You're gonna need it pretty soon."

An hour later, Hawk and Primrose dropped over a jog of rocky hills and into the yard of a combination store and saloon.

The *pulperia*'s main building was a barrackslike, two-story adobe with a second-story balcony wrapping around the front and both ends. The owner probably rented out the upstairs rooms to freighters. Two heavy-axled wagons sat, tongues hanging, ash bows exposed, before the low adobe wall fronting the main building.

As Hawk and Primrose rode into the hard-packed yard, cleaving the small herd of goats and chickens, a skinny, stoop-shouldered Mexican sauntered out of a stable, smoking a brown-paper cigarette and glancing up at the riders beseechingly.

"Getting late. You spend the night?" he asked in broken English.

"Not tonight," Hawk said, looking the place over, eyes picking out every object behind which a man might seek cover during a lead swap. The pine smoke drifting from the main building's big fieldstone chimney was laced with the smell of grilled chicken.

"Business, she's slow," the Mexican drawled, removing the cigarette from his lips, turning his head to follow Hawk and Primrose across the yard. "I give you special deal, uh? Free pussy!"

"Not tonight," Hawk repeated, and spurred the grulla into a trot.

Riding to his right, Primrose said, "What're you thinking?"

"I'm thinking Flagg and his boys will stop there for the night. Flagg's getting old. I'm guessing he won't be able to pass up a real bed and a free female."

They rode for a while.

"I know him," Primrose said.

Hawk looked at him, silhouetted against the sinking sun. "What's that?"

"Flagg was a guest of Major Devereaux's at Fort Bowie a few times. Apparently, he and Devereaux were at West Point at the same time. I've played cards with the man. He has political ambitions. Rumor has it he could very well be the next territorial governor."

Hawk lifted a shoulder and looked over his horse's head.

"You can't kill him, Hawk."

"The man's been warned, but he still intends to kill *me*."

Primrose didn't say anything for a time. He glanced at the falling sun to his right, then turned to Hawk. "I can't help you kill him. He's just doing his job."

"And he's a friend of your father-in-law's." Hawk grinned. "That's okay. I'll kill the son of a bitch myself."

When he looked over at Primrose riding along beside him, the lieutenant, sagging forward in his saddle, appeared pale, as though he were having a bout of the ague.

"Just stay out of my way," Hawk warned, "or I'll kill you too."

They rode for another twenty minutes, traversing a jog of mesquite-covered hills rising to steeper mountains in the southern distance. Hawk dismounted, climbed a knoll, and glassed his back trail. Seeing no sign of Flagg or Sheriff Killigrew and their six mercenaries, he turned to Primrose, who was sitting a square, flat-topped rock lower down the slope. Hands on his spread knees, the lieutenant studied the ground as if looking for something he'd lost.

"This is where we part company, soldier." Hawk gained his feet and walked past the lieutenant toward the two horses ground-tied at the bottom of the hill, their tails swishing in the early evening light, flies buzzing around their heads.

"Do you have to do this?" The lieutenant's voice was somber.

Hawk returned his field glasses to his saddlebags. "I see no other way to get them off my trail."

He mounted up and looked at Primrose. He looked young and miserable, sitting on that rock.

"What're you going to do?" Hawk asked.

Primrose had slipped his Army Colt from its holster. He brought it up as if it weighed a ton, aimed it at Hawk. He curled his lip with savage resolve as he ratcheted back the hammer. "I can't let you do it, Hawk."

"I know you can't," Hawk said, feeling genuine sympathy for the kid. "But you don't have a choice."

He reined the horse around so hard that the grulla pawed the air. He put the steel to him, and the horse lunged off its rear hooves into an instant gallop, thundering around the hill and heading back the way he'd come. Hawk didn't look back, didn't see the lieutenant sitting his rock, stewing, staring at the empty place Hawk had just vacated, cocked revolver aimed at nothing.

Fifteen minutes later, Hawk was glassing the *pulperia* from a notch in the basalt ridge just south of it. The grulla was tethered in a hollow at the bottom of the ridge. As he peered through the lenses, Hawk curled his upper lip in a grim smile.

The *pulperia*'s owner was no doubt very happy this night. Ten horses milled in the corral flanking the main building. A skinny Mexican boy in white slacks, sandals, and a dark brown poncho was hauling water from the well. Another, shorter kid was forking hay through the fence slats.

Smoke puffed in earnest from the building's rock chimney, while five men milled on the front ramada, spilling into the yard — laughing and smoking, glasses in their hands. They were rough-looking Mexicans, revolvers and long-bladed *facóns* jutting from sheaths on their hips, thighs, and from shoulder rigs under their arms. One man, hearing something from the second story, looked up and, cupping a hand around his mouth, shouted encouragement in Spanish. He and the other men in the yard laughed.

A man yelled something through one of the second-story windows — Hawk couldn't make out the words — and the men in the yard laughed harder.

Flagg and Killigrew were probably in the bar drinking or upstairs getting their ashes hauled. Hawk wasn't so much concerned about them as the scalp-hunters. Fighting men, they wouldn't be easy to take down.

Let them keep drinking. Let the light fade, and he'd have the drop. . . .

Hawk made a thorough reconnaissance of the place, noting the arroyo behind it, then scuttled a few feet down the ridge, rose, and jogged to the bottom, taking long strides, his spurs chinging, boots lifting sand. He stowed the field glasses in his saddlebags, sat down to remove his spurs, shucked his rifle, tugged his hat brim low, and jogged west along the base of the ridge.

By the time he'd stolen around behind the main building and dropped into the ravine, the sun was down, but the sky remained pale. The brown ridges were mantled in umber. There'd be enough light for another forty-five minutes or so.

The Henry in his right hand, keeping his head low, he jogged through the ravine, the low sides canting shadows onto the sandy bottom and swallows wheeling over his head. The ravine's sides dropped, the cut rising to level, brushy ground about thirty yards behind the *pulperia,* a few barrel cactuses and pecan trees towering over the blocky shapes of disintegrating chicken coops and abandoned shacks. The place at one time had probably been an abbey or a monastery.

To Hawk's left were the corrals in which

the horses ate and drew water, a couple rolling in the dust, the dust rising in a soft brown cloud above the corral. On his right, a girl cried out softly. There was the wooden clatter of logs tumbling. Beyond the chicken coop, grown up with brown scrub, stood another tin-roofed structure resembling a stable. From there, a man's guttural voice warned the girl in Spanish to be quiet and pull her bloomers down.

Hawk moved right through the knee-high brush, crouched over his Henry, until he'd gotten the chicken coop and scattered pecan trees between him and the main building. As he continued across the yard and through the pecans, the building, resembling a stable, slid up before him.

It wasn't a stable, but a simple, roofed shed. The side facing Hawk was open. Inside, split logs were stacked. Sitting on the stack, half-reclining, was a dark-haired girl. Between her flailing legs was a man in a short leather jacket and buckskin breeches, a steeple-crowned sombrero hanging down his back. On the back of his wide cartridge belt was a black knife sheath trimmed in silver.

The girl kicked feebly at him, struggling, as he pulled her underwear down her thighs. Hawk's Spanish was poor, but the girl seemed to be telling the man she wasn't one of the *putas,* but a simple errand girl. If he took her like this, her mama would have to send her to a convent.

"Please don't ruin my life!"

The man ripped the underwear with one enraged jerk, and tossed it into the brush. The girl sobbed and continued pleading as he bent his knees, opening the fly of his breeches. He thrust himself at the girl once, twice, grunting savagely.

As he thrust the third time, Hawk's knife careened end over end and buried itself hilt-deep in the man's back, cleaving bone with a crunching thump.

17.

TO KILL OR
NOT TO KILL

The girl must have thought the man between her legs was leaning down to kiss her. She turned away, pursing her lips and punching his head with her fists. Arching his back and breathing sharply through gritted teeth, he stepped back from her, turning slowly as he reached around with his right hand, clawing for Hawk's bowie.

Hawk bolted into the shed, raised his rifle barrel over his right shoulder, and brought the butt soundly against the sighing man's face. He heard the nose snap. Lowering the Henry, he jerked the man into the brush behind him and looked at the girl.

She'd risen onto her elbows, her face a brown oval framed by straight black hair in the weak light. She was breathing loudly, brows furrowed with shock and confusion.

Hawk pressed a finger to his lips. In halting Spanish, he told her he was a friend here to rid the *pulperia* of the others like this one.

He jerked his head at the man lying unmoving in the brush. He could hear the man breathing, but barely.

"*Sí*," the girl said quickly, raking a deep breath.

She jumped off the woodpile, her dress dropping over her bare thighs, and dropped to her knees beside her attacker. She plucked the man's *facón* from its sheath at the back of his cartridge belt, held the blade up before her face, then looked at Hawk.

"*El perverso es el mío!*" she hissed. The pervert is mine!

Hawk lifted his left cheek as she pulled the man onto his back and jerked his shirt away from his crotch, but turned away when she went to work with the knife. Crouching, he glanced around the yard, then ran to the main building's heavy-timbered back door.

He turned his head to the gray wood, listening. Inside, glasses thumped on tables and men spoke loudly in Spanish. Spurs chinged on the floorboards. A cork was popped from a bottle. Coins clinked. Someone sneezed; someone laughed and blessed him.

Hawk didn't think about his next move. In such a situation, when he were badly outnumbered, spontaneity and lightning force were the best courses of action.

He turned the doorknob, shoved the door

open an inch, then kicked it inward with savage force and took two long strides inside, his green eyes raking the room from the sun-seared planes of his implacable face.

He lowered his rifle, his left hand caressing the forestock while his right thumb raked back the hammer. At the same time, his brain registered the bar to his right, the round tables before it, positioned around ceiling joists, and the stairs rising on his left.

A half second after the door had slammed the back wall, startling one of the half-dozen men up from his table, a frown crumpling the near-black skin between the man's eyes, Hawk squeezed the Henry's trigger. The gun boomed. A man sitting near the stairs, who had bolted to his feet clawing a Navy Colt from a shoulder holster trimmed with shiny black Apache scalps, howled and goose-stepped backward, chest geysering blood.

The man hadn't hit the floor before Hawk, taking two more steps into the room and calmly levering the Henry, slid the barrel right and continued firing until seven cartridge casings danced on the floor around his boots. Gun smoke webbed before him. Inside the cloud, the scalp-hunters groaned and grunted and cursed, tumbling like cans shot from fence posts.

Only one of the Mexicans fired a return shot, the bullet plunking into the bar as he fell facefirst into his table, man and table going down together in a thundering roar of breaking wood and glass and splashing liquor.

Holding the Henry's barrel straight out before him, Hawk looked left. The stoop-shouldered Mexican he'd seen earlier lay facedown on the floor, hands on his head. Before the bar, one of the scalp-hunters gave a death rattle; another rolled over, and a boot thumped the floor. Voices rose from outside and upstairs.

Hawk wheeled and took the stairs two steps at a time. Outside, men shouted and pistols popped as boots clacked on flagstone.

Hawk gained the top of the stairs and dropped to a knee as a gun flashed before him, barking loudly, the slug whistling past Hawk's left ear and thumping into a ceiling beam. Fifteen feet down the hall, a pale, stocky figure moved behind the wafting powder smoke, the wan candlelight glinting off a silver-plated pistol and off the heavily pomaded hair of Flagg's partner, Sheriff Spade Killigrew.

Hawk fired in the general direction of the

glints — two quick pops of the Henry. The shooter groaned and stumbled through an open door.

Shouting curses through bared teeth, Killigrew thrust his pistol out the door and fired another stray shot. Hawk triggered the Henry, the hastily aimed round hammering through the sheriff's forehead, just above his right eye and thick, black brow. The man grunted and fell into the room with a heavy thud. A girl's shrill screams rose from the room as Hawk ejected the spent cartridge, which clattered down the steps behind him.

At the end of the hall, a door slammed. At the hall's left side and about thirty feet from Hawk, another door opened and a big man stormed out, bearlike and naked, wearing only a sombrero and a neckerchief, extending a sawed-off shotgun in one hand, a sawed-off rifle in the other.

As the man, raging like a bull stampeded off a cliff, triggered the shotgun and rifle at the same time, the rifle's crack barely audible beneath the barn-blaster's cannon-like roar, Hawk dropped. His chest slammed the floor.

He rolled left into an alcove. The shotgun roared again, the rifle booming a half second later. The .00-buck and .44 slug blew a small crater out of the floor where

Hawk's chest had hit.

Hawk rolled back out into the hall, propping himself on his right shoulder, and levered five quick rounds into the big naked bear's chest and belly. The man threw his arms out, dropping the shotgun and triggering the rifle into the rafters, as he staggered backward, his enraged bellows growing louder, mouth forming a big, pink O in the lower center of his square, bearded face.

Impossibly, the man got his feet under him. Blood painting his torso and spraying the walls and doors to either side, he lowered the short-barreled Winchester, clumsily levered a shell.

"¡Muero, tú mueres, amigo!" I die, you die, friend!

Hawk held his own rifle steady on the man's face. His shot echoed the big man's own. As the man's slug sang over Hawk's head, Hawk levered another round, fired again as the big man stumbled back, falling, the second shot taking the man through the soft underside of his chin.

As the man fell, Hawk's bullet ripped out the top of the man's shaggy head, thumping into the door at the end of the hall, spraying the panels around the hole with blood and brains. Outside, a rifle cracked and a pistol popped, the last shot ricocheting with an angry *zing.*

The big man had no sooner hit the floor than Hawk was up and running, leaping the quivering, bloody mass of the big Mex's naked body, and smashing his foot against the blood-washed door. As the door exploded inward, shards of frame flying around the dim room pungent with marijuana smoke and sex, Hawk sidestepped right and dropped to a knee, snapping the Henry up and snugging his finger against the trigger.

To his right, a naked whore sat up in one of the room's two beds. Her russet hair was piled atop her head, sheet drawn up to cover her breasts. Straight across the room, a tall man, shirt untucked and in stocking feet, was halfway through the shuttered window. He carried a gun in his right hand; his cartridge belt dangled from the other.

"¡Por favor!" the whore cried, extending her right hand beseechingly.

"Stop, Flagg." Hawk aimed his rifle at the back of the man's head.

Flagg froze. He faced the balcony, his shoulders tensing.

Hawk drilled a round into the window casing. Flagg jumped with a start and turned around slowly, his eyes lighting on Hawk's Henry. The lawman dropped his revolver and cartridge belt.

"You got me, Gideon."

"Thought I told you to go home."

Flagg shrugged, lifted a corner of his mouth. "You got me."

Hawk waved the Henry's barrel. "Get over here."

Flagg's broad right cheek twitched. His patchy silver beard stood out against his red face. "What're you gonna do?"

"Get over here."

Slowly, holding his hands up, palms out, Flagg walked toward Hawk.

"Por favor," the whore kept begging Hawk thinly, holding the sheet up to her breasts with both hands.

Hawk stepped sideways and jerked the Henry toward the door. "Out. Down the hall." He'd use Flagg as a shield against the men who'd been milling around outside when he'd entered the building. He could have killed Flagg and leapt off the balcony, but the gunfire told him several men were still out there. Since they were here for him, he didn't have much of a chance.

He strode up behind the lawman, rammed his rifle's butt between the man's shoulder blades, throwing him brusquely forward. "Move!"

Continuing to prod Flagg's back with his

rifle, Hawk followed the lawman down the dim hall to the stairs, candles smoking and sputtering around them, the smell of blood hanging heavily. Flagg was five steps down the dim staircase, Hawk two steps behind him, when a figure appeared at the bottom of the stairs, silhouetted against the main room's back wall.

Hawk stopped, snapped his rifle to his shoulder, aiming over Flagg's left shoulder, tightening his trigger finger.

The figure he'd drawn a bead on flung a rifle out from his side, opening the palm of his free hand. "Gideon, it's Primrose!"

As if through a spyglass, the lieutenant's shape took form — the sun-seared, pink-splotched face, auburn goatee and side-burns, tan kepi shoved back on his head. He no longer wore the bandages around his forehead, or his blue tunic, which he'd replaced with a deer-hide poncho he'd bought from a trader he and Hawk had met along the trail.

Incredulity spiked Hawk, evoking a skeptical chuff. So the lieutenant had been what all the shooting was about. . . .

"Well, well," Hawk said, poking the Henry's barrel into Flagg's back, getting him moving again. "To what do I owe the honor?"

"Thought you could use a hand," Primrose said, taking a step back from the stairs.

Hawk studied the lieutenant, smoke still trickling from the barrel of the soldier's carbine. At the bottom of the stairs, keeping his Henry's barrel snug against Flagg's back, Hawk turned his head, swept his gaze around the room.

Besides the six men he'd killed himself, two others lay near the front door. The stoop-shouldered barman had risen from behind the bar planks. Crouching, one hand on the bar top, he stared at the three men gathered at the bottom of the stairs, his expression switching back and forth between fear and derision.

Hawk grabbed the collar of Flagg's shirt, thrust the man brusquely toward the front door, prodding Flagg's back with his rifle as he crossed the blood-washed room, stepping over bodies and raking his gaze around cautiously. He stepped over one of the dead men lying near the front of the room, and followed Flagg out the door and onto the patio.

More dead men out here, two lying atop one another as if dropped from the sky. To his left, a groan lifted. Keeping the Henry trained on Flagg, Hawk slipped his Russian from its holster and sidled over to the wounded man lying near a potted orange tree beside an adobe balcony pile. The man was sliding his hand toward a revolver in blood pooling on the patio's cracked flags.

Hawk stopped the hand's movement with a shot through the man's head, the flat crack of the Russian sounding like a cannon in the silence that had followed the fusillade.

"You left one alive," Hawk said as the lieutenant's gaunt frame appeared in the doorway.

Primrose glance around. His gaze lighted on Hawk. "You owe me, Gideon. You'd be dead by now if I hadn't followed you here."

"I'm fresh out of medals, soldier." With his left hand, he shoved Flagg out into the darkness of the yard. "Now, if you'll excuse me, I've got one more bit of business."

"You owe me, Hawk," Primrose repeated, grabbing Hawk's right sleeve. "Let him live. I'll take him back to Arizona. Till then, we'll keep him bound."

Hawk studied the lieutenant, his green eyes flashing angrily in the wan lamplight slicing through the door. Hawk opened his mouth to object, but said nothing. He closed his mouth, his chest rising and falling. He looked at Flagg, who regarded the lieutenant as though trying to place him. Then Hawk returned his eyes to Primrose.

"He's your pet, Lieutenant. You tend him close, or I'll put him down in a heartbeat."

With that, Hawk lowered his rifle and strode off in the night.

18.
A MEXICAN UNDERSTANDING

"So, let me get this straight, soldier," said D.W. Flagg when they were riding later that night under a sky full of stars. "You came down here to retrieve the payroll money you lost, and entangled yourself with a kill-crazy ex-lawman."

Hawk rode point along the deep-rutted wagon road cleaving the rocky, desert terrain. Flagg and Primrose rode behind him, Flagg's wrists locked with his own metal cuffs, his ankles bound to his stirrups. He'd obviously had his share of *aguardiente* and marijuana back at the *pulperia,* and he hadn't yet sobered. In fact, he'd gotten more and more talkative the longer they'd ridden through the dark Mexican hills.

More and more brash.

"Didn't know who he was till we'd been traveling together for a spell," Primrose said grimly, staring into the night beyond Hawk. "Besides, we have similar objectives."

"Oh?" Flagg laughed. "Your objective is to get the money back, show your father-in-law what a great soldier you are. Command material! What's Hawk's objective?"

"Killing," Hawk said, glancing over his shoulder at Flagg riding off his grulla's right hip. "And I'm beginning to think I made a big mistake, not killing you back at the roadhouse."

"See what I'm talking about?" Flagg said to Primrose. "Only man who could take down all those scalp-hunters — and Sheriff Killigrew — single-fucking-handed, is a kill-crazy son of a bitch like Hawk."

"The lieutenant didn't do half bad himself," remarked Hawk, swaying easily in his saddle. They'd been holding their horses to walks to avoid trail hazards concealed by the darkness, but there was no need to hurry. They had only another hour or so to El Molina, and it was relatively early.

Primrose felt his ears warm slightly from chagrin. "I had only four men to contend with," he said. "And they were all heading inside to deal with you."

Flagg turned to the young lieutenant, the lawman showing his white teeth in the darkness. "He's teaching you right well, eh, Lieutenant?"

Primrose turned to the lawman, his calm

voice belying his irritation. "I was only trying to get to you before he did, Marshal.
Are you wishing I'd lingered?"

Flagg turned his head away and spat. He
pulled back on his reins, stopped his dun.
The lieutenant did likewise, glancing at
Flagg curiously.

Holding his voice low, the lawman said,
"You're cavortin' with a known criminal,
soldier. You shoot the son of a bitch, and I
might forget about that."

"Without him, I have little chance of
retrieving the payroll money."

"With him, you're breakin' the law."

"I figure, just being down here, I'm breaking the law. I might as well break it with a
man who can help me fulfill my objective."

Flagg canted his head to one side. "Let's
say you get the money back. What're you
gonna do then?"

Primrose didn't say anything for a moment. He adjusted his hat's angle, sighed.
"I'll cross that bridge when I come to it. In
the meantime, Flagg, I'd appreciate you not
complicating matters. When Gideon Hawk
has vowed vengeance on someone — like
he's vowed vengeance on the gang we're
after — he'll let no one stand in his way.
Including me . . . and you."

"Come along, fellas," Hawk called. He'd

stopped his grulla about thirty yards up trail and turned him sideways — a tall, broad-shouldered rider silhouetted against the towering rocks and shimmering stars. "You don't want me to start suspecting a mutiny."

Primrose glanced at Flagg, who returned the look, snorted wryly, and heeled his horse forward.

The three rode for another forty-five minutes before the tinkle of a piano and muffled laughter and the smell of wood smoke and latrines rose on the breeze. Hearing whoops and the celebratory reports of several pistol shots, they rode over a pair of rocky hills and descended to the village sprawled across a hillside falling to a round mountain lake, the dark water shimmering in the light of the recently risen moon.

A wooden sign, broke off at the post and wedged between a piñon tree and a boulder, announced EL MOLINA in sun-faded red letters.

They rode along the winding main street, whores calling softly from balconies while drunk miners and vaqueros retched or fornicated in dark alleys or — as in one case — on the flat bed of a wagon parked along the street. More pistol fire rose — quickly fired rounds indicating an angry lead swap. A woman screamed.

Before Hawk, a stout shadow crossed the street, holding a dead chicken, head down, in each hand. The squat man turned his head toward the three newcomers, and stopped before a cement stock trough on the right side of the street. He spread his arms wide, chickens dangling, and puffed a fat stogie.

"Yanquis, no?"

Flanked by Flagg and Primrose, Hawk stopped his tired grulla, whose stomach had been grumbling since they'd left the *pulpería,* and stared down at the man.

"I have a special rate for Yanquis . . . and a special place," the man said, grinning beneath his mustache, hublike cheek nobs rising into his eye sockets.

"Special place to get our throats cut, no doubt," growled Flagg.

"No, no, Señor. *Safe* place. No other place is safe for gringos. As long as you pay American money, I give you American comforts, such as rye wheeskey, hot baths, and I have one white girl. Quiet place. Not on main street. And I lock my doors at night. You will be safe from bandits."

Flagg was about to say something else, but Hawk cut him off. "You have a stable?"

"A very large, very clean stable, Señor."

"Fresh hay and oats, clean water?"

"The freshest hay and oats, the cleanest water. I haul it myself from the lake."

Hawk studied the man for a moment. "Lead the way."

"You crazy, Hawk?" Flagg said. "You're not going to fall for that old trick?"

"Shut up," Hawk said, kneeing the grulla down a dark alley on the heels of the squat, bowlegged Mexican.

They rode downhill, shod hooves clacking on intermittent stretches of cobbled ground, for about fifty yards. The Mexican suddenly threw his head up, singing a Mexican tune about a girl named Maria and a bottle of wine. A half second later, three sombrero-hatted silhouettes rose on the tiled roof to their right.

Starlight winked off gun barrels.

Hawk jerked back on the grulla's reins, reached across his belly for the Russian .44. Thumbing the big pistol's hammer back, he extended it out and up from his right shoulder. The Russian popped once, twice, three times, smoke and fire jetting from the barrel.

Because Flagg and Primrose's horses had kept moving up behind him, nudging the grulla, Hawk missed his third shot. The bushwhacker was startled enough by his gunfire, however, that he hesitated, ducking and fumbling with his rifle. As the other two dry-gulchers fell ass-over-teakettle from the tiled roof, landing with a thumping clatter on the cobbled ground, skulls cracking like dried gourds, Hawk fired again.

The third man groaned and stepped back from the roof's lip. He sank to one knee, folding an arm over his belly. Again, the Russian barked. The man flipped straight back against the tiles. From below, only his boot soles were visible, two small arrows pointing toward the stars.

Flagg cursed and held his jittery mount's reins taut.

"What the hell?" said Primrose through clenched teeth.

Hawk holstered the near-empty Russian and drew his Colt. At the first shot, the Mexican had thrown himself belly-down on the ground. Now he lay on his left hip, propped on his left arm, staring up with black eyes in which the moonlight shone like quicksilver. His body was rigid, mouth opening and closing without saying anything.

Hawk kneed the grulla forward, turned the horse sideways to the man, and aimed the cocked pistol at his head. "Now that we have that out of the way," he said levelly, "let's get back to business. You try anything like that again, I'll cut your oysters off and feed them to you raw. Do we have an understanding?"

The man's mouth opened and closed. His throat made a wet noise as he swallowed. He turned his head to the dark, oblong humps of the two dead men, and he crossed himself. "We have an understanding, Señor."

"Now, I hope you really do have a room for us, and a stable for our horses, or I'm going to get downright annoyed."

"*¡Sí, sí, sí!*" the man said, sticking his cigar back into his mouth, standing, and picking up his chickens. He waddled down the hill. "The very best in El Molina!"

"Christ," Flagg growled, his sweated face glistening in the moonlight. "What'd I tell you?"

Hawk holstered the Colt and spurred his horse ahead. "The devil you know, Flagg. The devil you know . . ."

They continued following the Mexican down the hill, winding around hillocks and old sod and adobe mining shacks, most of which appeared abandoned, to a large adobe house about fifty yards from the lakeshore. A boat was pulled up on the rocks out front of the place, clothes of all shapes and sizes strung on a line to the left. The house had several sets of narrow, stone stairs, balconies, and patios. Somewhere on the other side of the house, a lusty cat was screeching.

Someone strummed a guitar, and in several visible windows, lanterns shone.

They turned the horses into the corral flanking the house, with the squat man's assurances that he'd tend to the mounts himself as soon as he'd seen Hawk and his two companions to rooms. Hearing voices inside the main part of the house, Hawk insisted the man take them inside through an outside stairs, preferably to an isolated part of the house.

"*Sí, sí, sí,*" the man said, sweating now and breathing nervously.

"And don't spread it around you have gringos staying here," Hawk growled as he followed Flagg and the squat man up a narrow, winding staircase at the building's rear. "That would annoy me too."

"*Sí, sí, sí.*"

Inside a dark hall, the squat man paused to scratch a lucifer to life on his sandal bottom. He lit a short piece of candle he'd fished from his pocket. He held the sputtering candle high and continued walking in his shambling, heavy-footed gait.

Muffled voices rose from below, and the guitar had gotten louder. A couple of girls were giggling. The cat had stopped screaming.

"What about this room here?" Hawk said, pausing at a door on the right side of the hall. A crucifix was mounted over the door. On both sides of the door hung blurry tintypes, one of an old woman and one of a gray-bearded, slit-eyed man. On the floor was a straw mat, as if for scraping dirty sandals.

The squat man turned, cleared his throat. "That . . . is my room, sir."

"Open up. We'll take it."

With a sigh, the man produced a key from his pocket and opened the door on a simple but amply furnished room with a small desk and a brass bed, a bureau, washstand, and two shuttered windows. There was a gun rack with three old-model rifles and a shotgun. On the floor were two thick rugs.

When the squat man, still breathing hard from nerves and the climb up the stairs, had lit a bracket lamp and two candles, Hawk plucked the key from his hand and shoved him toward the door. "Bring up some extra bedding, three plates of food and coffee, and a jug of good whiskey." He grinned without mirth. "You'll be sampling each in our presence, so don't even think about hauling out the rat poison."

"*Sí, sí, señor*," the squat man said wearily, and ambled toward the open door.

"And remember . . ." Hawk called to him.

"I am as silent as the dead Christ, Señor. . . ." The squat man left the room.

Hawk shoved Flagg down on the bed, unlocked the left handcuff.

"What now, Hawk?" the lawman asked.

"Shut up."

He jerked Flagg onto his back, closed the cuff around the brass frame at the head of the bed, and locked it. Flagg grunted and cursed. "~~Goddamn~~ you, Hawk, you can't —

Hawk slammed his Russian's barrel across the lawman's right temple, knocking him flat on his back. Flagg sputtered and sighed, and his body relaxed. Hawk stood, holstered the Russian, and lifted Flagg's booted feet onto the bed, tipped the man's hat over his face.

"Christ," Primrose said, staring at Flagg with crumpled brows, "you have to hit him that hard?"

Hawk tossed the key on the dresser. "That was a love tap."

Later, when the food had been brought up, and they'd watched the squat Mexican, whose name was Guadalupe Reyes, take a liberal bite of the beans, corn, chicken, and tortillas, they ate. Then Hawk donned his hat and walked to the door.

"Where you going?" Primrose said.

He was sitting on the floor, his back to the wall by the washstand. Flagg had come around, but was wisely keeping his mouth shut.

"Gonna go out for a while, get the lay of the land."

Primrose started to get up. "I'll go with you."

"You stay with Flagg."

On one knee, the lieutenant stared up at him.

"Don't worry," Hawk said, opening the door and glancing cautiously up and down the dark hall. "If I find your money, I'll try to bring it back without any blood on it."

He clicked the door shut, and was gone.

19.
MOUNTAIN LION TAVERN

Hawk walked down the stairs in shadowy moonlight, one hand on his Colt's butt. At the bottom, he stopped and glanced at the lake.

The moonlight shimmered on its gently rippling surface. The breeze over the water felt cool against his wind- and sunburnt skin. The particular mix of smells — pure water, wet sand, and seaweed — brought back the many afternoons he'd spent fishing with his son along Wolf Creek, which meandered through the prairie grass and cottonwoods not far from their house in Crossroads, Dakota Territory.

Hawk glanced over the dark hulks of the adobe houses and stables and boulders rolling up the hill toward the main part of town, from which the sounds of revelry rose faintly among the occasional snaps of gunfire. He turned and walked down to the lake, and looked around.

Seeing no one else along the shore, he kicked out of his boots and stripped off his dusty clothes, which he shook out and piled on a boulder. Naked, he walked across the wet sand, the earth feeling good beneath his bare feet, the breeze combing his dry, dusty skin that hadn't seen a bath in weeks.

Up the hill in the distance, someone played the guitar faster, and a man sang along, stomping his foot. The sound was nearly covered by the lap of the wavelets against the sand and rocks.

Hawk waded into the water, the coolness inching up his shins and thighs. He plunged in, his heart wrenched by the refreshing chill closing around him, instantly relieving the burn of the dust, wind, and searing desert sun. He'd never been much of a swimmer — hadn't swum, in fact, since he was a kid — so his strokes were awkward, but he swam out until, looking back, the shore was a thin black line. Above the line, the lights of Reyes's adobe winked dully.

He turned, took a deep breath, and swam back. When his feet touched the sand and small, sharp rocks, he crawled five yards and lay for several minutes, belly down, on the shore, the water lapping around him. He tried to summon the thoughts and feelings of his child self, swimming in a prairie pothole on a warm summer day.

No cares. Only the moment.

Then he thought of Jubal, saw a perch burst from a brown-green creek at the end of a fishing line, the cane pole in Jubal's hands bowing sharply. But the image vanished, replaced in Hawk's mind by the boy's body falling, the noose around the boy's neck drawing taut as the horse galloped out from under him. . . .

"You have good sweem?" It was a woman's voice — high-pitched and husky at the same time, buoyant with humor, thick from drink.

Heart thudding, Hawk looked up sharply, digging his fingers into the sand. She stood silhouetted before him — a curvy young woman in a thin, multicolored skirt cut well above her knees. She wasn't wearing a blouse, and her breasts, around which several silver necklaces were draped, were pear-shaped and full, jouncing slightly as she breathed.

Hawk glanced at his gun belt, coiled atop his clothes on the boulder, ten or so feet away.

"Don't be alarmed. Guadalupe send me for you. He want you be happy."

Hawk released a silent, relieved breath. Seeing no reason to be modest before a whore, he stood, towering over her, looking down. She was brown-skinned, black-eyed, thick hair curling over her shoulders.

He brushed water from his eyes, the breeze chilling him and drying him at the same time. "Tell Guadalupe I'm happy."

"Free of charge. The *puta gringa* is occupied."

"Not interested."

He walked around and grabbed his underwear off the boulder.

"Why not interested? I Guadalupe's best whore. I please men, even Yanquis, all across Sonora!"

Hawk was stepping into his underwear. "I'm sure your reputation precedes you, but I'm not interested. Nor in the *puta gringa*. You might as well go back to the hotel and make ole Guadalupe some money."

Fists on her hips, she watched him dress. Finally, as he sat down to pull on his boots, she gave an angry chuff, wheeled, and stomped toward the hotel, her silver necklaces jingling faintly, her feet padding softly across the sand.

Hawk's shirt and hair were nearly dry by the time he reached the town's main thoroughfare. The street twisted between lantern-lit adobes bustling with activity. Men and women laughed loudly or grunted with animal passion in the whores' cribs clustered here and there about the street.

Occasional pistol shots resounded. Coins clanked. Roulette wheels ticked. In an alley to Hawk's right, men were fighting — shadows jostling, knives flashing in stray lamplight. Spanish curses rose on enraged shouts and snarls.

Hawk walked on, duster thrown back behind his pistols, keeping his eyes peeled for a large group of gringos, his ears pricked for English. Occasionally, he peeked through a cantina's dust-streaked window, but he saw no groups of Americans larger than three or four.

He came to the main square and paused near the stone fountain. Somewhere off to his right, a priest was crouched over a prone, writhing figure, offering last rites. A recipient of one of the fired bullets, no doubt. But it wasn't the dying man who held Hawk's interest. Standing just right of the fountain's stone angel, his reflection angling across the shallow, murky, straw-flecked water within the large, stone bowl, he stared at a cantina on the left side of the square, alone on a trash-littered lot.

A shingle hanging beneath the patio's brush arbor, and flanked by post-mounted torches, announced TABERNA DEL LEÓN

MONTAÑA.

It was a big, sprawling place, busy as an anthill slathered in honey. Amidst the din, Hawk's ears picked up several bits of shouted English.

Hawk turned away from the fading sighs of the dying man and the whispered prayers of the priest, and strode toward the cantina. As he passed between the torches, heading for the front door, he raked his gaze across the dimly lit front patio. Seeing only drunk Mexican miners, border banditos, vaqueros, and a couple of near-naked whores, he pushed through the batwings and stepped inside.

A few steps beyond the door, pushing through the crowd and swinging his gaze around, he stopped suddenly, his heart catching, his eyes narrowing.

Near the back of the big, wooden-floored room were nearly a dozen well-armed Americans in dusty trail garb. They sat at several tables near the room's back left wall, not far from a beehive fireplace. They seemed to be associating with the dozen *federales* spread about the square or round, rough-hewn tables. In fact, five of the Americans, including a honey-haired girl in a calico shirt and overlarge canvas trousers secured with a rope belt, were sitting with three *federales.* Laughing and drinking and smoking fat cigars, they seemed to be having a good time.

Anticipation tingling, Hawk pushed on down the pine bar, jostling and being jostled, and found a vacant spot to stand near the far end. It took nearly a minute to catch the harried apron's eye; he gestured for two tequila shots.

He threw back one shot and turned sideways, facing the doors across the room but watching, from the corner of his right eye, the American border toughs and the *federales* they were mixing with. He turned his attention to a curly-headed little Mex who'd leapt onto the counter about ten feet away. Swaying drunkenly, the man acted out a story Hawk couldn't make out from this distance, triggering finger pistols and laughing.

Someone pushed against Hawk's right shoulder, and he turned to see the girl from the bandits' table trying to squeeze between him and a bulky Mexican miner, to get to the bar.

"Move your ass!" she grumbled. Her angry eyes met Hawk's. They slid away, slid back. Her brows straightened out, and she gave him a quick, female study, a faint flush rising in her cheeks.

"What do you want?" Hawk said above the noise. "I'll order for you."

She continued to study him. Her hair was lushly tangled about her head, hanging like corn shucks to her shoulders. She was dusty and sunburned, she smelled like leather and horses, and her clothes sagged on her slender frame.

Still, she was one of the most beautiful women Hawk had ever seen. Beautiful and — judging from what Primrose had told him about the lovely bushwhacker who'd expertly flung lead at his unsuspecting men — deadly.

She smiled with only her turquoise eyes, keeping her lips straight. "Americano, eh?"

"That's right."

She blinked slowly. "Order me a bottle of wine, and tell the greaser to hurry the hell up. I'm thirsty and tired of their tequila and that sow piss they call whiskey down here."

Hawk turned and gestured for the wine. The girl tossed him a coin, and he tossed it to the apron, who set the straw-basketed bottle on the bar. Hawk gave it to her.

She stared at him, tipping her head back, her straw sombrero dangling between her shoulder blades. The corners of her full mouth rose slightly and her eyes slitted. *"Gracias."*

Hawk pinched his hat brim.

The girl turned away and pushed through the milling crowd to her table.

Hawk sipped his shot. It being a week-niqht, the crowd slowly dispersed, tables gradually opening up, the din softening.

Hawk ordered another shot and sat down at a table near the bar. He angled his back to the northeast corner, half-facing both the door on his left, and the gringos and the *federales* on his right. The crowd's roar had softened enough that he could hear the *federale* commander — a fat major with a flat, pockmarked face and with his leather-billed hat pushed back on his thick, black curls — when he stood and gathered two large money sacks about his shoulders.

The man lifted a glass to one of the Americans — a tall, steel-eyed hombre with wavy, sandy hair and matching mustache. "To our mutual endeavor, Señor Waylon."

The steel-eyed gent, with a slightly skeptical cast to his gaze, raised his glass and nodded. The major tossed back his shot and dropped his empty glass on the table, picked up another full glass amongst the myriad empties, held it up to the girl.

"And to the beautiful gringa, Señorita Saradee, who has found fit to bless our humble country with her presence."

The other *federales,* bleary-eyed from drink, hair hanging in their eyes, yelled their appreciation as they raised their own shot glasses, and joined the major in tossing back a drink in the pretty bandit's honor. The girl herself puffed out her cheeks like a bored kid in her teens, and sank down in her chair. She tipped the wine bottle to her lips, taking a liberal swig, scarlet liquid streaming down her chin.

"And do not worry about your *dinero,*" the major continued to the steel-eyed gent sitting beside the girl. The major patted the money sacks hanging down his chest from the rope around his shoulders, the U.S. markings clearly visible on the face of each pouch. "I will stow it safely away, to be divided later with the rest. You are in a very dangerous part of Mexico, the hills honeycombed with thieves. We wouldn't want all your work to come to nothing!"

Guffawing, the major tugged his hat bill down, gestured to his underlings, and swaggered drunkenly across the room toward the front doors.

The other *federales* gained their own feet clumsily, scraping their chairs back and donning their hats, taking up their rifles and adjusting their cartridge belts on their hips. They bent their own drunk-weary legs for the front door, the dozen or so remaining customers suddenly falling silent and watching the staggering, well-armed *soldados* with expressions of dread and disdain.

The batwings hadn't stopped shuddering in the Mexicans' wake when the other gringos, scattered about the back of the tavern, got up from their own tables and converged on the larger table, where the steel-eyed gent and the girl sat side by side, smoking and scowling down at the scarred planks.

The group had a private conference, most of which Hawk couldn't hear. It seemed as though the gang had been double-crossed, but intended to even the score in the near future. When the steel-eyed gent had settled the others down, including the girl, who seemed the most discontent of them all, several of the hard cases made for the stairs at the back of the tavern, yawning and grumbling.

When the majority of the men had climbed the stairs, no doubt repairing to rooms they'd rented earlier, leaving only five men at the table with the girl and the steel-eyed gent, Hawk felt a sudden quickening of his pulse and an itch in his trigger fingers.

Five drunk hard cases were manageable.

After the shooting, he'd slip out and return for the other men later.

But what about Primrose's money?

Through the fatigue of the long day's ride, his mind was slow to work through the problem. He was about to throw the rest of his third tequila back when he glanced over at the girl's and the steel-eyed gent's table. The pretty bushwhacker was sitting back in her chair, arms crossed on her breasts, staring at Hawk with a faintly coquettish smile.

The steel-eyed gent was turned toward her, talking quietly but vehemently, gesturing with his hands, his big face flushed with anger.

Ignoring the man beside her, the girl suddenly reached forward and picked up her wine bottle. She held it out toward Hawk in salute.

Holding up his shot glass, he returned the salute. At the same time, the steel-eyed gent stopped talking and slitted his eyes at the girl. He followed her gaze to Hawk, and the steel-eyed gent's face flushed crimson.

Hawk threw back his tequila, set the glass on the table. He didn't look directly at the steel-eyed gent, but held the girl's gaze as she tipped back the wine bottle, taking another long pull, wine dribbling down her chin. She set the bottle on the table, smacking her lips and wiping her chin with her left hand.

As the steel-eyed gent sat stiffening beside her, staring coldly at Hawk, she said loudly enough for Hawk to hear, "I bet *he* wouldn't have let himself get hornswoggled by those greasers."

The steel-eyed gent stared at Hawk, lips bunched beneath his mustache. The other five men at the table had turned to regard Hawk as well, frowning.

Holding his smile, Hawk shuttled his eyes to the steel-eyed gent's.

Suddenly, the man stood, his chair flying ten feet out behind him before catching a floor knot and overturning with a wooden bark. As the man wheeled from the table and sauntered toward him, Hawk gained his own feet slowly, sliding his duster flaps behind his revolvers.

20.

BUSHWHACKING
BEAUTY

"Don't you know it ain't polite," the steel-eyed gent growled through gritted teeth, stopping ten feet from Hawk's table, "oglin' another man's woman?"

Hawk shrugged a shoulder. "She was the one looking around."

The steel-eyed gent glanced at the girl still sitting at the table behind him, slumped down in her chair. Her arms were still crossed on her breasts, and her eyes were bright with anticipatory glee.

"He just ordered me a bottle of wine, Waylon," she said, chuckling. "You can't blame him for staring at me, can you? All the men stare. I don't think it was my tits he was staring at, though. At least, not *only* my tits. That's why I didn't take my usual offense."

Waylon turned back to Hawk, nostrils flaring. "That a fact?"

"Besides, he looks like one tough son of a bitch. I can't help admiring a tough man,

when they seem so damn scarce these days."
Brazenly she ran her gaze up and down
Hawk's tall, broad frame.

"Tough, you say?" Waylon sneered. He
flung his frock's lapels back from his
matched Remingtons. "Let's judge by how
long it takes him to die with two .44 pills in
his gut."

Waylon took one step farther back from
the table and spread his feet in the gunfight-
ing stance.

"Will you be comfortable shooting from
your position?" he asked Hawk. "Or would
you like to move out into the open?" He
gestured at a gap between the tables.

The girl was walking up behind the man
called Waylon. "No shooting," she said
poutily, moving between Waylon and Hawk.
"I want to see you fight like real men, with
your fists."

Hands resting on the butts of her own
pistols, she stood sideways between the two
men, smiling like a schoolgirl awaiting a
fresh glass of sarsaparilla.

"Suits me," Waylon said, raising his brows
at Hawk.

Hawk's face was expressionless. "What
does the winner get?"

"Why, me, of course!" Saradee intoned,
twirling on one foot and striking a lusty

pose, eyes glittering with a beguiling mix of girlish excitement and danger. Cocking a foot and sticking her chest out, hands on her pistol butts, she said, "Would you like to see *exactly* what the lucky winner shall enjoy?"

"Keep your shirt on, Saradee!" Waylon snapped, quickly unbuckling his shell belt. "This son of a bitch isn't going to be enjoying anything but a long, cold snuggle with the snakes."

The Mexicans who'd been sitting around Hawk had hustled out of the way but remained nearby, drinks in their hands and drunken grins on their faces. Nothing like watching two gringos going at it. The other hard cases who'd been sitting at Waylon's and Saradee's table had gained their own feet and come over, eyes bright with interest.

Most of the other drinkers remained at their own tables, only vaguely interested. No one came in from the patio, where a slight din still rose. Fights in El Molina were as common as bedbugs in the mattress sacks.

His eyes holding Waylon's fixed glare, Hawk unbuckled his own cartridge belt. The girl took Waylon's belt, then came over and held her hand out for Hawk's. Hawk turned around and set the belt and both holstered revolvers on the bar behind him.

Holding his gaze with a sly one of her own, she stepped around him and set Waylon's coiled gun belt at the end of the bar, several feet from Hawk's. While Hawk removed his hat and duster, and Kilroy removed his hat and frock, the other men from her table cleared the area around the two challengers.

Saradee shuttled her glance from Kilroy to Hawk. "Any knives, boys?"

When Kilroy had removed a knife from each boot well, Hawk removed his own bowie from the sheath between his shoulder blades, and set it with his Colt and his Russian. Waylon handed his own knives to Saradee. When she'd put them up with the hard case's revolvers, she backed away from the makeshift fighting ring and hopped up onto a table. She crossed her ankles, leaned forward, hands on her knees, and grinned with delight.

The challengers squared off, circling. Hawk studied his opponent.

The man had had too much to drink. He could barely stand, much less sidestep and feint. He should have told the girl to go to hell, and used his guns. He might have had a chance. As it was, Hawk was going to make mincemeat of the man's face, and he couldn't help smiling at the prospect.

Waylon stopped suddenly and jabbed his left fist at Hawk. Hawk didn't bother to dodge; still, the shot glanced off his right cheek, the pain barely noticeable amidst the hate surging in his veins.

In his mind's eye, he saw Waylon shooting into the Army detail, as though at ducks on a millpond, and he let the man lunge at him again. Hawk felt Estella Chacon fall slack and dead in his arms. He stepped away from Waylon's right roundhouse, pivoting on the ball of his foot. Waylon's roundhouse whistled through the air over Hawk's left temple, and the hard case staggered from his own momentum.

Hawk thrust his left fist at the man's right shoulder, to straighten him, then broke Waylon's nose with a short, crisp jab.

The nose lay flat against the man's hard face, blood gushing like wine from a cut flask. The man grunted and, stumbling backward, limbs akimbo, sucked air into his mouth. When he released it, frothy bubbles sprayed from both his nose and his lips, frothing his mustache and painting his shirt front.

"Jesus Christ!" exclaimed an observer to Hawk's right, leaping toward Waylon.

"Wait!" Saradee shouted, holding up a hand.

The hand held the man as though by puppet strings; he stopped, retreated to where he'd been standing with his compatriots. Waylon caught himself, straightened, and lowered his hands from his face, spraying blood with each exhalation.

His gaze found Hawk's. A faint smile touched his lips, and his eyes narrowed. He flicked his right wrist as though snapping out a handkerchief. Into that hand, a steel stiletto appeared from a sleeve slide, the razor-sharp blade flashing in the room's torch and lantern light.

He hadn't even started to move it toward Hawk before Hawk was on him, lashing out with his right boot. The boot smashed the hand; the blade flew and clattered off a wall. Hawk punched the dumbfounded hard case low in the man's gut. As Waylon folded, Hawk smashed his right fist into the man's left ear, and Waylon's breath whoofed out in a fresh spray of blood and spit.

He dropped to his knees.

Hawk lifted him by his shirtfront and, his face a grinning mask of fury, assaulted the man with a combination of brain-numbing blows to his face and temples. The blows didn't continue long. In less than a minute,

Waylon's back hit the floor with a wooden boom.

Hawk stood over him, opening and closing his skinned fists at his sides, his chest rising and falling sharply. He silently commanded the man to get up, but in a few seconds, it was obvious Waylon was finished.

Suddenly, Hawk was aware of the other men moving toward him, enraged snarls reddening their faces. Chairs and tables scraped the floor.

Hawk turned to face them. He glanced at his cartridge belt on the bar. He started moving forward, but stopped when Saradee yelled, "Fair fight, boys! Don't get your backs up!"

Two of the men only slowed their steps, but they kept moving toward Hawk. One slid his long-barreled revolver from his holster. He stopped when Saradee blew a hole in the floor, nipping his right boot sole. The man hopped on the other foot, cursing.

The girl ordered him and the other more aggressive hombre to haul Waylon up to his room and tend to his injuries. Reluctantly, staring coldly at Hawk, they obeyed. When they were gone, she told the other three men — more closely aligned with her than Waylon, it appeared — that she wanted some privacy. They got a bottle from the bar and headed upstairs, chuckling and glancing back at her and Hawk over their shoulders.

Saradee bought a fresh bottle of tequila and, balancing two shot glasses in her other palm, turned to Hawk. She gave him the cool up-and-down again, said, "It smells like blood in here. Let's go outside and have a drink."

Adjusting his cartridge belt on his hips, Hawk watched her turn and walk away. He wasn't sure why, but he followed her. When they sat across from each other at a small table by the square, she splashed tequila into each shot glass and sat back in her chair.

She dug a cigarillo from her shirt pocket, poked it in her mouth. Hawk held up the candle burning in the middle of the table, and she leaned forward, dipping the cigarillo's end in the flame. She puffed smoke, sank back in her chair, blew a lungful at him.

"Where'd you learn to fight like that?"

"I've always had a bad temper."

The tip of her wet, pink tongue touched the right corner of her mouth, where it found a tobacco crumb. She licked the crumb into her mouth, bit down on it gently, a curious cast to her penetrating gaze. "Where are you from?"

"Here and there." Hawk sipped his tequila. From the shadows around the patio, the girl had attracted several lascivious stares. "You?"

"Here and there. What're you doing in Mexico?"

"Look, it's getting late. If we're going upstairs, let's get a move on. If not, I'll buy another bottle and head back to my pallet."

The girl chuckled huskily, blowing smoke. Suddenly, the laughter was gone, and so was her smile. Curling her upper lip angrily, she snarled, "Listen, you uncouth dog, I'm not a whore. If you want me, you're gonna have to romance me a little. Is that asking so ~~god-damn~~ much?"

Hawk arched an eyebrow, glanced around at the Mexicans smoking and drinking in the wavering shadows. Several were passed out on the floor. One sprawled across a table. Several more ogled Saradee and whispered.

"Romance?"

She leaned forward. "You saw the *federales* walk out of here earlier?"

Hawk stared at her.

"They've got something of mine." Her eyes flicked across his arms and shoulders again, his bloody hands on the table. "You're gonna help me get it back."

"If I don't?"

"You'll stay a poor, wandering bandit, only one step ahead of the law, for the rest of your life." Saradee sank back in her chair and puffed the cigarillo. "And you'll never know the sweet bliss of *me*."

Hawk gave her an up-and-down similar to the ones she'd given him. He felt only hatred for the bushwhacking beauty, but he managed a lusty grin. *"Mierda."*

"The night is young," she said, throwing back the tequila. "Let's have some fun." She stood, set her right hand on the rail separating the patio from the street, and leapt as if her feet were springs. A moment later, she was jogging across the square.

Hawk snorted wryly, threw back his tequila, and followed her.

Since their own mounts were spent, Hawk and the girl secured two horses from a livery stable near the square — a couple of long-toothed nags typical of the liveries in this neck of the woods — and rigged them out with ancient Mexican saddles with big, dinner-plate horns.

The poor horses and even poorer tack didn't matter, Saradee assured him. They didn't have far to ride, and if they implemented her plan the way she intended, they wouldn't need speed either.

Hawk followed her over some dark hills and across a trickling stream. For a short time, they seemed to be following the fresh trail of a full dozen horses. Then they left the road the previous riders had followed, and cut cross-country.

About four miles from the village, they drew rein on the shoulder of a low rimrock. Hawk followed the girl's gaze to several pinpricks of flickering orange light a good mile south, on the low slope of a high, serrated ridge silhouetted against the moonlit sky. Squinting, Hawk made out the pale walls of a fortlike adobe structure sprawled across the base of the slope.

"Waylon said the *federales* had taken over an old ranch," Saradee said.

Hawk nodded, smiled to himself.

The girl gigged her gray nag forward, and Hawk followed her across the narrow valley, making a beeline for the lights. They tied the horses to cottonwoods on a wash bottom, and walked over another rise to the base of a low rock wall at the southeast edge of the hacienda. They hunkered down, their backs to the wall.

The girl opened her mouth to speak, but

Hawk cut her off. "My turn to play the leader."

She closed her mouth, stared at him, her face nearly invisible against the wall's shadows. He could feel the crazy, passionate heat of her. "I want only to know where the greasers are keeping the money," she whispered. "So we can return for it later . . . when the pigs have left the pen."

"How do you know they're going to leave?"

"They'll leave. And for the job they and Waylon intend, they'll need every man they have. I doubt they'll leave many behind. But I want to be able to get in and out quick, so I need to know the layout of the place. Tonight, they're all probably drunk, most probably passed out."

She grabbed his arm, dug her fingers into the flesh. "You help me get the money, we'll split it between us." She smiled, white teeth standing out against the dark oval of her face. "With thirty-six thousand dollars split two ways, we'll have one hell of a high-stepping time in Juarez!"

Hawk returned the smile. "I knew I was going to like you."

"Later this evening, you're going to like me even better." Saradee threw herself forward, ramming her breasts against his chest, and kissed him hungrily. "And tomorrow, when we're on the trail out of here with more money than you've ever made in your life . . . even better!"

Hawk rose slightly, peered over the top of the stone wall. The hacienda's torches flickered beyond an old, once-irrigated hay field grown up with piñons, junipers, and greasewood shrubs. At either end of the big casa, the *federales* had erected two tall, wooden guard towers. The towers were little more than vertical silhouettes against the starry, moonlit sky.

Hawk couldn't tell if they were manned. Probably. This was, after all, Yaqui country.

The towers weren't the only obstacles. The casa was surrounded by a half-dozen outbuildings of various shapes and sizes, any or all of which could be housing men. True, a good many of the major's men might be drunk, but probably not all of them.

To try something like this, Hawk had to be as crazy as the girl. Then again, from her he might get some clues on how to take down the rest of the gang, not to mention the money Primrose was in such a fever about.

"Come on," Hawk said, and leapt the wall.

21.

FORAY BY MOONLIGHT

Knowing the old hay field was visible from the guard towers, Hawk and Saradee crabbed slowly through the tough brown brush and gnarled piñon saplings, making as little noise as possible.

With the moon bathing the land, it wasn't a good night for attempting such a feat, and Hawk was surprised when, reaching the overgrown pecan orchard on the other side of the field, they hadn't been detected from either tower.

Not only that, but he hadn't seen any shadows moving beneath the peaked roof of either structure. They were close enough to hear the creak and click of boots on the tower floors — if there had been any. But except for the howls of distant coyotes and the occasional screech of a nighthawk, the night was silent.

Obviously, no guards stood watch in either tower.

Hawk and Saradee hunkered down on their haunches, at the edge of the orchard, breathing hard from the crawl across the hay field. Hawk raked his gaze around the yard. Spying no movement, he glanced at the girl.

At the same time, each holding a revolver, they stood and ran between a long, L-shaped bunkhouse and a stable, paused for another look around, then ran across the hard-packed wagon yard to the base of a broad stone staircase rising to two oak doors recessed in a crumbling adobe wall. Hunkering down in the shadows, Hawk looked once more across the yard, glanced at the top of the torchlit steps.

Only the torch on the right side of the door burned; the other had gone out. Hawk was about to rise when a soft snore stopped him.

He frowned, stole slowly forward, and edged a look up the steps. At the top, a blue-uniformed man lay curled up before the doors, one black jackboot resting atop the other, both hands pillowing his face. A billed blue-and-red hat lay upside down before his curly head. A Winchester rifle leaned against the landing's adobe wall, right of the double doors.

"Shit," Saradee muttered in Hawk's right ear.

Hawk turned to her, put a finger to his lips. A place this size probably had several entrances, but there was the possibility Hawk and the girl would run into a conscious guard. Rising to a crouch, aiming his pistol toward the doors, he ascended the steps, walking slowly on the balls of his boots.

At the top, he stepped over the sleeping *federale.* Holding his cocked pistol on the man, he tried the left door. It opened with a hard pull. He peeked into a dark foyer, hearing and seeing nothing but shadows. Holding the door open, Hawk beckoned to the girl, who ascended the steps quietly, stepped over the sleeping *federale,* and ducking under Hawk's arm, slipped through the cracked door.

Hawk walked inside and let the door close quietly. The girl threw her arms around his neck with a husky chuckle, pressed her breasts against his chest. Her hot body fairly shuddered. "I like your style, killer!" She ground her crotch against his, bounced up and down on her boot toes. "Take me now. Right here!"

Hawk bunched his lips with fury. He grabbed her shirt in both fists. She laughed with delight. He shook her once, knocking her sombrero off and causing her hair to fly about her head. Before he could shake her a second time, boots clacked on the flagstone to Hawk's right.

Releasing the girl, he turned toward a nook. Stone steps dropped away into darkness. In the murk, a dark shape moved. Vagrant light flashed dully off metal, winked off the patent leather of a billed hat.

The man growled, drunkenly dragging his words. *"¿Quién está allí — Ramon?"*

Hawk grabbed the girl and stepped back against the wall on the right side of the nook. The girl snorted, chuckling harder. Hawk slapped his left hand across her mouth, pinning her head to the wall.

With his right hand, he reached up behind his neck and plucked his bowie from the sheath between his shoulder blades. The approaching man's steps slowed. Coming on ahead of him was the heavy stench of tequila and sweat.

As he made the top of the stairs, Hawk saw his shadow, the brown smudge of his face, red trimming his hat. Heard the scrape of metal against leather as the man shucked a pistol from a covered holster. As the man turned toward Hawk and the girl, he expelled air loudly.

Hawk had rammed the bowie deep into the man's soft belly. His pistol clattering to the flagstones, the man bent forward over the knife. Hawk removed his left hand from the girl's mouth. He took a fistful of the Mexican's tunic and, holding the man steady, twisted the bowie, directing the blade up beneath the sternum and ribs toward the heart.

Doing so, he whispered in the man's ear. His Spanish was rough, but he got it across that if the man told him where the U.S. money sacks were, he'd take the pain away. The man hissed and sputtered, finally lifted his head and rolled his eyes to indicate the hall behind him.

He dropped to his knees. Hot blood surged over Hawk's right hand and wrist.

Shoving the knife deep into the man's chest cavity, finding the heart, Hawk drove the man down until his back was snug against the floor, the man's legs bent beneath his butt. Hawk held the bowie firm until the body ceased quivering. He pulled the knife from the bloody wound, wiped the blade on the man's red-striped trousers.

"So much for not causing a ruckus," the girl whispered.

"Grab his feet."

Hawk had grabbed the dead *federale*

under his arms and was pulling him into the nook from which he'd appeared. Cursing and chuckling nervously, Saradee grabbed the dead man's ankles and helped Hawk haul the man down the dark steps.

In a minute, they were on a lower level of the hacienda. Several torches danced light across a stone corridor. There was the faint smell of gunpowder and wine.

Hawk left Saradee with the body and went exploring. A few minutes later, he returned, lifted the dead man again, and he and Saradee hauled the man thirty yards down the hall to a pair of stout wooden doors. Both doors had been thrown wide, showing only darkness between them.

Hawk and Saradee hauled the dead *federale* down two flights of wooden steps, into stygian blackness in which the smell of gunpowder and wine had grown pungent. At the bottom of the stairs they laid the body on the earthen floor, and Hawk lit a match.

The flickering flame showed a dusty cellar room lined with old oak wine casks, in some places three rows high. In one corner of the musty room sat a half-dozen crates marked DYNAMITE. A rat scrambled, screeching, over the casks above the boxes, and disappeared into a hole in the stone wall.

Hawk opened one of the unlocked crates. Neat rows of wine-red dynamite sticks stared up at him. In several other boxes, he found caps and fuses. Looking around at the other boxes, he found two long, rectangular, pine-slatted crates, the words VAN-NORSDELL BAR-V RANCH, TUCSON, ARIZONA TERRITORY stamped on all sides and on the lids.

These boxes too were unlocked. When Hawk opened one, a dozen Henry rifles, padded with straw and burlap, glistened up at him in the light of his fourth match. He ran a hand down a smooth, walnut stock. These *federales* — obviously more bandito than *federale,* though down here the two words were often synonymous — had intercepted a rifle shipment north of the border. With all this firepower — two dozen rifles *and* dynamite — they must have one hell of a job planned.

Hawk remembered all the salutes and backslaps in the tavern earlier.

"What the hell are these for?" he asked the girl.

Saradee ran her own hand down one of the rifle's brass finish. She glanced up at Hawk suspiciously. Then she smiled. "They're hitting a train bridge day after tomorrow. Stopping a government train loaded with a million dollars worth of gold bars heading for Mexico City."

"You and Waylon throw in with them?"

"Why not? The bean-eater major took our money to show he wouldn't be fucked with, but we're supposedly going to be splitting up the gold evenly. I don't believe a fucking word of it. He needs all the men he can find to take on the train and the soldiers guarding the gold, but he wants to share that gold with gringos like he wants a burning case of the pony drip."

She entwined her hands behind Hawk's neck and said softly, "That's why, lover, you and I are going to take the payroll money and hightail it. Thirty-six thousand is enough for us. Too much money would only make us fat and lazy. Besides, I have a feeling Waylon isn't going to live to see a penny of it. The bean-eaters have us outgunned."

Hawk kissed the crazy woman, nuzzled her neck. "Sounds like the right amount to me." He slid her hands apart. "We'd better hide that hombre over there. With luck, they won't miss him, probably think he got cold feet and lit a shuck."

Lighting several more matches, Hawk explored the entire cellar, finding a nook thick with spiderwebs and fetid with rat shit far in the back. That was where, in an old feed bin buried under half-rotten horse blankets and cracked leather harness, they hid the *federale's* bloody carcass.

When they'd covered the bin again with the blankets and harness, they retraced their steps upstairs and closed the double doors, then continued down the hall in the direction the dying *federale* had indicated.

Ten minutes later, a light glowed in the corridor before them. Voices rose. Coins clinked. A man laughed; another yawned loudly and in Spanish announced it was getting late.

A chair scraped. As others berated the man for his weakness, boot heels clacked and spurs chinged into the distance.

Hawk walked along the left wall and stopped beside an open arch through which the wan lamplight flickered. Hawk edged his left eye around the edge of the arch, peered through the open doorway.

Beyond was the casa's original kitchen and dining room area. Thirty feet away, a large, heavy table sat surrounded by high-backed chairs. Because of another wall, Hawk couldn't see the entire table, but in his field of vision were five half-dressed *federales.* Those he could see looked bleary-eyed, the light from a large, rock fireplace dancing across their swarthy, sweaty, unshaven faces.

The men were drinking and gambling, tossing coins and cards this way and that. Hawk didn't see or hear the major. Probably getting his beauty sleep for the big morning after next. Beans and pork bubbled in a big cast-iron pot suspended over the fireplace, sending out a spicy aroma. The smell of the food was tempered by the fetor of the *federales'* rancid perspiration. The bottles on the table were opaque. Probably mescal.

No wonder security was so lax.

Hawk raked his gaze around the joined rooms, searching for the payroll pouches. He doubted the major would leave the money in the hands of these glorified banditos. It looked as though the dying *federale* had duped him.

He was about to pull his head back from the arched opening when his gaze settled on a tall wooden cabinet standing against the wall behind the gamblers. It was a heavy, ornately carved piece, much scarred and shrouded in dust and cobwebs. At one time, it had probably held expensive dishes. Hawk doubted it held dishes now. If so, why the stout chain through its scrolled iron handles, and the heavy padlock securing both ends of the chain?

Hawk turned to the girl. "Blackjack."

"Let me see."

"Don't you trust me?"

She stared up at him, pupils expanding and contracting. She ran her eyes across his chest, lifted her gaze again to his face. "No!" She sidled past him, edged her own look through the arched doorway.

"The cabinet," Hawk said.

He pressed his back to the wall as, to his right, Saradee stared through the doorway. Her right hand fell absently to the butt of her .45 poking up on her right hip. Hawk closed his own hand over hers.

"You don't have a chance," he whispered in her ear.

She pulled back from the opening, looked at him. Her face was flushed and sweating. "Damn tempting to shoot every last greaser in the place, ain't it?"

For a fleeting moment, Hawk felt as though he were staring into his own anguished, kill-crazy eyes. It was an unsettling, dizzying sensation, like falling headfirst down a deep well.

As quickly as it came, it was gone.

"Remember the plan. We'll be back for it."

"Together?"

"Why not?"

She swallowed, took his hand. Together, they walked back the way they'd come. Outside, the guard was still sleeping, curled up and snoring. Hawk and Saradee stepped gingerly over him and descended the stairs.

Hand in hand, they walked back across the hay field.

Back at the horses, Hawk turned out his left stirrup and grabbed the big saddle horn. Saradee tugged his arm.

She stepped back, removed her hat, and shook out her hair. She began unbuttoning her shirt slowly. Staring up at him, she shrugged out of the shirt, dropped it, and stood before him bare-breasted. In the milky moonlight, her jutting nipples slanted shadows across the full, round orbs.

"You're man enough to beat the hell out of Waylon Kilroy, but are you man enough for me?"

When they'd finished coupling like wolves enraged by the moonlight, they dressed slowly, sweating and fatigued.

"We meet back here, morning after next," Saradee said, breathless. "First light."

"I'll be here. We'd better ride back to town separately, so no one gets suspicious."

She kissed him, entangling her tongue with his, then climbed into her saddle and reined her horse toward the main trail.

"Don't worry. I'll tell Waylon I drilled a bullet through your head." She laughed. "Later, lover."

She ground her spurs into the nag's ribs and headed off toward town.

22.

An Ear for Waylon

Back at Reyes's hotel, D.W. Flagg was trying to work his right hand free of the handcuff secured to the brass bed frame.

The deputy marshal gritted his teeth as he twisted and turned the hand while pulling it, careful to keep the cuff from knocking against the brass. He didn't want to awaken Lieutenant Primrose, who lay on his pallet against the wall to Flagg's right. A single candle burned atop the dresser near the door, the light flickering across the soldier's mussed auburn hair and weatherburned skin.

Chin to his chest, stockinged feet crossed, his upper body covered with a thin wool blanket, Primrose snored softly.

Flagg held the cuff taut against the frame and applied firm, steady pressure. Try as he might, and as sweaty as his hand had become from the effort of trying to free himself, he could not slip his knuckles through the ungiving metal ring.

No longer able to contain his fury, he cursed loudly and rapped the cuff against the frame with a shrill metal clang.

Primrose lifted his head with a start, uncrossing his feet and reaching for the pistol beside him. "What the hell is it?"

His nervous gaze swept the room, lighting on Flagg, red-faced and grimacing. "It's this damn cuff, Lieutenant. Get it the hell off of me!" He gave the cuff another loud wrap, the force of the blow causing the bed to bounce with a raucous wooden bark.

"Be quiet, Flagg. You're going to awaken the whole place!"

"You have no right to hold me here, Lieutenant! Unlock this ~~goddamn~~ cuff!"

In a nearby room, someone groaned. A voice called out from below.

Primrose gained his feet and aimed his revolver at Flagg, the lieutenant's own face now flushed with fury. "You're gonna bring the whole place down on us. Shut up!" He flicked the Colt's hammer back.

Flagg glared up at him. His cracked lips shaped a sneer. "Look at yourself, soldier. He's turning you into what he is — a cold-blooded killer."

"I haven't killed you yet."

Flagg laughed without mirth. "No, but

286

you're going to . . . as soon as he does. My blood'll be on your hands, same as his."

"He's not going to kill you. He's assured me that when our work is done here, he'll turn you loose."

"And you believe that vigilante?" Flagg shook his head. His temple was marred by the blue goose egg from Hawk's pistol barrel. "He has no intention of letting me live. He knows I'll be after him again."

Primrose lowered the gun slightly. "I won't let him."

"You'll have no choice. Anyone who gets in Hawk's kill-crazy way gets turned toe-down right quick, in case you haven't noticed."

When Primrose said nothing, Flagg added, "Look at yourself, Lieutenant. He's got you believin', just like him, that the end justifies the means. If you don't turn me loose, that money you're so intent on bringin' back to your dear old father-in-law will be awash in the blood of a deputy U.S. marshal!" Flagg shook his head and smiled savagely. "I guarantee it, Primrose. That bastard's going to kill me, sure as he's got me chained to this blasted bed!"

His face cast in troubled thought, the lieutenant lowered the pistol to his thigh. "If I let you go, will you leave the village, head back to the States, and cause no more trouble here?"

"Trouble?" Flagg chuffed, then chuckled. "Christ, yes! I know when I've been beat. I'll head back to Arizona, rest up, and take him down somewhere on the other side of the border."

Flagg studied the younger man's thoughtful countenance. "Don't worry, your dark secret's good with me. I won't mention anything to Devereaux."

Primrose cursed under his breath, turned, set his pistol on the dresser, and picked up the handcuff key. He walked to the bed, poked the key in the lock, and turned it. The cuff clicked and opened, and Flagg pulled his hand away, rubbed the wrist with the other hand.

"Thanks. Maybe you're a tad smarter than I'd given you credit for." The marshal stood a bit unsteadily, crouched over his saddlebags, and removed his cartridge belt. He wrapped the belt around his waist, loaded his revolver, then donned his hat and hefted his saddlebags over his shoulder.

"Remember, Marshal, you gave me your word you'd leave the village."

Flagg chuckled and pulled the door open. "Tell the son of a bitch good-bye for me, will you?" He looked up and down the dark hall, turned back to Primrose, and winked. "And tell him we'll be seeing each other again soon!"

With that, he went out, leaving the door standing wide behind him. Hearing the marshal's boots on the outside steps, Primrose closed the door and stared at it for a long time before collapsing onto the bed.

A few minutes after leaving Hawk, Saradee tossed her hair out from her neck and threw her head back on her shoulders. She sang as she rode:

The needle's eye doth supply
The thread that runs so true,
And many a man have I let pass,
Because I thought of you.

And many a dark and stormy night
I walked these mountains through;
I'd stub my toe and down I'd go
Because I thought of you.

When Saradee got back to El Molina and turned the nag back over to the livery barn, she started toward the Mountain Lion Tavern, heading through a dark, trash-strewn alley. The town had quieted considerably since she and her friend — Christ, she didn't even know his name! — had headed out to the *federale* camp.

Two Mexicans stepped out of the shadows before her, knife blades gleaming in their fists. One of them, his drink-glistening eyes shifting back and forth between Saradee's eyes and her breasts, said something in sneering Spanish. The other man laughed and lunged toward her.

Saradee made short work of the two drunks, her pistols cracking sharply, the echoes absorbed by the mud and adobe walls rising on both sides.

Her gun smoke billowing in the darkness, she was about to step over the two dead men when an idea spoke to her.

She crouched and slipped a razor-sharp stiletto from the death grip of one of the would-be attackers. A minute later, she dropped the man's bloody ear in her neckerchief, and folded the neckerchief away in her pocket. Whistling softly the song she'd sung on her way into town, Saradee continued to the Mountain Lion.

The sweet-musty fragrance of marijuana rose from the dark patio upon which only a few man-shaped silhouettes slumped in the darkness. Inside, a skinny boy in burlap rags was scrubbing Waylon's blood into the warped pine floorboards. Of the six men inside, three belonged to Saradee's own gang. Two others looked like Mex miners, the third a crowlike, addlepated beggar muttering into his empty stone tankard.

"Whiskey," Saradee told the barman sweeping lazily behind the bar. "Something a little better than the poison you usually serve."

The barman just stared at her, uncomprehending. Too tired to dicker, she settled for the first bottle the man set on the bar. She tossed him a couple coins, popped the bottle's cork, and moseyed over to the table where the two men from her group sat. J. J. Beaver Killer was playing solitaire, and Jimbo Walsh was cleaning his pepperbox revolver, the pieces of which he'd placed on a blue neckerchief atop the table. Between the men were several empty shot glasses. Watching Saradee come over, Walsh grinned knowingly.

"Have you some fun tonight, Boss?"

She stopped before their table and took a long slug of the whiskey. "Where's Waylon?"

"Upstairs with a bottle. Turkey cleaned him up, straightened his nose while me and Dog-Tail held him down. You know they don't even have a sawbones in this town?" Walsh shook his head, then held the revolver to his right ear, listened intently to the click as he slowly thumbed back the hammer. "This is one uncivilized race. Makes our Injuns look like learned men from Yale."

He'd said this last while staring at the half-Cheyenne across from him, but Beaver Killer ignored him. The big Indian peeled a soiled pasteboard from the deck in his thick left hand, laid it on a six of clubs as the ribbons tied to the ends of his braids swished about the table.

Beaver Killer looked up at Saradee. "You ain't goin' up there, is ye, Boss?"

Saradee shrugged and splashed whiskey into one of the Indian's empty shot glasses. Splashing some into one near Walsh's revolver parts, she curled her lip in a sneer. "I got Waylon eatin' out of my corset."

She turned and headed for the stairs.

Walsh called. "How we gonna play it . . . day after tomorrow?"

Saradee hesitated. She'd already figured how *she* was going to play it — or *not* play it. How her men and Waylon's played it, she no longer cared. She curled her lip again, and her blue eyes glittered devilishly. "As soon as you get your hands on one of them gold bars, pick out one of Waylon's boys or one of them greasers, and just start shootin'."

With that, grinning as she thought of her

men and Waylon's and the greasers cutting each other down while they scurried about the gold bars spilled like jackstraws around the train wreckage, she turned and climbed the stairs.

She stopped before the door of the room that she and Waylon had rented earlier, and knocked twice. "Waylon, honey?"

She turned the knob, pushed the door two feet open, and peeked inside. The room was lit by one dim lantern on a stand beside the bed. Waylon sat atop the bed, his head and shoulders resting against the headboard. He wasn't wearing a shirt. His face was criss-crossed with heavy bandages, one of which held his broken, lumpy nose in place. His eyes, big and purple as ripe plums, were swollen nearly shut. His lips were swollen too, and blood trickled from one of the open cuts, dribbling slowly down his chin. The blood glistened in the lantern light.

Slowly, as if the movement were a strain, Waylon turned his head toward the door. The lantern light found what little of his eyes showed between the puffy lids. They glittered like small metal filings.

Saradee stepped into the room and closed the door. "How we doin', sugar?"

Kilroy stared at her. In his left hand, he held a whiskey bottle. On the bed near his right lay one of his shiny Remingtons. His hand closed over the gun's ivory grips, and he picked up the revolver and aimed it at Saradee, thumbing back the hammer.

"*Puta* bitch."

"What?"

"I'm gonna kill you right where you stand."

Saradee frowned. "Why?"

"You set me up to fight that big son of a bitch when you knew I'd drank half the tequila in El Molina. Then you *left* with him." He moved his head a little, stared down the barrel.

"Waylon — honey, sweetheart — don't be silly. That son of a bitch was starin' at my tits half the night, and I was tired of it. I wanted you to punish him for me. You know — like a man is supposed to do for his woman. In my own juiced state, I didn't realize that you too were three sheets to the wind."

Kilroy held the gun steady, aimed at her head. His face was a dark checkerboard around the white, blood-spotted bandages.

"Here — I've got a little present for you," Saradee said, reaching into her pocket.

Kilroy's gun hand tensed. She stopped, then, moving more slowly, reached her left hand into a pocket of her canvas trousers that bagged on her lithe frame while still, somehow, revealing her delectable curves. Her breasts swelled against the calico blouse she'd stolen from the miner she'd killed.

Out came her hand with the folded neckerchief. Moving toward the bed, she slowly lifted the folds of the bloodstained cloth, then crouched down before Kilroy, extending her open left hand in which the severed ear lay — blood- and dirt-streaked, with several fine brown hairs angling out from its edges.

"The bastard ain't hearing so good down in hell," she said. "Thought you might want to dry this and wear it around your neck."

Kilroy looked up from the ear. He breathed through his mouth, his chest rising and falling sharply. His slitted eyes were puzzled.

"Stabbed him three times in the heart, gave him to the liveryman's hogs." She shrugged and set the ear and neckerchief on the stand beside the lamp. "Just my way of sayin' I was sorry for hornswogglin' you into a fight when you was drunk." She kept her eyes downcast but threw her shoulders back, pushing out her breasts. She made her voice small with contrition. "I hope you'll forgive me, honey."

Kilroy stared up at her, his slitted eyes

roaming that incredible body. Finally, he cursed through his sore teeth and depressed the Remington's hammer. Leaning the bottle against his side, he swept the covers back with his right hand, revealing the lower half of his body clad in long underwear. "Get in here."

Hawk got back to Reyes's hotel only a few minutes after Saradee returned to her and Kilroy's room over the Mountain Lion. He unlocked the door of his room, unholstered his Russian, and stepped inside.

Holding the door open, he raked his gaze around. A nearly expired candle offered as much shadow as light.

Primrose was the only one here. The lieutenant lay on the bed, hands behind his head. He stared up at Hawk, pushed up on his elbows.

"Did you find the money?"

Hawk nodded, holstered the Russian.

Primrose sat up, his voice excited. "You did?"

"Located it. We'll get it day after tomorrow."

Hawk tossed his hat onto a hook by the door and walked to the washstand. He tipped water from the pitcher into the tin basin, splashed water on his face.

Behind him, Primrose said with chagrin, "You, uh, gonna ask about Flagg?"

"I figured you'd let him go." Hawk removed his shirt and neckerchief, and scooped water over his neck. He tipped his head back to work the kinks out. "To tell you the truth, I was getting bored with his conversation."

"What happens between you two must be between just the two of you. I want no part of it." Primrose paused, then added haltingly, "He's going to try and kill you again."

Hawk toweled his face. "I know."

Primrose studied him, brows ridged. "That doesn't really trouble you, does it? You don't fear death . . . care not whether you live or die."

Hawk tossed the towel across a chair and began removing his cartridge belt. He stopped and stared at the wall. "We all gotta die, Lieutenant."

23.
THE TRUCE

Someone rammed their fist against a door — three hard thumps. Each was a lightning bolt lancing Kilroy's brain. His eyes snapped wide. Or as wide as he could get them in his current condition. The cuts and bruises, not to mention his broken nose, made him feel as though he were wearing a plaster mask lined on the inside with sharpened steel spikes.

"Boss, the greasers are here!" yelled Turkey McDade on the other side of the wood. "They said you agreed to take a morning ride with 'em."

Kilroy groaned. It took him several seconds to climb his way up from the excruciating pain in his face and head, and to locate the place in his brain that controlled his voice. His mouth tasted as though a scorpion had crawled inside and died only after giving his tongue several sharp stings. "Shit."

"You okay, Boss?"

Kilroy groaned, spat. "Tell 'em I'll be down in a minute."

Boots thumped off down the hall. The vibration in the floor caused an empty whiskey bottle to fall off the other side of the bed and to hit the floor with a glassy thump.

It rolled around the warped floor for a few seconds before another groan sounded from inside the room. Down around Kilroy's crotch, something moved beneath the blankets. Awkwardly, he threw the covers back to reveal Saradee's head and shoulders, her hair shining in the full light angling through the deep-set windows flanking the bed.

Outside, birds chirped and wagons clattered. A horse whinnied.

Saradee lay facedown on Kilroy's bare belly. She was naked, and her hair was fanned out across her shoulders and his hips. Her back angled down to her flaring hips and pert, round butt. In her right hand, she held one of her silver-plated .45s down near Waylon's right knee.

Probably practiced her French on him last night while holding the damn six-shooter, only resisting the temptation to shoot off his manhood because his men were near.

The nastiest *puta* down here couldn't hold

a candle to Saradee.

Kilroy reached down, grabbed the revolver from her limp hand, and lightly tapped the barrel against her head. "Get up. *Federales,* remember? We're ridin' out with 'em to the train bridge."

She groaned and turned over. "Huh?"

"We're ridin' out with the *federales* — and I use that term loosely — to make sure they don't pull anything funny settin' those dynamite charges."

She rolled onto her back, her bare breasts flattening slightly across her chest, and pressed a hand to her temple, wincing against the hangover. Even in that position, those orbs were still full, round, and magnificent.

"I'll wait here," she said, smacking her lips. "You can tell me about it."

Kilroy got up and, feeling as though someone had taken a sledgehammer to his face, stooped to pick up his balbriggans. Imagining the trainload of gold bars took some of the sting away. He couldn't quite fathom being as rich as the *revolucionarios'* gold would make him — if he lived to get his hands on it, that is — but he was willing to take a shot at the train anyway. It seemed that the greasers had the technicalities mostly worked out; they just needed more shooters.

"Sure . . . you stay and sleep," he told Saradee, and chuckled.

He was pulling on his jeans when Saradee's eyes snapped wide. She wanted nothing to do with the gold, but if she didn't ride out with the gang, they might get suspicious and foil her plans to abscond with the payroll loot.

She stared thoughtfully at the ceiling. "Reckon I'd better see to my own interests," she said through a yawn. "Wouldn't want you and the greasers throwin' in against me." She dropped her long legs over the side of the bed and stretched catlike. Rising, she kissed Waylon's nose, enjoying his pained yelp, and began gathering her strewn clothes.

Ten minutes later, they descended the Mountain Lion's stairs, both moving stiffly, Kilroy looking like the sole survivor of a stagecoach's plummet from a thousand-foot cliff. He hadn't had time to freshen his bandages, and they now showed as much red as white. His snuff-brown hat, the crown pancaked in the Colorado style, was tipped back on his head as if to ease the strain on his nose.

As the two crossed toward the front of the room, past the tables upon which the chairs were upended for sweeping, and past the floorboards stained brown from Kilroy's spilled blood, the outlaw paused at the bar to order a fresh bottle. He popped the cork as he and Saradee walked outside, where the *federales* sat their horses before the patio, left of Saradee's and Kilroy's own gang. The north-of-the-border bandits sat their own mounts with stiff expressions on their hungover countenances, sliding sneering looks at their Mexican counterparts, as if barely able to stomach sharing the same street.

The *federales* returned the looks with even more bitter expressions of their own.

Kilroy tipped back the bottle, taking a long pull. Instantly, the invisible nails piercing his nose and cheekbones dulled enough to lighten the red pain-veil over his eyes.

He followed Saradee into the square, where Major Valverde intoned, "Señor Waylon and the magnificent Saradee, how good it is to see you both this lovely morn — !"

Feeling his face warm with embarrassment and keeping his eyes down, Kilroy walked passed the major's tall, cream stallion, heading for the riderless horse beside that of Turkey McDade.

Valverde sucked a surprised breath. "Madre Maria, Kilroy, what happened to your face?"

Chuckles rippled through the dozen or so *federales* gathered behind Valverde and his scarecrow lieutenant, Juan Soto. Tenderly, Kilroy toed a stirrup, grabbed the horn, and swung onto his horse. He took the reins from Turkey McDade and glanced over the tightly grouped Mexicans.

At the back of the group lay a wagon, two mules in the traces, and several crates piled in the box and secured with ropes. Two baby-faced *federales* in baggy uniforms with hats that seemed to swallow their curly heads sat in the driver's box, sweating and looking edgy. They were no doubt hauling the dynamite for blowing up the bridge.

Kilroy brought his gaze forward to Valverde and Soto.

The major's brown eyes were bright with glee. Beneath the brim of his ratty, straw sombrero, Soto's eyes were their usual diamondback-flat, but the man's bony shoulders jerked with silent laughter.

In spite of the havoc the sore muscles wreaked in his face, Kilroy grinned. "This is my celebration face," he told Valverde. "Now, why don't you and your esteemed lieutenant lead us to the party?"

Chuckling, Valverde glanced at Soto. The lieutenant raised his right hand and twirled it, then swung his horse around. As he and Valverde headed through the group of men behind them, the group parted, half the men backing their horses toward the fountain. They apparently meant for the Americans to ride in the middle of the group, with Valverde's men at both the front and flank. The wagon, with its deadly munitions and nervous pilots, would bring up the rear.

Kilroy cursed and gigged his horse after Valverde, Soto, and the half-dozen men riding directly behind the two leaders.

When they were riding through the mountains east of town, following an old mining trail, Kilroy leaned over to Saradee sitting her piebald off his right stirrup. "I unloaded your pistols earlier, while you were using the thunder mug," he said quietly. "You might want to go ahead and load them now."

"I did," she said, smiling. "You might wanna take a peek at your own hoglegs. I unloaded them last night while you snored."

Kilroy flushed behind the bandages, and shucked a Remy from his right holster. He opened the loading gate and spun the wheel. He glanced at Saradee, and his nostrils flared.

Plucking cartridges from the loops of his shell belt, he quickly loaded each revolver.

When he'd spun the second one's cylinder and dropped it back in its holster, he stared straight over his horse's ears at the dusty, blue-clad back of the soldier riding ahead of him.

He leaned slightly toward Saradee and said through the side of his mouth, "I know you and me have sort of fallen out of trust with each other, but now might be a good time to call a truce."

Saradee pooched her lips out and stared at Valverde and Soto leading the group up a low rise through pines. The morning sun burned the green, ankle-high grass growing around rocks and boulders.

"I'll spread the word to my boys, if you'll spread the word to yours."

"Consider it done." Kilroy leaned back and plucked his bottle from his saddlebags. It was already half empty. "If we play this right, you and me could be one hell of a lot richer than we ever thought possible."

"What about the major?"

Kilroy took another pull from the bottle and returned the cork to the lip. He lifted a shoulder. "He's got us outgunned by only four men. I've played against worse odds than those in Kansas!"

"Yeah, but did you win?"

■ ■ ■ ■

The trail the group followed dropped gradually until two low sandstone walls, spiked with mesquite and piñon, rose on both sides of a rocky arroyo. The ravine's stony floor was threaded by a thin trickle of springwater. Ahead, two train trestles, supported by stone and wood, arced across the canyon.

The group rode under the first trestle, the wooden braces smelling of sun-scorched oak and creosote, and continued for a hundred more yards. Valverde held up his right hand in the shadows cast by the second trestle. Kilroy lifted his gaze to the ties and tracks a hundred and fifty feet above.

A pale-green lizard lodged in the rocks of one of the pilings stared down at the newcomers, flicking its tongue.

Valverde turned to Kilroy, who'd ridden up off his left flank. "A wonderful place for a horrible accident — wouldn't you say, Señor Waylon?"

Kilroy's eyes were still roaming the stone pilings between which heavy wooden beams were crisscrossed like the flat irons of a jail cell.

He sat up straight in his saddle. "Tomorrow morning, huh?"

"The train is due to pass at six a.m.," said Juan Soto.

"Although you probably know our trains here in Méjico tend to run not always on time," added Valverde. He shrugged. "Still, we will be here by six, just in case."

"How do you know it's going to cross the arroyo on this trestle," said Saradee, more to look interested than for any other reason, "and not the one we just passed?"

Valverde looked at her, his eyes dropping momentarily to her shirt, then back up to her face. "A very good question, Miss Saradee, which shows you are much more than just *muy bonita*, uh?" He grinned from ear to ear, his lips showing red against his broad, pockmarked brown face. "In their haste, the railroad built the original trestle on a fault line. Very bad. So, last summer, they had to reroute. This is now the trestle that is used to cross the arroyo."

He turned southward, pointing. "As you can see, the tracks climb a medium-steep hill as they approach the trestle, so the train will be going very slow, just creeping along. For that reason, I wish to blow the bridge only when the locomotive has crossed. That way, we can be assured of as many casualties as possible. Still, since the rear cars will be far from the bridge when it blows, many of the guards will jump to safety."

"And put up a fight," Kilroy said, casting his gaze toward the south end of the bridge. "Just how many guards are we talking about?"

"My informant has told me between fifty and sixty. Half will no doubt die when the bridge blows. The others will be disoriented and, as you can see, there isn't much cover on that side of the arroyo. With as many men as we have, they should give us little problem."

"Peek them off," said Juan Soto, grinning around a small, black cigarette, "like dooks off the meal pond."

"Pretty as a picture," said Saradee. "What happens when we've killed all the guards?"

"We dig through the wreckage, of course," replied the major. "When we have found the gold, we take it back to our headquarters for a big fandango — the largest in the land! The next morning, when we are clear-eyed, we will split up the gold and the money we, uh" — placing the end of a fist to his mouth, he gave a dry cough — "found stashed in the mine of Juan's father, Pedro."

Soto curled a lip at Kilroy.

"Then we'll be wanted on both sides of the border," said Turkey McDade, sitting his pinto behind Kilroy, sucking a quirley.

He laughed dryly, as did several other Yankees.

Valverde feigned surprise as he turned his white-ringed eyes to Kilroy. "You are wanted on the *americano* side of the border? Oh, my God — you did not tell me this! For what?" He laughed heartily and punched Kilroy's right shoulder.

The wagon clattered along the arroyo behind them. Valverde turned his head to look back the way he'd come. "It is about time!" he shouted in Spanish. "What have you drivers been doing — playing with yourselves? Hurry, we have a bridge to blow!"

Behind the dust veil lifted by the wagon, Gideon Hawk watched the Mexican and American bandits through field glasses.

24.

PRELUDE TO FIREWORKS

Hawk lay belly-down along the north bank of the arroyo, about fifty yards back from the first railroad bridge. His position was concealed by a boulder on his left and a spindly mesquite on his right.

"What's going on? What are they doing?" Lieutenant Primrose asked, hunkered down behind the boulder off Hawk's left hip.

"Don't get impatient, Lieutenant."

"What're we doing here?" Primrose's voice betrayed his frustration. "What the hell has this to do with retrieving the payroll money?"

"Nothing."

Through the first trestle's far-left arch, Hawk watched through the thinning dust veil as the group of American outlaws and Mexican *federales* made way for the wagon. The wagon stopped in the shade of the second bridge.

Last night after they'd made love — if you

could call it love — Saradee had told Hawk the bandits' plan. So he pretty much knew what was happening now, as she and the steel-eyed gent, Kilroy, and the two *federale* leaders sat their horses while the fat major berated the wagon drivers, cheeks puffed, his right fist in the air.

The two young drivers scrambled down from the wagon seat, one quickly crossing himself, and ran back to the end of the wagon. As one of the wagon boys tossed a tarpaulin aside and rummaged around in a wooden crate, Hawk lowered the glasses and turned to Primrose.

"I told you to stay in the village, Lieutenant. Nasty habit you've developed — followin' me."

"Where's the money?"

"At the *federales'* camp. Don't get your underwear all twisted. By this time tomorrow, you and the loot will be on your merry way back to Arizona and the big party Major Devereaux will no doubt throw in your honor."

"Why wait till tomorrow? Most of the *federales* must be *here*. How many could be left at their camp?"

"There'll be even fewer there tomorrow."

Primrose gritted his teeth as Hawk casually cleaned the field glasses with his shirt-tail. "While they and those killers are busy out here, I say we go to the camp and secure those greenbacks!"

"Go ahead," Hawk said, training the glasses again at the commotion at the base of the second bridge. "I got work to do."

Hawk adjusted the binoculars' focus until the arches of the second trestle swam sharply into view. Above the heads of the milling Americans and the *federales,* three men scaled the wooden cross-struts. The men climbed slowly, carefully, carrying small burlap sacks as preciously as newborn babes.

Hawk lowered the binoculars and retreated behind the boulder. As he wound the leather lanyard around the glasses and slipped the glasses into their velvet-lined case, Primrose stared at him, bemused.

"How do you plan to do it?"

"Do what?"

"I take it you didn't ride out here to enjoy the Mexican countryside," Primrose said, lifting one cheek and slitting one eye. "Kill them. *All* of them."

Hawk rose and carried the glasses back to their horses ground-tied at the base of a knoll.

"If you intend to hold the money hostage," Primrose said, "it isn't going to work. In spite of how you are, or what you might think of me, I don't value the money more than life. I won't help you take them on."

"Don't need your help," Hawk said, pulling a burlap knapsack from his saddlebags. "Got all the help I'll need right here."

He carried the sack over to the boulder and sat down beside the lieutenant. He laid the sack beside him, then kicked his boots out, crossed his ankles, and rested his back against the boulder. He tipped his hat brim over his eyes.

Primrose opened the sack and peeked inside. Staring up at him were three bunches of hide-wrapped dynamite, complete with caps and fuses. Four sticks composed each bunch.

"Christ," Primrose said. "Where in God's name did you get that?"

"Lady luck," Hawk said, yawning and crossing his arms over his chest. "I didn't get much sleep last night, Primrose. Wake me when the hard cases have moseyed, will you?"

Eyes closed, half-dozing, Hawk heard the horses and the wagon clatter away down the arroyo.

Primrose tugged on his sleeve. "They're gone."

Hawk poked his hat brim up and turned to peer down the ravine. Moving much more quickly now, the driver and his partner conversing loudly and laughing, the wagon disappeared around a bend. The hard cases left only dust and the smell of fresh mule and horse plop in their wake.

In the brush of a nearby hillside, a wild pig squealed. The sun beat down like a glowing hammer.

Hawk stood, removed his duster, shoved his arms through the straps of the knapsack, securing the pack between his shoulder blades, and stepped carefully down the arroyo's low, steep bank.

"For Christ sakes," Primrose said behind him.

"You must be half-Mex," Hawk said, striding toward the trestle, "all your talk about Jesus."

It took him a half hour, climbing amongst the beams in the hot sunshine, to attach the dynamite charges to the trestle braces with the thin rawhide ties he'd procured from Guadalupe Reyes's livery barn. When he finished, he climbed down, jumping the last three feet, his boots kicking up dust amongst the rocks at the arroyo's floor. His sweat-soaked shirt clung to his back and chest, and sweat dribbled through the dust on his dark, chiseled face.

Primrose stood holding Hawk's duster in one hand, the reins of both horses, standing hang-headed behind him, in the other. "What now?"

Hawk grabbed the duster and squinted at the sun. "Time for lunch." He tossed the duster over his bedroll, swung into the grulla's hurricane deck, and gigged the horse toward town.

In El Molina, they had lunch in a little cantina not far from Reyes's place, then took a two-hour siesta with the rest of the village, the lieutenant curled up on the floor of their room while Hawk slept on the bed. The shutters were thrown open to the muffled screech of gulls and the fresh breeze off the lake.

The heat and the breeze made Hawk dream about walking along a lake near Crossroads with his wife, Linda, and he woke smiling. As he stared at the cracked adobe ceiling flecked with fly shit and soot, the present returning to him slowly and heavily, the smile faded. He stomped into his boots and went down to the lake for another swim.

Late afternoon found him and Primrose back at the same cantina in which they'd had lunch, drinking tequila and what passed for beer down here — yeasty and warm. When it grew dark and the miners came in from the mines, dusty and jubilant and getting drunk quickly on the cantina owner's home-brewed whiskey, Hawk and the lieutenant ordered platters of pork with all the trimmings. When they finished eating, they ordered more beer and tequila, sat on the small front veranda, and kicked back in their chairs.

The light faded and the stars kindled. The smell of mesquite smoke and spicy cooking odors grew strong on the breeze. Occasionally, a gull screeched or a distant coyote yammered. Dust from the steady stream of horseback riders and wagons sifted constantly, as did the smell of tobacco and liquor, horse shit and latrines. Pistols popped intermittently all across town.

The Mountain Lion Tavern sat kitty-corner across the square. Hawk and Primrose watched and listened as the gringo outlaws openly celebrated their coming fortune. They were only silhouettes from this distance — jostling shadows against the candles and lantern light — but Hawk could make out the long-haired Saradee gambling with a group near the square. She was the loudest of the revelers and, of course, at the center of the celebration.

Kilroy's tall, lean frame with his Colorado hat sat relatively quietly, kicked back in a chair. He was no doubt mentally licking his wounds, his bandages glowing in the shadows.

Hawk finished his beer and turned a glance through the open, glassless window behind him. Amidst all the brown Mexican faces and straw sombreros was that of a tall American in a cream Stetson, moving toward the cantina's crude bar from a back door.

Flagg carried a Winchester in his right hand. Raking the room, his nervous eyes met Hawk's on the other side of the open window. Flagg stopped, took one fluid step behind an adobe post from which a lantern burned. Hawk's right hand strayed to his Russian's butt, froze when he saw Flagg trying to keep the post between him and Hawk as the lawman retraced his steps to the back door and ducked outside.

"What is it?"

Hawk looked at the lieutenant, the young officer's brows arched with curiosity, his eyes glassy from drink.

Hawk drained his beer, stood, and stretched. "Time for bed."

The next morning, Saradee awoke in the

predawn dark, got up, threw her shirt around her naked shoulders, and lit a lamp. She dropped the mantle over the flame. Before she waved out the match, she used it to light a half-burned cheroot lying with several others in the ashtray on the bedside table.

Puffing smoke, she regarded Waylon still snoring on the bed, the fresh bandages Saradee had used to dress his wounds glowing in the guttering lamplight. If anything, his nose was even bluer than it had been yesterday, the bridge expanding into his swollen eyes, giving his face a bearlike appearance.

Saradee stuck the cheroot in her teeth, went to her cartridge belt draped over a chair back, and made sure both pistols were loaded. Satisfied, she climbed onto the bed and walked her fingers up the outlaw's battered face, lightly flicking his lips.

"Wakey, wakey, little one," she sang. "It's moooorninggggggg."

A half hour later, she and Waylon were riding at the head of the gang, trotting their horses into the lightening eastern horizon. They were riding in the direction of the two train trestles, where they'd agreed to meet Valverde, Soto, and company.

A metallic clang sounded beneath Saradee's horse. The horse lunged sideways, dropping its right shoulder. "Damn — look at that!" Saradee said as the chestnut limped forward and stopped.

Kilroy checked down his own mount and turned toward Saradee. "What is it?"

"Threw a shoe."

"You didn't check your shoes before we pulled out?"

Saradee snapped a sharp look at him, an angry flush rising in her cheeks. She didn't say anything. She didn't have to. Kilroy knew that look, wished he could take that last question back. After all, he had been the one who'd called the truce.

Chagrined, he began to swing down from the saddle. "I'll have a look."

"I have a hammer and nails in my saddlebags. I'll reset and be along in a few minutes." Saradee glanced at the others clumped around her. "You boys go on."

"Sure you don't need a hand, Boss?" asked Jimbo Walsh.

"What — because I don't have balls I can't hammer a few nails into a horse's hoof?"

Walsh raised his hands, palms out. "Whatever you say, Boss. See you later!"

He gigged his horse ahead, waving the others on. Kilroy's gang followed suit. Kilroy himself was the slowest to pull out, casting faintly skeptical glances over his right shoulder. Fifty yards away, he jerked his hat brim down, turned to look over his horse's head, and urged the horse into a gallop behind the others.

Saradee had busied herself with hammer and nails. Now, as the gang galloped off, hooves clomping into the distance, she turned her head to look after them. She gave a wry snort and picked up the thrown shoe, the nails of which she'd loosened this morning, when the other gang members were making sure their own nails were firmly set in their horses' hooves.

It took her only a few minutes to reset and hammer the shoe. She swung onto her saddle, turned the chestnut off the trail that she and the gang had been following, and spurred it into a westward, cross-country gallop.

Forty-five minutes later, she reined up before the cottonwoods where she and her mysterious friend had agreed to meet.

Having expected him to be waiting for her, Saradee looked around. No sign of him. Around her, shadows angled out from the shrubs and land formations as the top of the huge, molten sun inched above an eastern rimrock.

She dismounted, glanced toward the *fed-*

erale headquarters hidden behind a jog of purple-pink hills. Pacing back and forth beside her horse, she lit a fresh cigar and peered north toward town.

On the side of a hillock, a small herd of deer grazed the dew-silvered bunch grass.

"Bastard," she whispered when she'd waited a full fifteen minutes. "~~Goddamn~~ bastard," she repeated, louder this time.

She dropped the cigar butt, mashed it out with her boot toe, and her heart hammering, mounted up and digged the chestnut into a ground-eating gallop.

She crossed the hay field in less than a minute. She shucked her Winchester from the saddle boot, cocked it one-handed, and rested the barrel across her saddlebows.

But she met no resistance at the hacienda's main gate. In fact, she saw no other person in the courtyard — other than a blackened, desiccated human hanging spread-eagled from a large wooden cross near a chicken coop. Horses stared at Saradee over the top rails of a distant corral, and a few chickens pecked in the yard churned with fresh tracks, littered with fresh horse apples.

Saradee dismounted and, holding the Winchester at low port, mounted the same steps she and her "friend" had mounted before, entered the casa by the same door. She stopped, listened, hearing nothing but the muffled buzz of flies in the dank air in which the fetor of unwashed men and spilled booze mixed with the lingering smell of a spicy Mexican breakfast.

Saradee walked along the hall. After three steps, she broke into a run, turning sharply into the room where she and the broad-shouldered hombre had discovered the chained and padlocked cabinet.

Six feet inside the room, she stopped dead in her tracks. She didn't hear the sharp intake of her own breath. The cabinet padlock hung open, three bullet holes through its steel face. The doors were open a foot.

Saradee walked heavy-footed across the room, opened the doors.

The cabinet was empty.

Not empty.

A large piece of yellowed paper lay on the third shelf from the top. Saradee picked it up, raked her enraged gaze over the sketched likeness of the mysterious stranger and the words GIDEON HAWK, ROGUE LAW-MAN in large block letters beneath the even larger letters announcing WANTED: DEAD OR ALIVE.

25.

SHOOT-OUT IN ARROYO DEL MOLINA

"I reckon this is where we finally part ways, Lieutenant," Hawk said an hour after they'd retrieved the payroll money from the *federales'* encampment — a relatively easy job, since the three skinny kids Valverde had left to garrison the place had run at the first bullet fired over their heads.

Hawk raised his canteen to Primrose. "Here's hoping you have a nice ride back Arizona way."

The Army pouches were draped over the hips of the lieutenant's Indian pony. "Why don't you leash that wolf of yours, Hawk, and ride back with me?"

Hawk lowered the canteen from his lips and corked it. "Job to do."

Primrose dropped his eyes, then stuck out his right hand. "Well, I can't wish you luck, because I won't condone what you do, but I will thank you for your help."

Hawk shook the lieutenant's hand. "Don't

mention it." He reined the grulla eastward, stopped, and turned back. Primrose hadn't moved. "Remember to watch your backside, and stay off the main trails. You're carrying a heap of money in a very poor country."

Primrose smiled with half of his mouth. "Don't tell me you're worried about me."

"Just don't want all my work to go for nothing." Hawk pinched his hat brim, then reined the grulla around and gigged it into a gallop.

He stopped the horse a half hour later, as the sun rose above the horizon. Looping the reins over a mesquite branch, he shucked his rifle and climbed a hillock. Near the crest, he hunkered down and cast his glance over the other side.

Fifty yards from the base of the hill, the arroyo snaked through spindly cottonwoods and willows. Southeast, the two trestle bridges stood silhouetted against the brightening eastern sky. Man-shaped shadows milled around the base of the one to which Hawk had attached the dynamite.

Directly south, on the other side of the arroyo, the outlaws' horses stood swishing their tails and grazing at the edge of the arroyo's southern fork. One man-shaped shadow stood crouched near one of the horses, no doubt hobbling its feet. Another horse shook its mane and whinnied.

Hawk gritted his teeth, hoping the grulla didn't answer. It didn't.

Hawk waited, watching from the hillock's brow with only his naked eyes, not wanting to risk a sun flash off his binoculars. In the quiet morning air, he could hear the outlaws' muffled conversations. Occasionally, someone chuckled. Rifles were cocked with metallic scrapes, and then boots barked on wood as the outlaws began spreading out upon the unused train bridge.

No one, apparently, had noticed Hawk's dynamite fixed to the trestle's wooden braces. If the sun was higher, they no doubt would have.

Slowly, quietly, he slid a fresh shell into his Henry's breech. He waited until the men hobbling the horses had joined the others on the bridge, then backtracked down the hillock. Holding the Henry in his right hand, he ran crouching across a sage-stippled flat to the boulder that he and Primrose had hidden behind yesterday.

He pressed his left shoulder against the rock, peered around it to the bridge. A fat man dressed in *federale* blue and a tall man in a black duster stood in the center of the bridge, over the others kneeling or lying prone, facing the other bridge, rifles in their hands. The fat man was Valverde. The tall man in the black duster, Waylon Kilroy. The American outlaw kept turning his bandaged face toward the arroyo, no doubt looking for the girl.

At the moment, she was probably discovering the message Hawk had left in the *federales'* makeshift safe. Which meant she could be along anytime.

Hawk hoped the train would be along sooner. He didn't want the crazy girl throwing a horse apple into his rain barrel, and he couldn't take a shot at his dynamite charge until the outlaws' attention was on the oncoming treasure train.

Involuntarily, Hawk followed Kilroy's glance along the arroyo. Yep, Saradee's arrival here before the train would be damned unfortunate.

Hawk hunkered down with his back to the boulder, settling in, waiting.

The sun climbed steadily, the day heating up, shadows slowly dissolving. Hawk's anxiety increased as well. Mexican trains were notoriously late, but by his calculations, this one was nearly an hour behind schedule.

The thought had no sooner passed than a distant whistle sounded. The raspy wail rose again, following by the distinctive chug of a steam locomotive. Atop the trestle bridge, Valverde shouted orders in Spanish.

Hawk glanced around the boulder. The bridge's rock and adobe arches glowed in the brightening sunlight. Atop the bridge, all the men were facing up the arroyo, away from Hawk. All, that is, except Kilroy, who remained standing on Hawk's side of the bridge, raking his anxious gaze across the country down arroyo and over Hawk's head.

Hawk ducked back behind the rock. Shit.

The train whistle rose louder, echoing. The steam locomotive rasped, chugged, couplings jostling as the train snaked around a slow, curving incline. The wheels screeched upon the morning-cool rails.

Keeping his head low, Hawk glanced around the right side of the boulder, a foot above the ground, brown brush and a sage clump shielding him from the bridge.

The train came into view, climbing the slight grade toward the far bridge — a hundred yards away and closing, little more than a dark, rectangular centipede from this distance, a shadow creeping through the clay-colored hills.

Muffled clicks sounded behind Hawk, almost inaudible behind the train's whistle and its rushing wheeze as it climbed the hill. Frowning, Hawk looked behind him. He saw nothing at first, but the clicks became soft thuds. Hoof falls.

Dread pinched his lower gut as his eye found a shadow moving through a crease in the sun-parched, yucca-stippled knolls in the northwest. Horse and rider were moving toward him — *galloping* toward him.

Saradee's hair bounced upon her shoulders, her straw sombrero showing bright tan in the sun's intensifying light, stirrups winging out from her horse's ribs. Riding low in the saddle, she lashed the horse's hips with her rein ends.

Hawk raked out a curse, thumbed back the Henry's hammer, and turned toward the bridge, snaking the rifle around the right side of the rock and resting his elbows in the brush. He doffed his hat, snugged his cheek to the stock.

As he slid the barrel over the rightmost dynamite pack, four feet from the top of the bridge, a voice called, "Hey!" In the upper periphery of his vision, he saw Kilroy bolt toward the side of the bridge, snapping a rifle to his shoulder.

Hawk steadied his aim, took a slow, deep breath, released it, and squeezed the trigger. Dust and wood splinters puffed six inches right of the dynamite.

The locomotive shrieked, chugged, its

funnel-shaped stack lifting sooty black smoke skyward.

A half second after Hawk's rifle had barked, Kilroy triggered his Winchester. The slug cracked into the boulder a foot left of Hawk's head. Ignoring it, ignoring Kilroy's exasperated shouts and the other men beginning to rise from the bridge floor, ignoring the sound of the approaching rider behind him, Hawk levered another round into the Henry's breech, and planted the bead on the dynamite. A quarter second before he fired, Kilroy drilled the rock beside Hawk, and Hawk nudged his own slug two inches wide of the explosives.

Cursing under his breath, he quickly ejected the spent shell, snapped the stock to his cheek. Kilroy fired again, the slug spanging off a small rock two feet in front of Hawk.

As Hawk laid the bead on the dynamite, adjusting for distance, the hoof thuds behind him grew louder, and he could hear the jangle of bit chains.

Kilroy fired another round, blowing up dust before and to the right of Hawk, who lowered the Henry slightly and blinked dust from his eyes. As more men began shouting in English as well as Spanish, and as the train's engine was twenty feet from the farther bridge, Hawk aimed quickly, squeezed the Henry's trigger.

The dynamite detonated with the boom of a ten-pound howitzer.

Kaa-booooom!

The sound was multiplied twice in the next second as the other two packs of dynamite exploded into angry red flame, blowing the braces apart and shredding the railroad ties above.

Hawk had positioned two packs on either side of the arch. Now, as the packs blew in a chain reaction started by the first explosion, blowing the floor of the bridge skyward, the fault lines in the middle arch separated. Sounding like giant eggs cracking, they yawned.

The middle arch collapsed, and the entire bridge fell like a house of cards. Men, rifles, and railroad ties from above tumbled with the falling rock and adobe and burning wooden braces, to the rocky floor of the arroyo. Debris rained into the wash, blowing up dust and rocks and causing the ground beneath Hawk to lurch and roll.

Ammo popped in the fire. Men who'd survived the fall, only to burn in the flames, screamed.

The locomotive and wood-mounded tender car chugged onto the second bridge, bugling shrilly, black smoke puffing sky-ward.

Two *federales* had survived the fall and the flames. One hobbled toward the far side of the arroyo, toward a rifle lying in the dust.

Hawk glanced over his right shoulder. Seeing no sign of the girl, he jacked a fresh shell and shot the wounded *federale,* then turned the rifle back to his left, to one of the American hard cases crawling toward Hawk, dragging his broken legs, his face a circle of smeared red.

The man raged, awkwardly aiming a pepperbox revolver. Hawk drilled a round through his chest, blowing him back against the bloody, twisted corpse of Major Valverde.

Behind Hawk, a boot crunched grass and gravel.

Hawk rose, spun around. The girl was six feet behind him, standing sideways and extending one of her beautiful Colts straight out from her shoulder. Hawk dropped his Henry and drew his Russian.

He figured he'd die before he could raise the pistol.

He was wrong.

The girl stared down the barrel of her own revolver, thumb on the cocked hammer, but she did not fire. Her eyes were stony, and her nostrils flared slightly, tawny hair winging out in the breeze.

Hawk extended the Russian beside the girl's own extended Colt — an unmatched set, with the barrels pointed in opposite directions. He ratcheted back the hammer and stared into her eyes.

Nearly a minute passed, and neither fired.

Behind Hawk, dying men groaned. The fire cracked and popped. Saradee's horse milled in the arroyo to Hawk's left, nickering and shaking its head at the flames.

"You double-crossed me, lover," Saradee said.

"That's assuming we ever had an alliance."

"We had one hell of an alliance. Don't you remember?"

Beneath the grime of his flat-brimmed hat, Hawk's eyes were hard. She adjusted her grip on her gun. "Where's the money?"

"Where it belongs."

She curled her lip. "You and me could have had a hell of a good time with that lucre." She glanced at the yawning maw of Hawk's Russian, and the corners of her mouth rose further. "Reckon we got us a Mexican standoff, lawman."

"I reckon."

Depressing her Colt's hammer, she lowered the gun to her side.

She stepped forward, turned her head slightly, and kissed the barrel of Hawk's revolver. A gentle, lingering, open-lipped kiss. She glanced along the barrel at him, her eyes sharp with challenge.

Hawk's finger tightened on the trigger but, as if a pebble were lodged between the trigger and the steel band of the trigger guard, it locked just short of firing.

Saradee's smile broadened, her eyes sparkled knowingly. "Some other time, lover." She stepped back, turned, and walked westward along the arroyo bank, hips swaying deliciously, round bottom straining the seat of her black denims. She turned into the arroyo, mounted her horse, and rode off down the ravine.

Slowly, Hawk lowered the Russian.

On the other side of the arroyo, enraged voices rose. Hawk looked that way. Two other survivors of the bridge explosion were scrambling up the butte at the far end of the now-demolished bridge.

Hawk holstered the Russian, picked up his rifle, and ran across the arroyo and up the other side. He caught the two *federales,* both carrying two of the new Winchester rifles Hawk had seen in the headquarters basement, at the bottom of a brushy swale.

As they began scrambling single-file up the swale's far, low bank, Hawk held his Henry straight out from his right hip. "Turn around and die like men!" he shouted in Spanish.

They froze. As one, they jerked around, fumbling with their rifles.

After levering two quick shots, the *federales* tumbling back down the rise, Hawk turned and walked back across the arroyo littered with burning bridge debris and bodies. Movement to his right caught his eye.

Between two piles of burning lumber, a tall, hatless, soot-covered figure staggered toward Hawk. Kilroy tripped over one of his fallen gang members, regained his balance, and raised a pistol toward Hawk.

Dropping to one knee and snapping the Henry to his right shoulder, Hawk levered three quick shots to Kilroy's one, the outlaw's slug slicing across Hawk's raised left elbow. Hawk's own slugs formed a tight, three-point star above the bridge of the outlaw's broken nose.

Dropping his pistol and loosing a clipped scream, Kilroy staggered straight back and fell on a burning timber. The fire instantly engulfed him, his face melting like wax behind the wild, crackling flames, the man's black boots jerking spasmodically.

The fire wind was fetid with the smell of burning flesh and creosote.

Hawk lowered the rifle, peered through wavering heat toward the far bridge. The train chugged northeastward, climbing another dun-colored rise as the black line of it thinned with distance.

Hawk climbed the arroyo's northern bank and, resting the Henry's barrel across his right shoulder, tramped back toward his horse.

Keeping his rifle in his right hand, Hawk mounted the grulla. He was about to tap his spurs to the mount's flanks, when a figure stepped out from behind a cottonwood tree. The man held a rifle over his shoulder. He wore a big, cream Stetson. His silver-flecked mustache stood out against his lean, lined face.

Hawk swung the barrel toward Flagg.

The lawman's eyes dropped to it. "Had you in my sights, Hawk. All the time you were shooting at the bridge, I could have drilled you."

"Why didn't you?"

Flagg lifted a shoulder. "Didn't see the point in stopping a cold-blooded killer from killin' cold-blooded killers. Besides, I get the distinct impression that letting you live would be worse punishment than putting a bullet through your head."

Hawk stared at the lawman, slowly lowered his rifle. "You do the badge proud, Flagg."

Flagg slitted his eyes. "We'll meet again, Hawk."

Flagg backed away, keeping his eyes on Hawk's rifle. Twenty yards away, he turned and disappeared in a fold in the hills. A minute later, the lawman reappeared, galloping a steeldust northwest toward El Molina.

Hawk laid the Henry across his saddlebows, keeping his finger through the trigger guard. He lowered his black hat, glanced at the black smoke and the flames.

A horseback figure on the other side of the arroyo caught his eye. Saradee climbed a low, southern rise, stopped at the crest, and turned her horse back toward the arroyo — horse and rider silhouetted against the brassy desert sky.

She stared down the hill and across the arroyo at Hawk. Hawk stared back at her. Finally, she turned her horse, heeled it down the other side of the hill and out of sight.

Hawk turned the grulla and spurred him north.

ABOUT THE AUTHOR

Peter Brandvold was born and raised in North Dakota. He currently resides in Colorado. Visit his Web site at www.peter brandvold.com or send him an e-mail at pgbrandvold@msn.com.

The employees of Thorndike Press hope you have enjoyed this Large Print book. All our Thorndike and Wheeler Large Print titles are designed for easy reading, and all our books are made to last. Other Thorndike Press Large Print books are available at your library, through selected bookstores, or directly from us.

For information about titles, please call:
(800) 223-1244

or visit our Web site at:
www.gale.com/thorndike
www.gale.com/wheeler

To share your comments, please write:
Publisher
Thorndike Press
295 Kennedy Memorial Drive
Waterville, ME 04901